SHIVAJI MAHARAJ
The Greatest

SHIVAJI MAHARAJ
The Greatest

Dr. Hemantraje Gaikwad

Published by
PRABHAT PRAKASHAN PVT. LTD.
4/19 Asaf Ali Road,
New Delhi-110 002 (INDIA)
e-mail: prabhatbooks@gmail.com

ISBN 978-93-90378-98-2
SHIVAJI MAHARAJ The Greatest
biography by Dr. Hemantraje Gaikwad

Edition
2026

Paperback Price
₹ 500.00 (Rupees Five Hundred only)

Printed at
R-Tech Offset Printers, Delhi

This book is dedicated to the

- Nationalism
- Diplomacy
- Management
- Strategy
- Foresight
- Will power

and

- Tenacious Personality of **Shivaji Maharaj** which every Indian should imbibe in him.

Foreword

'Shivaji Maharaj, the Greatest' is a compilation of facts from various resources, books, encyclopaedia, museums and wikipedia.

I have not made any new or original discovery or found a new reference. I have only assembled great incidences and great acts by great men and have compared them with Shivaji Maharaj.

My aim in writing this book is very simple—to give Shivaji Maharaj his due status in world history. Though the concept of this book developed first in English, my well wishers insisted that I first bring out the book in Marathi and accordingly the Marathi edition was published in 2012. The book won the Granthalaya Bharatiya Puraskar, Nagpur. The second edition came out in 2014, the third edition in 2018 and the fourth edition has been published in 2020.

Whilst writing the first edition, I corresponded with many publishers and writers to take permission to include passages, figures, pictures and maps in my book. Most of the publishers, authors and copyright owners were pleasantly surprised that I have shown the courtesy to seek permission.

The first person I approached was Shriman Vijayrao Deshmukh, author of Shakakarte Shivrai. He stays in Nagpur but was in New Mumbai due to a marriage ceremony. He called me there. We are aware of the hustle and bustle of Indian marriage ceremonies. I was amazed at the number of people who came to seek his blessings but he ignored all of them and heard me politely. He assured me that this is a monumental work.

He also gave me permission to take any reference, passage and map that I may desire from his book, Shakakarte Shivrai. From this day onward till now Shriman Vijayrao Deshmukh is my guru and has guided me in all my writing. I am indebted to him.

After that I contacted the authors/publishers of 'Shivaji kon hota?' (Who was Shivaji?) by Shri Govindrao Pansare. Shriman Jaisinghrao Pawar author of 'Shivchhatrapati: ek Magow' ('Shivchatrapati: an analysis'), publishers Shri Bhave of 'Chhatrapati Shivaji Maharaj' written by late Shri K.A. Keluskar, Smt. Gayatri Pagdi and Shri Priyadarshan Pagdi the grandchildren of Setu Madhavrao Pagdi and Shri T.V. Jadhav author of 'Shrimant Yogi'.

Besides all the above, I would like to record the help offered by Dr. Sachidanand Shevde, author of 'Shivaji chi yuddhneeti' (Shivaji's battle tactics); the publishers of 'Shivajiche Armar' (Shivaji's Navy) Smt. Swati Joshi; 'Shivkalatil Durg ani Durg Vyawastha' (Forts and fort administration in the time of Shivaji Maharaj) by Shri Mahesh Tendulkar; the author of 'Madhya Yugeen Bhartacha Itihas' (Medieval History of India) by Shri J.L. Mehta.

One of them refused to give permission in writing, saying, 'Our books are reference books and anybody is allowed quote from them as long so you give credit, to the book and authors.'

But one instance that I will not forget is my interaction with the Hon. Secretary of Maratha Mandir Shri R.R. Gawade, who took a lot of pains to allow me to take passages from Shriman Shejwalkar's book 'Shri Shivchhatrapati: Complied History of Shivaji-Foreword, Outline and References'.

Similarly Shri M.M. Karnik, President and Smt. M.P. Patil, Secretary of Maharashtra State Literature and Culture Mandal took great efforts to allow me to use paragraphs from Shri S.V. Awaleskar's 'Raigad chi Jeevan Katha' (The story of Raigad) and Dr. V.G. Khobrekar's 'Shivkal' (The Times of Shivaji). I am greatly indebted to all of them.

Besides these, my family and friends stood rock solid behind me in my endeavour. First and foremost among them are Dr. (Mrs.) Maitri Gupta and Shri Yogesh Gupta. Since last 50 years they have been with me through thick and thin. Sometimes it seems they are more concerned about my well being than even me, myself.

My psychiatrist friend Dr. Rajan Prabhu who was instrumental in me going to Raigad in 1980 for the first time. He has always been with me during my trying times. He always says that 'I have been his most difficult patient'. And he is quick to add 'It is just a joke'. But he knows that I know that, 'It is not a joke'.

But the person whom I must thank most is Prof. P. K. Ghanekar. Since last ten years, when I took my baby steps in the study of history, he has held my hand and guided me. He is a walking–talking encyclopaedia on Maratha History. He has written more than sixty books and I have liberally taken paragraphs from them. Though we are both almost the same age, he has been a kind and tolerant teacher to an over enthusiastic and blustering student. He has imbibed in me the art of writing history where every sentence needs a reference. A big 'thank you' to him from the bottom of my heart.

I am also grateful to Shri P.K.B. Chakravarty for giving me inputs for the betterment of the book and writing an endorsement for the back cover.

Similarly I wish to thank Dr. S.M. Sapatnekar, ex-Director of Haffkine Institute for guiding me for the past 50 years in every aspect of my life.

I also wish to thank Babasaheb Purandare for all his help in writing the book and in making of the documentary 'Shivaji Maharaj—the Greatest' which is available in Marathi, English, Hindi, Sanskrit, Kannada and Bangala. He has blessed me in the documentary and they are his exact words, that I have used as a preface of the book. Babasaheb Purandare has explained Shivaji Maharaj to each & every child through his tableau 'Janta Raja' and has delivered 22,000 lectures on Shivaji Maharaj, from the age of

20 yrs to 97 years. A commendable task indeed!

Last but not the least, I wish to thank my family for the understanding that they have shown, my ophthalmologist wife Dr. Pushpa, my homoeopath son Dr. Gaurang, my dentist daughter Dr. Gunjan and my son-in-law Harshal.

I am greatly indebted to them.

Prelude

On 4th March, 1980, my friend Dr. Rajan Prabhu and I were interns at Grant Medical College when we decided to visit Raigad for the tricentenary celebrations of Shivaji's death anniversary.

Prime Minister Indira Gandhi was the chief guest at the function and in her speech she said, "I think Shivaji ranks among the greatest men in the world. Since we were a slave country, our great men, whatever their standing has been, somewhat played down by the world history. Had the same person been born in a European country, he would have been praised to the skies and known everywhere. It would have been said that he had illuminated the world." *Lokrajya*, April 1985.

She came and went by helicopter. Incidentally, that was the first time I saw a helicopter at close quarters and in all its dusty glory. When her helicopter flew into the clouds, my thoughts also started soaring in the sky and remained there for thirty years before they could crystallise into a book form.

It is heartening to note that Shivaji is on the list of people who have the suffix 'the great' added to their names.

List of the greatest people of the world

Similarly, there is another list of 100 great people of the world (Appendix B) and contains the names of :

Painters like Michelangelo,

Inventors like Leonardo Vinci,

Philosophers like Plato,
Religious men like Buddha,
Warrior kings like Alexander

We shall not discuss the first four categories. We shall restrict ourselves to kings, warriors and conquerors. There is still another list of the ten greatest warriors—Alexander, Caesar, Hannibal, Richard, Leonidas, Spartacus, Saladin, Miyamoto Musashi, Audie Murphy and San Tsu.

Of these, the first four will be compared with Shivaji while the next three will be discussed in brief.

Three key words

The three key words we shall concentrate on are: 'GREAT', 'WARRIOR' and 'KING'.

We shall discuss various events in Shivaji's life and compare them with great events that have occurred all over the world. We shall use thirty criteria and discuss whether Shivaji deserves a name in the list of 'great warrior kings of the world'. We shall then discuss the 'greatman' and the 'greatness theory'.

We shall then take eight foreign representatives and two Indian warrior kings and compare them with Shivaji. The two Indian warrior kings are Akbar and Aurangzeb.

The best comparison would be between two contemporary kings, i.e. Aurangzeb (R1658-1707 A.D.) versus Shivaji (1637-1680 A.D.). The next best comparison would be between two kings separated by a century but in the same geographical region, i.e. Akbar (1542-1606 A.D.) versus Shivaji (1637-1680 A.D.). This we shall take up even before Aurangzeb to describe the background of Shivaji.

The eight foreign warrior kings are

Alexander, 356-323 B.C.
Caesar, 100-47 B.C.
Hannibal, 247-183 B.C.
Attila, 406-453 A.D.
Richard the Lion, 1157-1199 A.D.

William Wallace, 1270-1305 A.D.

Adolphus Gastavus, 1594-1632 A.D.

Chenghis Khan, 1162-1227 A.D.

It may not seem fair to compare Alexander (356-323 B.C.) with Shivaji (1627 -1680 A.D.), but as shall be described later, the battle tactics and siege technology of Alexander (356-323 B.C.) was more advanced than the battle tactics and siege technology of Shivaji (1627-1680 A.D.).

As we shall see, the British, Portuguese, Dutch and French who toured India in the 17th century compared Shivaji with many brave warriors, including the eight listed herewith.

We shall also discuss how Shivaji experienced events of world-shaking magnitude in one lifetime, how he had almost no weakness and how his aim in life was make his kingdom strong and his countrymen free of social ills.

We shall first study Shivaji and then compare him with eight foreign and two Indian warriors.

Thirty Criteria

The thirty criteria we will use are tabled below:

1. The Background
2. Shivaji's Childhood
3. Shivaji and David and Goliath
4. Shivaji and Thermopyle
5. Shivaji and Guerrila war
6. Shivaji and Sack of Surat
7. Shivaji and Troy
8. Shivaji's Forts and Great Wall of China
9. Shivaji and the Great Escape
10. Shivaji and Navy
11. Shivaji and Magna Carta
12. Shivaji and Geneva Convention
13. Shivaji and Religion
14. Shivaji and Diplomacy
15. Shivaji and Crisis
16. Shivaji and Liberty, Equality, Fraternity
17. Shivaji and Marathi Language

Contents

The Background

Dharmayuddha

Hindu military science recognised two kinds of warfare—the *dharmayuddha* and the *kutayuddha*. *Dharmayuddha* is war carried on the principles of Dharma, meaning here the *Ksatriya* Dharma or the law of kings and warriors. In other words, it was a just and righteous war which had the approval of society. On the other hand, *kutayuddha* was unrighteous war. It was a crafty fight carried on in secret. The Hindu science of warfare values both *niti* and *shaurya,* i.e. ethical principles and valour. It was, therefore, realised that the waging of war without regard to moral standards degraded the institution into mere animal ferocity. A monarch, desirous of Dharma *vijaya,* should conform to the code of ethics enjoined upon warriors. The principles regulating the two kinds of warfare are elabourately described in the *Dharmasutras* and *Dharmashastras,* the epics (*Ramayana* and *Mahabharata*), the *Arthashastra* treatises of Kautilya, Kamandaka and Sukra. Hindu India possessed the classical fourfold force of chariots, elephants, horsemen and infantry, collectively known as the *chaturangabala.* To the Hindus, war was but a game of chess. (chess also goes by the old name of *chaturanga*).

The fourfold way to *moksha* inculcated by the Hindus only stressed on different means of escaping life. This was the very antithesis of positive activism of the invading Muslims. To make matters worse, the leadership then was in the extremely incompetent hands of, for example, Ramdev Rao of Maharashtra, who, despite his pedantic titles (*gurjara-kunjara-dana-kanjirava; telinngatunga-taruanmulanamatta-danavala; malavapradipa-samana-malayanila, etc.*), as Rajwade has observed, was an unmilitary king. According to the Paithan copper-plate inscription, Ramdev granted three villages to 57 Brahmins on the condition that (among other indications of good behaviour) they should use no weapons! This stipulation, indeed, was superfluous for the people for whom Hemadri had already prescribed an engrossing round of rituals in his *chaturvarga*—Chintamani. Its Vrata, Dana, Tirtha, Moksha and Prayaschitta Khandas left little room for trifling duties like the defence of the state. Karma was not as yet the action of the *Gita*, but only one class of ritual.

Marco Polo, who sojourned through the land between 1288-93, speaks of the people as 'going to battle with lances and shields, but without clothing,' and are a despicable unwar-like race. They do not kill cattle, he further observes, nor any kind of animals for food; but when desirous of eating the flesh of sheep or other beasts, or birds, they procure the Saracens, who are not under the influence of the same laws and customs, to perform the office.'

Before the advent of Islam (1000 A.D.) the vassals of a weak king would declare independence with the central power helpless to prevent it. A powerful general used to dethrone a weak king and raise his own kingdom. This had been the fashion in which a new power was established. The new king inherited the existing army and the bureaucratic structure automatically.

Jihad

In 1000 A.D., India was possibly the richest country in the world. Such a country presented an irresistible target for the ravanging Mongols and their descendants, who settled in present-day Afghanistan, Uzbekistan and Tajikistan, all within comparatively easy reach of north-western India. The Hindus did not lack in bravery on the battle-field. Even so, there were seven reasons for the victory of the Islamic invaders. The first reason was the concept of *jihad*.

The Muslims are commanded by the Quran to wage an everlasting war against the infidels and are assured victory in the struggle.

1. On infidels is the curse of Allah (The Cow: 161).
2. Allah is an enemy to infidels (The Cow: 15).
3. The worst of beasts in Allah's sight are the ungrateful, who will not believe (Spoils of War: 55).
4. Oh ye who believe! The non-Muslims are unclean (Repentance:17).
5. Oh ye who believe! Murder those of the disbelievers and let them find harshness in you (Repentance: 123).

Since humans do not like harming innocent people, *jihad* is nothing but an inducement to murder and plunder non-Muslims for the sheer crime of not believing in Muhammad. It is called a 'holy war'. Those who return home victorious, come laden with booty, which includes wealth and non-Muslim women for concubinage and free seduction, but those 'crusaders' who are killed 'in the way of Allah' go straight to paradise where young virgins of exquisite beauty and pretty boys anxiously wait to serve them! Even more stunning is the fact that while every code of moral conduct treats murder, rape, plunder, lechery as sins, Islam counts them as acts of piety.

Illegitimate sex amongst Muslims is *haram*, but for a *mujahid*, taking up non-Muslim women as concubines in a *jihad* is Legitimate. Carnal gratification, man's greatest desire, is the first temptation that the concept of *jihad* carries. A Mujahid, i.e. the Islamic warrior, who at that time suffered pangs of sexual starvation in the arid land of Arabia, was promised plenty of sensual enjoyment as a reward for participating in the carnage whether or not he survived the rigours of the battlefield. If he (a *mujahid*-Islamic warrior) got killed, he was assured that the *houris* awaited his glorious company in *jannat*, i.e. paradise, and if he survived, he had a share in the plunder, which included women of the infidels. Islam has prescribed flogging, and death by-stoning for sexual offences, such as fornication and adultery because it holds such acts as unlawful when committed out of wedlock, but when a Muslim 'fights in the way of Allah' to murder the infidels and plunder their property, then the Quran relaxes this rule:

"And anyone of you who has not the affluence to be able to marry believing free women in wedlock, let him take believing handmaids that your right hand owns... so, marry them, with their people's leave and give them their wages honourably as women in wedlock, not as in licence or taking lovers" (Women, IV: 25). These verses demonstrate beyond a shadow of doubt that amongst Muslims, the Quran forbids sexual intercourse outside wedlock: marriage is a must for the fulfilment of sensual desires, but this law is blown off by the wind of change when it comes to a *mujahid* (the holy warrior).

Muslim War Tactics and Strategy

The second reason as discussed above was, no doubt, the cruel and rapacious methods of warfare for which the Hindus had no answer. Combined with this was the fact that the war tactics and strategy of the Muslims was far more advanced than that of the Hindus. The reason for this is easy to understand. Since 1100 A.D. during the Crusades, the Muslims under Saladin had fought against the Christians under top-class warriors like Richard the Lionheart. The Crusaders had, in turn, honed their war tactics from a long line of warriors dating back to the Roman centurions. The Muslims who invaded India had already learnt stealth, deceit and organisation from blood-thirsty warlords, like Chenghis Khan and Timurlane.

"The Mongols, Persians, Parthians, Turks, Sogdians, Bactrians and Scythians (or Tartars) all use the same fighting tactics. To pass over details, they are most dangerous when they seem to be flying in headlong riot. For turning round on their horses, although they are going at full gallop, they fling their javelins with such deadly aim that they can transfix the eyc of an enemy...if they invite battle with six thousand troops, they are sure to have twenty thousand hiding in ambush; and in the rear of these again, several thousands more are held in reserve, that they may support the advance-guard in case of a reverse, or rally them, if routed. Such reserves often turn defeat into sudden victory by checking the pursuit, by restoring the fight through their freshness and unimpaired vigour, and by compelling the weary enemy to retire...On advancing to the attack, Mongol generals extend one or both wings in the endeavour to outflank and encircle the enemy."

In short, even during war, to the Hindus, valour and honour were important and both these were trampled under the Muslim juggernaut of plunder, rape and massacre. The Hindus were so short of tactics that very often all the battle meant for the Muslims was to find the king or *senapati* and kill him. This happened both when Hemu's eye was pierced by Akbar at second battle of Panipat and when Sadashiv Bhau got off his elephant at the third battle of Panipat.

"The Hindu rulers used to be astonishingly ignorant of the border situation. Their enemy would catch them unawares, often marching in over 200 miles in their territory and only then would they wake up to the situation. Besides, whatever may be the outcome of the battle, it is the land of the Hindus which was defiled.' (Shriman Yogi p...)

"A Hindu Power had certain distinguishing traits. It is not as if they did not emerge victorious in a war against the Muslim invaders. There have been many victories. But their victories did not destroy their Muslim opponents. The latter's territory did not diminish, his power was not erased. The victor's territory did expand. Even though victorious, the victor became weaker and stayed so. In short, it is plain that they faced total destruction in defeat and weakening in victory" (Shriman Yogi p...).

Royal Library of Alexandria

To get some idea of the Muslim fanaticism, let us have a look at their attitude to any book other than the Quran.

The Royal Library of Alexandria, or Ancient Library of Alexandria, in Alexandria, Egypt, was one of the largest and most significant libraries of the ancient world. It flourished under the patronage of the Ptolemaic dynasty and functioned as a major centre of scholarship from its construction in the 3rd century B.C. until the Roman conquest of Egypt in 30 B.C. The library was conceived and opened either during the reign of Ptolemy I Soter (367-283 B.C.) or during the reign of his son Ptolemy II (283-246 B.C.).

In 642, Alexandria was captured by the Muslim army of Amr ibn al-Aas. The longest version of the story is in the Syriac Christian author Bar-Hebraeus (1226-1286), also known as Abu'l Faraj. He translated extracts from his history, the *Chronicum Syriacum* into Arabic and added extra material from Arab sources. In this *Historia Compendiosa Dynastiarum*, he describes a certain John Grammaticus (490–570) asking Amr for the 'books in the royal library'. Amr writes to Omar for instructions and Omar replies: "If those books are in agreement with the Quran, they are superfluous and we have no need of them destroy them, and if these are opposed to the Quran, they are heresay and we don't need them; destroy them."

So, all the texts were destroyed by using them as tinder for bath houses of the city. Even then it is said to have taken six months to burn all the documents.

Hindu Attitude to Conversion

The third was the Hindu attitude to conversion. In their aim to make the whole world Islamic, the Muslims, after every victory, gave their prisioners two options—Islam or death. With a sword hanging on their neck, naturally few of any Hindus could resist conversion. Two of the rites of conversion were circumcision and the eating of beef. But once converted, even though by force, these new converts realised that all doors to revert back to Hinduism were closed to them. Once it sunk in that they were forever imprisoned in Islam, they had no alternative but to co-operate with their new brethren. Some went a step further and decided to take revenge on the Hindus who prevented them from re-entering

Hinduism. When the Muslims learnt this, they took up conversion with greater zeal and on a larger scale. This gave rise to a unique situation for the Muslim invaders gained in strength with every battle for their war prisoners more than made up for their own soldiers who died on the battlefield. So, however bravely the Hindus fought, they inadvertently landed up making the Muslims stronger with every battle. Every prisoner, once he converted, was welcomed with open arms and given respect and self-esteem, not to mention the fact that he was free of all barriers of caste and taboos of religion.

The best example of this was Malik Kafur, who became Alauddin Khilji's general. On being converted, he became a fanatic Muslim and it was this Malik Kafur who defeated Ramdeorao Yadav of Devagiri and sent him in chains to Delhi. Muzaffar Shah who destroyed the Somnath Mandir was born a Hindu Brahmin as also Timmappa Bahrud, who helped establish the founder was Malik Ahmad Nizam Shah.

Hindu Attitude towards Their Women

The fourth reason was the disgusting attitude of the Hindus towards their women. The Muslim invaders kidnapped Hindu women and raped them not only to satisfy their lust and leave a permanent scar of terror, but they more importantly did so to increase the population of Muslims. Islam had sanctioned the Muslims four legal wives but there was no restriction on cucubines obtained as spoils of war. These Hindu women who were forced into harems became mere objects of lust. Though this happened because of the failure of their menfolk on the battlefield, what was shocking was that because they had been deflowered and despoiled in captivity, the doors of Hinduism were forever closed to them. The Hindus never made any attempt to release them from their misery. When the Muslims realised that once a Hindu woman's chastity was plundered, she became their property forever, their rapacious nature knew no bounds. Sir Jadunath Sarkar writes that the men were lucky to die on the battlefield, but it was the women who bore the brunt of the Muslim wrath. These were no ordinary women; they were royalty, wives, sisters and daughters of kings and princesses. But they were all reduced to objects of lust for a night or two, and then they spent the rest of their loveless listless lives in harems guarded by eunuchs.

Sects and Bisects of the Hindus

The fifth reason was that the Hindus were a divided lot. One trait was common to all the sects of the Hindus, namely their antipathy towards all the rest. Besides this suicidal exclusivism, the psychological effect of the total teaching of Hinduism was devitalising. The caste that a person was born in decided the work and status as an adult. Islam preached equality and unity in work and prayer. Merit rather than birth decided status in life and even a slave could become a ruler and establish a dynasty. On the other hand, if a Hindu was a natural swordsman, but was born in a potter family, there was no way he would be allowed to fight because that was the prerogative of the Kshatriyas. On the other hand, if a Kshatriya was blessed with good litrerary skills and had an aptitude for mathematics, he was obviously well suited for studying the Vedas and astronomy. But he was forced only to fight even if he had no stomach for it because the study of *Vedas* and astronomy was the absolute realm of the Brahmins.

The exclusivism of the Hindus was so fragmentary that it did not stop at compartmentalising them into four castes, but each caste had sub-castes and each sub-caste had sects, sub-sects and its accompanying hierarchy. Thus, it was not as if all Brahmins were a united lot. In fact, the two main sects—the Deshastha Brahmins and Konkanastha Brahmins—despised each other. The oneness in Islam was based on the fact that they were required to pray together five times a day facing Mecca and eat together from a large plate which made fighting together and dying together on the battlefield easier. There was no one unifying factor that could identify the Hindus. In fact, when the Muslims invaded a kingdom, the king and his army (i.e. the Kshatriyas) fought them tooth and nail, but the rest of the Hindu population went about their daily chores for the caste system had imbibed in them that fighting had nothing to do with them. And perhaps, even if they were in anyway motivated to fight, they had neither the training nor the arms.

Petty Jealousy of the Hindus

The sixth reason was the petty jealousy that the Hindu kings bore against each other. India was, at this time, a chaos of warring kingdoms, more interested in settling scores with their neighbours than in unifying against the invaders. The best example was the unique feud between Prithviraj and his father-in-law Jaichand. Jaichand was enraged that his daughter Sanyogita had eloped with Prithviraj. He must have had his reasons for disliking Prithviraj. When Muhamed Ghori invaded India in 1191, Prithviraj defeated him in the first battle of Tarain. Ghori asked forgiveness, Prithviraj as per the *yudhniti* instilled in him, spared his life and allowed Ghori to go back to Ghazni. Ghori swore revenge, came back in 1192 and attacked Prithviraj in the second battle of Tarain and demanded that Prithviraj convert to Islam. At this juncture, Jaichand not only refused to make common cause against the foreign invader, but actually gave away secrets that eventually caused the defeat of Prithviraj. Jaichand disregarded the fact that very soon it would be his head on the block. And, surely enough, he was defeated by Ghori at the battle of Chandawar in 1194.

Similarly, in 1310, when Marwaharan Kuleshwar, the ruler of the Pandya kingdom of South India died, his two sons Verwarman and Jatawarman fought for the right to rule, which was fair and natural. But what was despicable was that Jatawarman asked for the help of Alauddin Khilji to get full control of the kingdom. It never struck Jatawarman that the ascendancy to the throne was an internal dispute and had to be sorted out internally. Alauddin Khilji was an outsider, the follower of a blood-thirsty religion that thrived on plunder, rape and conversion. And rather than give up a part of the kingdom in return for help rendered, it was better to make some sort of a settlement with his own brother. At least, his brother would never enslave him or rape his daughters; sooner or later, Khilji would. But the Hindus had no sense of unity or social cooperation and were willing to forge alliances with foreigners against their own family. The Muslims, on the other hand, cut the throats of their brothers, back-stabbed their cousins, murdered their uncles and imprisoned their fathers. They fought viciously and ruthlessly within themselves for the right to rule, but there is no record of a Muslim ruler collabourating with a Hindu ruler against a Muslim ruler. The *Mahabharata*, no doubt, taught that "when we fight amongst ourselves, we are one hundred against five, but when we fight against others, we are one hundred and five against the rest." But this was only in theory and it was the Muslims who practiced it rather than the Hindus.

Idol Worship by the Hindus

The seventh reason was the innocent belief of the Hindus in their gods and their Brahmins. The Hindus were often defeated even before the battle started. The Muslims destroyed the temples and amassed great wealth from them. The Hindus humanised their idols: their gods ate and drank and even otherwise behaved like people. The Hindus thought that if the Muslims could destroy their living Gods, how could the Hindus dare to fight with them (Shriman Yogi p.)?

The Brahmins

The social leadership of Hindus, i.e. the Brahmins were not only apathetic, but rather bowed before the Muslim invaders and their sycophancy was pathetic, e.g. one of them had a bright idea that if there was an *Upanishad*, then the victorious Muslims also deserved an *Upanishad* on Allah and, accordingly, they penned the '*Allaho-Upanishad*'.

They also reasoned that though Sanskrit was a rich and beautiful language, it is necessary that for it to reach its rightful status it needs official sanction of the rulers and, therefore, Urdu verbs were included in letters, correspondence and treatises.

Hindu Brahmins refused to work at the *durbars* of Hindu *rajas* and preferred to be appointed as court pandits of Muslim kings. Pandit Jagannath, the creater of such prose like *Rasgangadhar*, and poetry like Gangalhari, Lakshmilahri was established at the *durbar* of Shahjahan. When a Hindu raja of Jaipur requested him to come to his court, he sent a pithy reply, "My needs can be fulfilled only either by Dilleshwar or Jagdishwar. The other *rajas* can at best only provide me with enough money for my salt and pepper."

Invasion of Mahmud Ghaznavi

The major Islamic invasion of India started with Mahmud of Ghazni. From the above description, it is then not surprising that Mahmud Ghaznavi's armies so easily defeated the Indian kings. Mahmud began a series of seventeen raids into north-western India at the end of the 10th century. His first expedition in 1000 A.D. was directed against the frontier towns. His sixteenth expedition was the plunder of Somnath temple (dedicated to Shiva) in 1025 A.D., situated on the sea coast of Kathiawar. Mahmud of Ghazni attacked this temple and looted it of gems and precious stones. He then massacred the worshippers and had the temple burnt. It was then that the famous Shivalingam of the temple was entirely destroyed.

The temple and citadel were sacked, and most of its defenders massacred. Mahmud personally hammered the temple's gilded *lingam* to pieces and the stone fragments were carted back to Ghazni, where they were incorporated into the steps of the city's new Jamiah Masjid.

After looting the Somnath temple, when Mahmud was going back to Ghazni, the Jats attacked his army. So, to punish the Jats, he returned and defeated them in 1026.

The objective of Mahmud's expeditions was to plunder the riches of temples and palaces. He was not interested in expanding his empire to India.

The Sultanates that Ruled India

The Sultanates that ruled India later are enumerated below:

1. Qutub-ud-din Aibak and Altmash (1206- 1235 A.D.)
2. Razia Begum (1236-1239 A.D.)

3. Ghias-ud-din Balban (1266-1286 A.D.)
4. Khilji dynasty (1290 -1320 A.D.)
5. Tughlaq dynasty (1320-1414 A.D.)
6. Firoz Shah Tughlaq (1351-1388 A.D.)
7. The Saiyads and the Lodi Dynasties (1451-1526 A.D.)
8. The Bahmani kingdom (1347-1526 A.D.)
9. The Empire of Vijayanagar (1336-1565 A.D.)

The Mughal Dynasty

10. Zahir-ud-din Babur (1526-1530 A.D.)
11. Nasir-ud-din Humayun (1530-1540 A.D.)
12. Sher Shah Suri and his successors (1540-1555 A.D.)
13. Akbar the Great (1556-1605 A.D.)
14. Jehangir and Nurjahan (1605-1627 A.D.)
15. Shah Jahan (1627-1658 A.D.)
16. Aurangzeb Alamgir (1658-1707 A.D.)

Babur at the First Battle of Panipat

Babur's Mughal forces consisted of between 13,000 and 15,000 men, mostly horse cavalry. His secret weapon included 20 to 24 pieces of field artillery, a relatively recent innovation in warfare.

Lodi's primary weapon of shock and awe was his troop of war elephants—numbering anywhere from 100 to 1,000 trained and battle-hardened pachyderms, according to different sources.

Ibrahim Lodi was no tactician—his army simply marched out in a disorganised block, relying on sheer numbers and the aforementioned elephants to overwhelm the enemy. Babur, however, employed two tactics unfamiliar to Lodi, which turned the tide of the battle.

The first was *tulughma*, dividing a smaller force into forward left, rear left, forward right, rear right, and centre divisions. The highly mobile right and left divisions peeled out and surrounded the larger enemy force, driving them towards the centre. At the centre, Babur arrayed his cannons. The second tactical innovation was Babur's use of carts, called *araba*. His artillery forces were shielded behind a row of carts which were tied together with leather ropes to prevent the enemy from getting between them and attacking the artillery men. This tactic was borrowed from the Ottoman Turks.

Using his *tulughma* formation, Babur trapped the Lodi army in a pincer motion. He then used his cannons to great effect; the Delhi war elephants had never heard such a loud and terrible noise, and the spooked animals turned around and ran through their own lines, crushing Lodi's soldiers as they ran. Trumpeting, their eyes wide with panic, the elephants turned back and charged into their own troops, crushing scores of men underfoot. Their opponents had brought a terrifying new technology to bear—something the elephants likely had never heard of before!

According to the *Baburnama*, Emperor Babur's autobiography, the Mughals killed 40,000 to 50,000 of the Delhi soldiers.

The defeat of the Delhi Sultanate at the First Battle of Panipat is a crucial turning point in the history of India and was a major step towards the establishment of the Mughal Empire,

During this time, the state of the common man is well described in the following passage:

Athanasius Nikitin, a Russian merchant wrote in 1470-74: *"The land is overstocked with people," he writes, "but those in the country are very miserable, while the nobles are extremely opulent and delight in luxury. It is not difficult to distinguish between the opulent classes and the indigent masses; the former were mostly composed of the ruling Muslim nobles and the latter largely comprised the conquered Hindu subjects. The wealth of the rich was derived from the peaceful toils of the peasants, and the spoils of war, supplemented by the profits of such trade as then existed. But war was the most paying industry, especially when it was the enemies' countries that were more frequently devastated. Under the Bahmani Sultans, most of fighting was done on foreign soil. While, therefore, the 'overstocked' population supplied the man-power for the armies, those who survived the slaughter, or rather their masters were enriched beyond the dreams of avarice."*

How this wealth was expended might be gathered from the following description by Nikitin.

He found the Khorassanian 'Boyar' Merlik Tuchar, merchant prince, keeping an army of 2,00,000 men; Melik Khan, 1,00,000; Kharat Khan, 20,000; and many other Khans keeping an army of 10,000 men. The Sultan went out with 30,00,000 men of his own. *"They are wont to be carried on their silver beds* (palkis)*, preceded by some twenty chargers caparisoned in gold and followed by 300 men on horse-back and by 500 on foot, and by horn-men, 10 torchbearers and 10 musicians. The Sultan goes out hunting, with his mother and his lady, and train of 10,000 men on horseback, 50,000 on foot; 200 elephants adorned in gilded armour, and in front 100 horsemen,100 dancers, and 300 common horses in golden clothing; 100 monkeys, and 100 concubines, all foreign."*

The Khandagale Elephant Episode

The Nizam Shah convened a *durbar* at Daulatabad. Along with other *sardars*, there were three families—the Jadhav family, the Bhosle family and the Khandagale family. The Jadhav family was related to the Bhosle family by marriage, i.e. Jadhavrao's daughter Jeejabai was married to Shahaji Bhosle, the son of Maloji Bhosle. After the *durbar* had dispersed for the day, the three families along with the other *sardars* came out. Suddenly, an elephant belonging to the Khandagale family went beserk and trampled to death some members of the Jadhav family. Enraged at the death of his family members, Lakhoji Jadhav's son Dattaji attacked the Khandagales sword in hand. Seeing him in this belligerent state, Shahaji Bhosle and his cousin Kheloji went to the defence of the Khandagales. So, instead of everyone trying to control a raging elephant, what erupted was a full-flegged skirmish where family and friends were at each other's throats. Things really got horrible when Shahaji killed his brother-in-law Dattaji Jadhav. This should have brought everybody to their senses but that did not happen for a furious Lakhoji attacked his son-in-law Shahaji and injured him on his arm so seriously that he fell down unconscious. Fortunately, by then, the Nizam came to know of this madness and he sternly intervened, putting a stop to this senseless and wanton killing.

The above episode clearly spells out the mentality of the Marathas. A slight affront even by mistake could make two related families draw daggers at each other. They would thirst for revenge for generations and, what is more, take great pride in it.

□

Shivaji's Childhood

Shivaji was born on 19th February, 1630 at Shivneri, Jaluka Junnar near Pune (*The Land & People*/JOS 1-6).

The Slaughter of the Jadhavrao Family

On 25th July, 1629, when Shivaji was still in the embryo, his mother had been shocked by the cold-blooded butchery of her father, her two brothers and a nephew in the Nizam Shahi court. It happened as follows.

Fatah Khan became the chief minister of the Nizam Shahi after Malik Ambar's death. However, because of the palace intrigues of Hamid Khan, Fatah Khan was arrested and imprisoned. Hamid Khan was appointed as chief minister and Mukkarab Khan was made Commander of the army. The arrest of Fatah Khan nade some of the other *sardars* and *amirs* insecure of their own future. One of them was Shahaji's father-in-law Lakhoji Jadhav Rao of Sindkhed. He was seriously thinking of cutting of ties with Nizam and joining the Mughals. But the Nizam's spies reported this possibility to him and the Nizam sent for Lukhoji Rao. Lukhoji Rao presented himself along with his three sons, Raghav, Achlogy and Yeshwant. As per the court etiquette of those times all four were unarmed when armed assasins fell upon them and ruthlessly killed them. Luckily Jadhav Rao's brother Jagdeo Rao and fourth son Bahadurji had not accompanied him to the Nizam court. They escaped along with Lukhojirao's wife Girijabai to Sindkhed and became Mughal *mansabdars*. (SHALT. meh. 114)

In 1633, Jijabai had nearly been captured by Mhaldar Khan,

the *quiledar* of Trimbak. In 1636, Shahaji (Shivaji's father) was besieged together with his family in the fortress of Mahuli and might have been slaughtered or imprisoned for life.

Shahaji was captured by Baji Ghorpade and brought in chains by Afzal Khan to Adil Shahi at Bijapur. (Stgm/hs sardesai/309)

Education of Shivaji

The *Shivbharat* says:

As Shivaji had turned seven, Shahaji thought his son was eligible to start studying the alphabet. He along with other boys of his age was handed over to a teacher and before the teacher was done with the first letter, this child would write the second. The teacher taught him the script which is the doorway to all disciplines. The Guru *took pride in this intelligent, well-behaved, handsome and charismatic little prince, who learnt the alphabet so quickly and he, in his mind, noted 'here is an extraordinary child'. (Shlat/mhn688)*

The Chitnis chronicle details the syllabus of Shivaji's studies—*reading-writing,* subhashit *(sayings), the* Ramayana, *horse riding, elephant riding, wrestling, archery, use of guns, fencing, vastu, astrology, gemology, magic, use and antidotes of poisons.* (*VD163)*

There is no letter at present available in Shivaji's handwriting to prove that he was literate but the fact that his father Shahaji and son Sambhaji were well versed both in Sanskrit and Marathi prove that it was most likely that he too was fairly adept at them.

More important, there is a letter dated 12 April, 1663 written by Philip Gifford from the Rajapur factory to Surat which said:

"*Yesterday a letter arrived from the Rajah written by himself to Rougy (Raoji) giving him an account that how he himself with 400 choice men went to Shastachan's camp.*"

That Shivaji could read is proved by a letter written from Danda Rajapuri, "*The envoy should be careful to deliver the letter into Shivaji's own hands, for we fear these Brahmins make letters to speak what they please.*"

During the sack of Sura, Shivaji sent a letter signed by him.

All the above points prove beyond doubt that Shivaji was

well educated by the standards of his times. As per the prevelant protocol, he did not read or write in his *durbar*, but had it read out to him. (CS/VD/163)

In his account of Shivaji's escape from Agra, Kafi Khan writes that while making his way to Maharashtra, Shivaji left an exhausted Sambhaji with a Brahmin living in Mathura with very specific orders. '*To keep Sambhaji with him until he received a letter in Shivaji's own hand.*' (mhn 687)

Shivaji and Bijapur Court

A custom was prevalent those days among the nobles to take their wards to learn the court etiquette and this was also a part of their education Shahaji also expressed his desire to Shivaji to accompany him to the *durbar*. But Shivaji refused. When this gave rise to talk in court circles, Shahaji's friends insisted on him to introduce Shivaji to the court. Hence, Shahaji pressed Shivaji to go to the court and he consented. However, when Shivaji accompanied his father to the court, he did not perform the usual obedience required by court etiquette, He made a slight *salaam* and seated himself. After this, Shivaji often accompanied Shahaji to the *durbar*. But, on every occasion, he contented himself with an informal *salaam*. This conduct naturally excited a suspicion in the mind of the Sultan and he called Shivaji and questioned him point blank about it. But Shivaji replied that at the critical moment, he becomes confused. The Sultan burst into a fit of laughter at this witty reply. (stgm/hss/83)

Shivaji Maharaj's Seal

The earliest available letter by Shivaji Maharaj is dated 28th January, 1646. The seal is at the head of the letter. The seal of Shivaji Maharaj with its Sanskrit inscription says:

"This seal of Shahaji's son Shivaji, waxing like the crescent of the new moon and revered by the world, shines forth for the welfare of his people."

At the bottom of the letter is the phrase, *maryadeyam virajate,* which means 'the letter ends'.

There are certain significant factors of Shivaji Maharaj's seal:

- Shivaji Maharaj's seal is the first seal in Sanskrit, his father Shahaji's and mother Jijabai's seal are in Persian;
- Shivaji Maharaj's father Shahaji was an important *mansabdar* of the Adilshahi. In a *farman* dated 28th March, 1644 Shahaji was called *farzand,* i.e., son and Maharaja. No other Hindu *sardar* is known to have been given the title of Maharaja. It is surprising that the son of such a loyal official should have his seal in Sanskrit.
- Shivaji Maharaji's seal was in use in 1646, i.e. when Shivaji Maharaj was seventeen-years old. It means that by then Shivaji Maharaj (or his parents and teachers) had decided on the course of his life before that.
- All the seals of the ashtapradhans, sardars and officials of Shivaji Maharaj are in Sanskrit proving that it was not a whim or fancy, but concieved with purpose and intent.

The Importance of Forts

He knew (or was taught either by his mother and elders) that the *jagirdars* and *watandars* were selfish and interested only in themselves. He made up his mind to depend on the common people. Three of his childhood friends made history—Tanaji Malusare, Yesaji Kank and Baji Pasalkar.

Shivaji was hardly fourteen-years old when he had the first bitter experience of displeasure at the Bhjapuri court. Adilshah suddenly declared Shahaji a rebel and, in 1643, ordered the seizure of his Pune jahgir. His *farman* to Kanhoji Jedhe said:

"Shahaji Bhosle has been excluded from the exalted court. Khandoji and Baji Ghorpade, with other wazirs *have been appointed to dislodge his agent, Dadaji Kondeo, who is towards Kondhna. Join them with your contigent and under their instruction chastise and annihilate, Dadaji Kondeo and other associates of that traitor (*haram-khwar*) and capture that territory."*

Dadaji Kondeo, the guardian of Shivaji, became a hunted man. Adil Shahi troops marched into the Pune Jahgir. In those days forts were rarely given as jahgirs. Jahgirs meant the title to use the land revenue of the villages. A *jahgirdar* had no effective means of resistance if his sovereign came down against him. Even at that young age, Shivaji must have deeply felt his helplessness in the face of the Adilshahi onslaught. (SMP/CS/10)

In 1646, Shivaji took his first Fort Torna from its Bijapuri commander by some cunning device without fighting. He found a treasure amounting to two lakhs of *hon*. (Saht/JS26)

In 1648, he took advantage of a family feud of Nilkanth Rao and got the control of Purander Fort.

Shivaji built his kingdom and government before visiting any royal court, civilised city or organised camp. He received no help from any experienced minister or general. His native genius alone and unaided, enabled him to found a compact kingdom, an invincible army and a practical and beneficent system of administration. (*Shivaji and His Times*, Jadunath Sircar, p. 304)

□

Shivaji and David and Goliath

Few times in history has a battle become 'a one-to-one fight between two warrior generals'. The biblical story of David and Goliath is one of them.

David and Goliath

The Philistine army had gathered for war against Israel. The two armies faced each other, camped for battle on opposite sides of a steep valley. A Philistine giant measuring over nine feet tall and wearing full armour came out each day for forty days, mocking and challenging the Israelites to fight. His name was Goliath. Saul, the king of Israel, and the whole army were terrified of Goliath.

One day David, the youngest son of Jesse, was sent to the battle lines by his father to bring back news of his brothers. David was probably just a young teenager at the time. While there, David heard Goliath shouting his daily defiance and he saw the great fear stirred within the men of Israel.

David approached Goliath, carrying his shepherd's staff, slingshot and a pouch full of stones.

David said to the Philistine, "You come against me with sword and spear and javelin, but I come against you in the name of the Lord Almighty, the God of the armies of Israel, whom you have defied."

As Goliath moved in for the kill, David reached into his bag and slung one of his stones at Goliath's head. Finding a hole in the armour, the stone sank into the giant's forehead and he fell face down on the ground. David then took Goliath's sword, killed him and then cut off his head.

Shivaji's Early Conquests

From 1646 to 1649, Shivaji Maharaj conquered the forts of Torna, Kondana and Purander. But the Adilshahi was too busy with conflicts with Aurangzeb who was the Mughal *subhedar* of the Deccan at that time. Day by day he became bolder and bolder and on:

15 January, 1656, Shivaji Maharaj captured Javali.

06 April,1656, Shivaji Maharaj conquered Raigad.

24 September, 1657, Shivaji Maharaj seized Supa.

30 April, 1657, Shivaji Maharaj looted Junnar.

24 October, 1657, Shivaji Maharaj took Kalian-Bhivandi.

05 January, 1658, Shivaji Maharaj vanquished Mahuli.

Aurangzeb's Advice to Adilshah

Aurangzeb would perhaps have attacked him with all his might, but Shah Jahan fell ill in Delhi. He hurriedly concluded a treaty with the Adilshahi government and left for Burhanpur on 20 March, 1658 to contest the Mughal throne.

Before leaving for Delhi, he gave some advice to Adilshah:

- *"Be diligent. Protect this country, expel Shiva. The son of a dog is waiting for an opportunity."*
- *"If you desire to enlist the services of the evil-intentioned and accursed Shivaji, who has trespassed upon some forts in the Konkan and raised the dust of rebellion, be sure to assign a* jahgir *in the Karnataka so that he will be far away from the imperial territory and will be unable to incite a revolt."*

With Aurangzeb out of the way, Adilshah decided to turn his attention to Shivaji. The *Tarikh-i-Ali* records it as follows:

"He (Shivaji) was extending the hand of repression and injustice like a greedy and hungry dog that does not feel satisfied with the bone it gets and wants more and was oppressing the faithful (Muslims) who were engrossed in prayer."

Appointment of Afzal Khan

After the king (Ali Adilshah) received the news—because

he thought that *'(the tree of) the observance of the Muhammadi faith (Islam) would not bloom without the water of his bloodthirsty sword and the thorny bushes of infidelity and polyethism (Hinduism) would not burn without the fire of the enemy-consuming sword.'*

Adilshah appointed Afzal Khan with 10,000 horsemen with the orders *"to fan the flames of anger and melt the balance of Shivaji's life in the crucible of destruction and to trample the harvest of his life under the hooves of horses."*

And cautioned: *"even if that black-faced infidel (Shivaji) sent a deceitful letter, he (Khan) must not listen to his false words of flattery and do nothing but fling the fire of death on the harvest of his life and pull down the fort of his life."*

Afzal Khan, on his part, bragged: *"Who is this Shiva? I will bring him back without even dismounting from my horse!"*

Who was Afzal Khan?

Afzal was a giant of a man, but not from an aristrocratic family. His father was a cook (*bhatari*). This inferiority complex made him ruthless, cunning and a back-stabber. His attitude can be gauged by the following delineation:

*Afzal Khan would describe himself thus:

'I am the killer of infidels and traitors, I stamp under my feet the idols.'

*Afzal Khan's seal boasted: *'If the great heavens desire, it may compare the greatness (piousness) of a pious man and the greatness (piousness) of Afzal then from the* japmala *(rosary) everywhere instead of the sound of Allah, Allah will emit the sound Afzal, Afzal.'*

Afzal, Shahaji, Sambhaji

It is worth noting that in 1638, Adilshah sent Afzal Khan against Bangalore. As usual, he was accompanied by a Hindu *sardar*, Kenge Hanuappa Nayak. On the way, they decided to attack Sira which was ruled by Kasturi Ranga. When Kasturi Ranga came to know of this attack on his kingdom, he realised that he was no match for the warriors of Islam. He asked for a meeting to decide the terms of the treaty. During the interview

Afzal Khan killed him alleging that Kasturi Ranga had intended to betray his trust.

Of course, this was a lie and as Sir Jadunath Sarkar puts it best: *'A defeated and submissive chieftain, away from his own army and unarmed, does not attempt murder in his enemy's den. He humbly seeks peace by every means in his power.'*

But far more chilling was the fact that Jijabai had an elder son named Sambhaji. He was a full-blown adult warrior in 1654 because he was part of the Kanakgiri siege and that without his father Shahaji. Chitnis Bakhar states that during the siege of Kanakgiri, Afzal Khan took a bribe from the ruler of Kanakgiri and did not send the promised re-enforcements to Sambhaji. In the ensuing one-sided skirmish that followed, Sambhaji was felled by a cannon shot.

As if this were not enough, the following passage will explain why the very mention of Afzal Khan raised the hackles of Shivaji and Jijabai: *In 1648, Mustafa Khan, an Adilshahi *wazir*, had laid siege to Gingee in Tamil Nadu. Shahaji was one of the *mansabdars* under his command. In the middle of the siege, Shahaji requested permission to withdraw with his force to his jahgir. Mustafa Khan refused. Adilshah asked Mustafa Khan to arrest Shahaji, But Mustafa Khan had pledged friendship with Shahaji and even sworn by his son's (Atish) head. He, therefore, diplomatically used Baji Ghorpade to arrest him when he was sleeping after a night of merriment.

Four factors contributed to Shahaji's arrest. His friction with Mustafa Khan, his increasing hold over the *mansabdars* in Karnataka, his own ambitions and aspirations. However, it would be correct to say that Shivaji capturing Kondana in 1647 was the proverbial last straw.

But what is significant here is that it was Afzal Khan who took Shahaji in chains from Gingee to Bijapur. In this interim period, Shivaji gave up the Kondana Fort and Adilshah took a benevolent view. Shahaji was put in prison and not killed.

But, Shahaji never forgot this insult by Baji Ghorpade and

Afzal Khan and wrote to Shivaji urging revenge *'if you are my true son'.*

- Further, a letter sent by Afzal Khan on 15th July, 1654 sheds light on his ruthlessness. The *mukadam* of Afzalpur had left his post and gone to another village during the sowing season. Afzal Khan reminded the *mukadam* that he regarded the farmers as his children and that the *mukadam* should go back to his village and oversee the cultivation. Afzal Khan also assured the *mukadam* all fairness and absolutely no harassment.

However, its his next statement he is shocking.

Afzal Khan warns the *mukadam*:

'if he does not resume his duties, he will hunt him down and cut him to pieces and crush him through an oil mill.' Further, he promises this gruesome punishment not only to the wrongdoer, but also to the families of all those who give him refuge.

*Before Afzal Khan set out from Bijapur, he spent a month enjoying in his harem. When it was time to go, he had all the 200 ladies of his harem killed so that they would not sleep with any other man.

Shivaji Picks up the Gauntlet

No wonder Shivaji said to his courtiers: *'I will not make a truce (with Afzal). Even after the truce, he will kill me as did my brother Sambhaji. Let us fight, whatever be the consequences. But no negotiations or truce.'*

Afzal Khan was a seasoned forty to forty-five-year-old general when set out from Bijapur in May 1659. Shivaji must have been about 29 year old. This was till then the largest army that invaded the infant *swarajya*. Afzal Khan as seen from the map did not march as the crow flies towards Raigad where Shivaji was based. He took a tortuous route eastward and desecrated the Vithoba temple of Pandharpur and the Tulzabhavani temple of Tulzapur. At Malvadi, he threw in chains Bajaji Naik Nimbalkar, the brother of Saibai the wife of Shivaji. Bajaji's ransom of 60,000 rupees was paid by Naikji Pandhre, mortgaging the *deshmukhi* of Phaltan with two Baniyas, Jaichandibhai and Babanbhai of Malwadi. After that he again turned westward and reached Wai. This he did perhaps because he was the *Mukasa* of Wai *pargana* in 1649.

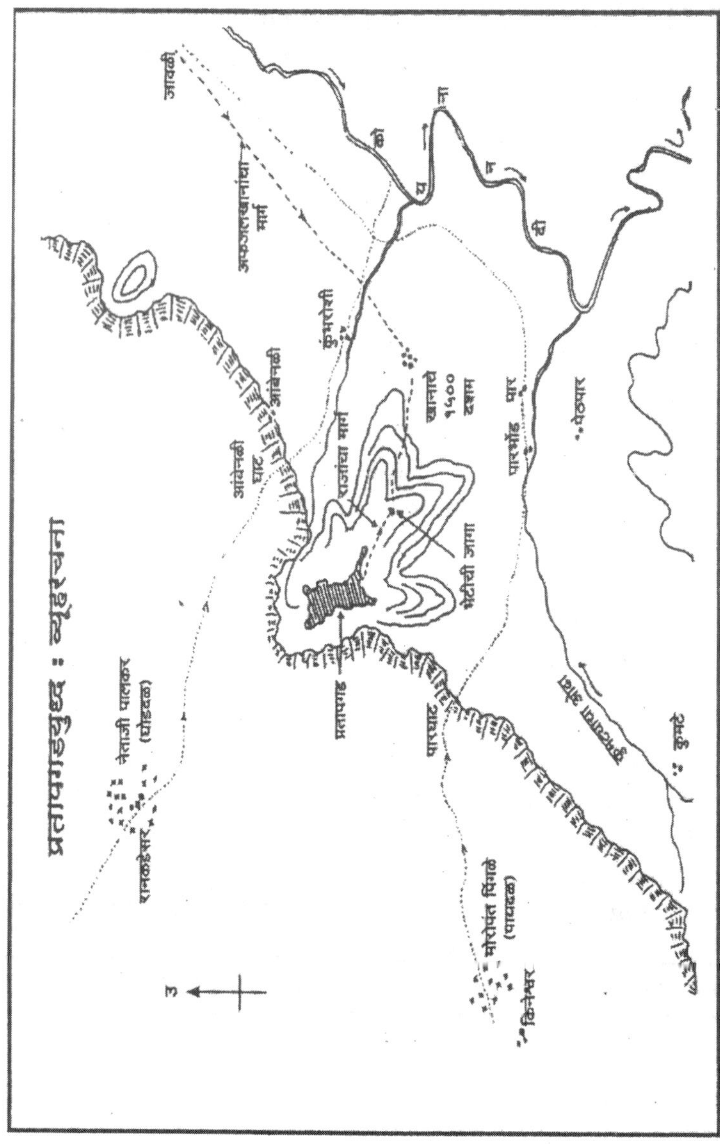

शिवकथाकार श्रीमान विजयराव देशमुखजी यांच्या आशीर्वादाने

The Adilshahi historian writes:

*"In a short time, the Khan made the country, seized by Shivaji, the riding ground (*jaulangah*) of his troops... The dust raised by the horses' hoofs of our heroes blinded the eyes of our enemies."*

But these acts of defilement only served to stiffen the Maratha resistance. A war of political liberation changed into a crusade.

On 16th June, 1659, Adilshah sent a *farman* to all the Deshmukhs of Maval.

"Shivaji out of thoughtlessness and evil propensities, has started troubling the followers of Islam. He has also plundered them...He has captured many forts in the royal territories... Therefore we have appointed Afzal Khan Muhamadshahi as subhedar *of the province and sent him with a formidable army...You should comply with whatever the Khan would write or tell you about the welfare of the state and royal policies. Whoever does not obey the orders of the Khan will have to face severe consequences."*

Kedarji Khopde and Khondoji Khopde joined the Khan.

Kanhoji Jedhe also received the *farman* which he took along with his five sons to Shivaji at Rajgad and said: *"I have come to fulfil the solemn oath that I made to Shahaji Maharaj. I place my* watan *at your feet."*

With this, he took some water and allowed it to flow to the ground as a symbolic gesture of renouncement. Other Deshmukhs also followed Jedhe's example.

Shivaji Invites Afzal Khan to Javali

As per the prevailing custom, Afzal Khan wrote a letter through his lawyer Krishna Bhaskar to Shivaji, the gist being:

"• *You have taken possession of many forts. (true)*
- *You conquered the 'mulk' belonging to Chandrarao More and the Siddi. (true)*
- *You have insulted, looted, humiliated the Muslims and destroyed mosques. (false)*
- *You sit on a throne, have your own seal and dispense justice. (true)*

- *Return the land to the rightfull owners or else I will attack you with my army of six kind of troops."*

The letter that Shivaji wrote is a classic example of diplomatic coaxing and flattery.

"• *You are incomparably powerful and strong. You have subdued all the chieftains of Karnataka. It is difficult for me to even look at you in the eye.*
- *Your existence has adorned the earth and you are free of all deceit.*
- *Come to Javali. It will incease my prestige. I will place my sword before you and hand over to you all the forts you have demanded."*

A Dutch letter dated 5th sent from Vengurla says his advisors suspected Shivaji of some cunningness and tried to dissuade him from going to the treacherous jungles of Javali. But the Khan was a megalomaniac and punished them. The nose of one was cut, the second was gibbeted on a spike and the third being Rustam-i-Zaman's brother was only rebuked.

The Meeting

The Khan agreed to meet Shivaji at Javali and camped at Par near Wai. Khan's emissary Krishna Bhaskar and Shivaji's emissary Gopinath Pantaji Bokil both decided the following conditions for the meeting on 10th November, 1659.

- The meeting would take place at the foot of Pratapgad.
- The shamiana would be put up by Shivaji.
- Both would be armed and accompanied by two armed attendants and envoys. Shivaji had selected Jiva Mahala while the Khan had Bada Sayed.
- Each would have ten bodyguards beyond the distance of an arrow shot.

As we saw before, the over-confident Khan had boasted that "he would capture Shiva without alighting from his horse."

Shivaji on the other hand, prepared for the duel in the following way:

- He wrestled with a *mavla* of the same size as Afzal. He even trimmed his beard so that the Khan would not be able to grip it.
- He found out who was to accompany the Khan and when he was told it would be Bada Sayed, who was an expert at *dandpatta* (long flexible sword), he selected the equally proficient Jiva Mahala.
- He wore an armour under his robe and a helmet under his turban.
- In his hand, he hid *wagh nakh* (tiger claws) and in his sleeve, he concealed a *bichwa* (dagger).
- And most important, he prayed to Goddess Bhavani.

The Khan reached the *shamiana* first. He was amazed at the rich trappings, but calmed down when he was told that the *shamiana* was a present for him from Shivaji. Shivaji entered the *shamiana* after some time. The Khan stood up, gave his sword to Krishna Bhaskar, spread out his arms in an inviting embrace and magnanimously said, "Oh son of Shahaji! Child! Rid yourself of pride in your wisdom and let me take your hand in mine. Come embrace me." As warned, Shivaji was amazed that his head barely came up to the Khan shoulders.

As per the then custom, they embraced first to the left, which went off well. Then they both swayed to their respective right. Afzal Khan encircled Shivaji's neck with his left arm and suddenly tightened his clasp in an iron grip while, with his right hand, he stabbed Shivaji with his dagger. Shivaji survived the attack, protected by the chain mail armour and his agility. He counter-attacked, passed his left hand round the Khan's waist and disembowled Afzal Khan with *wagh nakh* (steel claws). With his right hand, Shivaji plunged the *bichwa* into Afzal Khan's side. The wounded Khan relaxed his grip and came stumbling out of the *shamiana* shouting.

"Treachery! Murder! Help! Help!"

Krishna Bhaskar was the first to react. He unsheathed the sword that the Khan had given him and struck at Shivaji's forehead.

That incidentally was the only mark on Shivaji's body by which he was later identified by Jijamata after his escape from Agra. Bada Sayed was the next to attack Shivaji, but Jiva Mahala was quicker and he first hacked off Sayed's hand and then killed him.

Afzal Khan's palanquin-bearers tried to carry him away to safety, but Sambhaji Kavji beheaded the Khan and carried his head to Shivaji.

Shock and Awe

Soon after the slaying of Afzal Khan, Shivaji sped up the slope towards the Pratapgarh fort with his lieutenants and ordered cannons to be fired. This was a signal to his infantry, which had been strategically placed under the cover of the densely vegetated valley, to immediately attack Afzal Khan's forces. The carnage in the Bijapuri army was so terrible that *"all who begged quarters holding grass in their teeth as a mark of humility were spared. The rest (3,000) were put to the sword. The war booty was 60 elephants, 4,000 horses, 1,200 camels, 2,000 bundles of cloth and 10,000 in cash."*

With the death of Afzal Khan and the destruction of his army, the struggling Marathas emerged triumphantly from the critical danger they found themselves in. Shivaji's boldness, great daring, readiness to face risks even at great danger to his own life, his strategic planning and wise generalship, made a deep impression on friend and foe alike. In his first crisis, Shivaji showed that he was a born leader of men. In the struggle for an independent state, *Swarajya*, there was no turning back.

The killing of Afzal Khan made Shivaji the subject of awe all over India. (CS/SMP/103)

...was the most prominent action of the Great Sioux War of 1876.

In the Battle of Myeongnyan, on October 26, 1597, the Josepn Yi Sunsin fought the Japanese navy in the Myeongnyan Strait, near Jindo Island, off the south-west point of the Korean peninsula.

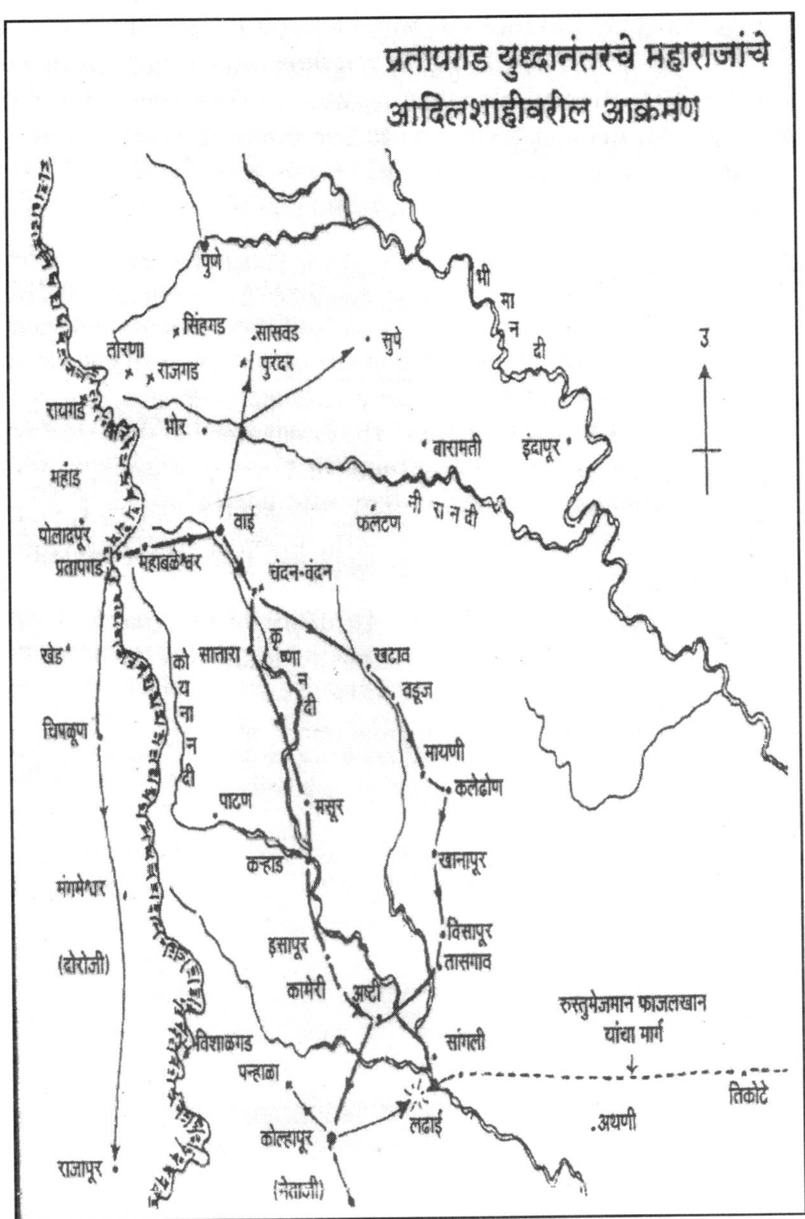

With 13 ships remaining from Won Gyun's disastrous defeat at the Battle of Chilchonryang, Admiral Yi Sunsin held the strait against a fleet of 133 Japanese warships and at least 200 logistical support Japanese. Many Japanese warships were sunk or disabled during the battle and the Japanese were forced to retreat. Given the disparity in numbers, the battle is regarded as one of Admiral Yi's most remarkable victories

The Battle of Rorke's Drift, 22-23 January. 1879, also known as the was a battle in the Anglo-Zulu War. Just over 150 British and colonial troops successfully defended the garrison against an intense assault by 3,000 to 4,000 Zulu warriors. The massive, bui piecemeal Zjjju attacks on Rorke's Drift came very close to defeating the tiny garrison but were ultimately repelled.

The Dunkirk evacuation, was the evacuation of Allied soldiers from rile beaches ... harbour of Dunkirk, France, between 27 May and the early hours of 4 June, 1940, because the British. French, and Belgian troops were cut off by the German army during the Battle of Dunkirk in the Second World War.

... total of 338,226 soldiers (198,229 British and 139,997 French) had been rescued by the hastily assembled fleet of 850 boats including the "little ships of Dunkirk", a flotilla of around 700 merchant marine boats, fishing boats, pleasure ... and Royal National Lifeboats Institution lifeboats—the smallest of which was the 14 ft 7 in (4.45 m) fishing boat Tamzine, now in the Imperial War Museum

The Battle of the Alamo (February 23 - March 6, 1836) was a pivotal event in me ... Revolution. Mexican troops under President General Antonio Loccz de ... Anna launched an assault on the Alamo Mission near San Antonio de Bexar ... day San Antonio. Texas. USA). All of Texian defenders were killed. ... by a desire for revenge, the Texloni defeated the- Mexican Army at the battle of San Jacinto, on 21 April, 1836, ending the revolution.

...ember the Alamo' became a war any of the ... army.

□

Shivaji and Thermopyle

Last Stands in History

Thermopyle
Custers last stand
Battle of Rourke's Drift
Battle of Myeongnyang
Wadborough Hill
Dunkirk evacuation in June 1940
Battle of Stow-on-the-World
Battle of the Alamo

Last Stand is a general military situation in which a body of troops holds a defensive position in the face of overwhelming odds. The defensive force usually takes very heavy casualties or is completely destroyed, as happened at Thermopylae or in Custer's Last Stand. Bryan Perrett suggests that although the majority of last stands throughout history have seen the defending force overwhelmed, on rare occasions, the outnumbered defenders succeed in their desperate endeavours and live to fight another day, and he lists the Battle of Rorke's Drift as one such engagement. Another example is the Battle of Myeongnyang.

Tactical Significance

A 'last stand' is a last resort tactic, and is chosen because the defending force realises the benefits of fighting outweigh the benefits of retreat or surrender. This usually arises from strategic or moral considerations, leading defenders to conclude that their sacrifice is essential to the greater success of their campaign or cause, as happened at the end of the Battle of Thermopylae.

The situation can arise in several ways. One situation is that retreat by the defending force would lead to immediate defeat, usually due to the surrounding geography or shortage of supplies or support, as happened to the Royalist infantry on Wadborough Hill after the Battle of Naseby.

Sometimes, rather than face annihilation at the hands of a pursuing victorious army, a rearguard will be tasked by the commander of the defeated army with hindering the advance of the victorious army. Even if the rearguard is destroyed in a last stand, its sacrifice may buy their commander time to disengage without losing the majority of his army as happened during the Battle of Roncesvalles or the Dunkirk evacuation in June 1940.

A last stand may also be the last pitched battle of a war where the position of the defending force is hopeless, but the defending force considers it their duty not to surrender until forced to do so, as happened to the last Royalist field army of the First English Civil War at the Battle of Stow-on-the-World.

At the End of a Siege

A siege may lead to a last stand by the defenders (see, for example, the Battle of the Alamo). Last stands at the end of sieges became less common after the Hague Conventions came in force. Before the 20th century, if a besieged garrison refused any offered terms of surrender and the attackers subsequently breached the defences, the defenders were only given quarter at the discretion of the attackers, something they were not likely to do if they perceived that by holding out, with no hope of relief, the defenders had needlessly squandered lives. Under the laws of war as they are now, "...it is especially forbidden... to kill or wound an enemy who, having laid down his arms, or having no longer means of defence, has surrendered at discretion; and to declare that no quarter will be given...", it is unlawful for an attacking force to kill a garrison if they attempt to surrender even if it is during the final assault on a fortified position.

Historical Significance

Last stands loom large in history due to the pull on popular imagination. Historian Nathaniel Philbrick argues:

Long before Custer died at the Little Bighorn, the myth of the Last Stand already had a strong pull on human emotions, and on the way we like to remember history. The variations are endless—from the three hundred Spartans at Thermopylae to Davy Crockett at the Alamo—but they all tell the story of a brave and intractable hero leading his tiny band against a numberless foe. Even though the odds are overwhelming, the hero and his followers fight on nobly to the end and are slaughtered to a man. In defeat, the hero of the Last Stand achieves the greatest of victories, since he will be remembered for all time.

Battle of Thermopylae

The Battle of Thermopylae was fought between Leonidas of Sparta, and the Persian Empire of Xerxes I over the course of three days 480 B.C., at the pass of Thermopylae ('The Hot Gates').

Vastly outnumbered, the Greeks held off the Persians for seven days in total (including three of battle), During two full days of battle, the small force of 7,000 led by King Leonidas I of Sparta blocked the only road by which the massive Persian army 1,00,000could pass. After the second day of battle, a local resident named Ephialtes betrayed the Greeks by revealing a small path that led behind the Greek lines. Aware that his force was being outflanked, Leonidas dismissed the bulk of the Greek army, and remained to guard the rear with 300 Spartans, who died with him, but only after killing 20,000 Persians.

Both ancient and modern writers have used the Battle of Thermopylae as an example of the power of a patriotic army of freemen defending native soil. The performance of the defenders at the battle of Thermopylae is also used as an example of the advantages of training, equipment, and good use of terrain as force multipliers and has become a symbol of courage against overwhelming odds.

Simonides composed a well-known epigram which was engraved as an epitaph on a commemorative stone placed on top of the burial mound of the Spartans at Thermopylae.

"Stranger, announce to the Spartans that here we lie, having fulfilled their orders."

I.e, Thermopylae asks the reader to make a personal journey to Sparta to break the news that the Spartan expeditionary force had been wiped out. The stranger is also asked to stress that the Spartans died 'fulfilling their orders'.

The Battle of Pavan Khind

When the citizens and court of Bijapur came to know of the killing of Afzal Khan and the routing of his army, there was first shock, followed by fear and later, rage. The whole Adilshahi began thirsting for revenge. But revenge meant sending an army to kill Shivaji and an army meant a general willing to pit himself against the cunning Shivaji. There was no one willing to pick up the gauntlet.

The Shivaji juggernaut was so all-conquering that he had subjugated Panhala on 28th November, 1659, the eighteenth day after the elimination of Afzal Khan. It was about nine o'clock at night when the fort came into Shivaji's possession and he was so excited that he inspected it by firelight.

It was in these circumstances that one of the courtiers advised Adilshah to depute Siddi Johar for the job. Siddi Johar was an Abyssinian slave who had usurped the fief of Kurnool, called himself the 'Lion of Kurnool' and defied the royal authority. Adilshah decided to be diplomatic. After all, desperate cicumstances needed desperate measures. He forgave Johar, gave him the title of Salabat Khan and an army of ten thousand and sent him against Shivaji.

Johar Lays Siege to Panhala

At that time, Shivaji was involved in a siege at Miraj. It is not clear whether Johar drove Shivaji to Panhala or Shivaji lured Johar to Panhala because it was at the periphery of his kingdom and fighting him there would lessen the chances of Johar devastating his kingdom. The siege started on 2nd March, 1660. Shivaji was sure that Johar would at the most have patience till the commencement of the monsoon. The monsoon normally made sieges impossible. Shivaji was not perturbed. After all, Panhala was well stocked for a siege of one year.

But, Johar turned out to be made of sterner stuff. He doggedly pursued with his siege, goading and cajoling his army to stay alert in spite of the torrential rains. He built shelters of palm fronds for his men. Shivaji sent small quick sorties, but they could not make a dent in the siege. Netaji Palkar, who was outside, did his best, but try as he might, he could not break the blockade.

At this point of time, two incidents occurred.

*Henry Revington, the crafty chief of the English trading station at Rajapur, was trying to clandestinely sell some mortar pieces to Adilshah. Normally, all the foreigners took a neutral stance of being traders and avoided getting entangled in local politics or war. But, Henry Revington with his colleagues, Gifford and Mingham, joined Johar and bombarded the Panhala fort with canons.

*Secondly, Shaista Khan was sent by Aurangzeb to subdue Shivaji. He reached Ahmednagar on 25th February, 1660 and Chakan on 21st June, 1660. Shivaji was now caught in a pincer attack.

Jijamata became so desperate that she decided to lead a force to try and break the siege of Panhala.

Shivaji Starts Negotiations

Shivaji now realised that rains would not make Johar budge from his positions and there was no chance of any help from outside. The only way out of the situation was to flee from Panhala. And he put into action a cunning plan of deception.

*He first deputed Gangadhar as his envoy to request Johar to plead on his behalf to Adilshah for mercy. Of course, Johar refused for he thought he had Shivaji trapped in a corner and there was no question of any kind of talks or mercy. He wanted an unconditional surrender. Shivaji then sent a message that he agreed to surrender and in keeping to the traditions, the time and conditions were negotiated.

*Shivaji had in his fort a barber named Shiva Kashid. He was of the same height and build as Shivaji himself. He also had a facial resemblance to Shivaji. Shivaji dressed him in his royal attire complete with jewellery and armaments and after prior intimation sent him in a palanquin to Johar's camp.

Shiva Kashid

While Shiva Kashid left by the main door of the fort, Shivaji along with about 600 members of the Bandal community left by a side exit (*chor dindi*) and proceeded towards Vishalgad, about 40 km north-west of Panhalgad. Since Shivaji had already intimated the Johar camp of his readiness to surrender, there was bound to be some amount of laxity in the siege.

Shiva Kashid's palanquin reached Siddi Jauhar's camp and there was great rejoicing. But, after some time, Fazl Khan, the son of the slain Afzal Khan, came into the tent. Now Fazl had seen Shivaji at Javali and, in fact, had accompanied Jauhar, only to take revenge of his father's death. He realised the person presenting himself as Shivaji was actually an imposter. He told Jauhar so. Jauhar's heart sank. His victorious moment turned to dismay.

To confirm the hoodwinking, news came that another palanquin was seen sneaking away in the direction of Vishalgad. In spite of realising that his three-month arduous siege had come to a naught, Jauhar gathered himself and sent his son-in-law Siddi Masud and Fazl Khan in pursuit of the real Shivaji fleeing towards Vishalgad. Shiva Kashid was killed by a spear thrust in his chest.

Jauhar thought even now all was not lost. After all, it was a dark moonless night and the skies were pouring. The ground was slushy and treacherous. The rivers were in flood and the path unbeaten. Shivaji had just a handful men and they were on foot while his men were on horseback and outnumbered them.

Baji Prabhu Deshpande

The way to Vishalgad was through a narrow ravine called 'Gajapur khind'. It was here that Baji Prabhu Deshpande, a Maratha *sardar* of Bandal Deshmukh, along with 300 soldiers, volunteered to fight to death to hold back the enemy to give Shivaji and the rest of the army a chance to reach the safety of the Vishalgad fort.

In the ensuing battle of Pavan Khind, Baji Prabhu Deshpande fought relentlessly. He was wounded but he held on and continued the fight until he heard the sound of cannon fire from Vishalgad, signalling Shivaji had safely reached the fort. He was at last killed by a Karnataki rifleman.

The result of this intense and heroic battle was the death of 300 Marathas and 1,286 of Adilshah's troops who were engaged in a fierce combat, allowing Shivaji to reach the fort safely on 13th July, 1660. (People from Bandal community were specially selected by Shivaji while escaping from Panhala for their knowledge of the region, rock-climbing skills and martial qualities. They had joined Shivaji in 1656, after the defeat of the Mores of Javali and within four years were willing to die for the cause.) Some of the notable people who died on that day were Siddi Halal and Siddi Wahwah. Though it was expected that Shivaji would reach Vishalgad in four hours, unknown to Shivaji and Baji Prabhu, Suryarao Surve and Jaswant Dalvi had laid siege to Vishalgad (on behalf of Johar) which Shivaji with his three hundred mavle had to fight through them. This took them sixteen hours instead of the expected four.

After the Afzal Khan episode, the sword of honour was given to the Jedhe family but after seeing the bravery displayed at the Panhalgad-Ghodkhind skirmish, the sword of honour was given to the Bandal family with the consent of the Jedhe family.

Siddi Jauhar, as expected, was a frustrated man. After the debacle at Panhalgad, he did not have the temerity to show his face to Adilshah and went directly to his fiefdom at Kurnool. Two months later, he committed suicide.

It is interesting to—Pavan Khind was a 'fight to finish' and ended positively with the objective of Shivaji reaching Vishalgad to fight another day being achieved. More importantly, there was no treachery.

□

Shivaji and Guerrilla War

During the medieval period, many important battles were fought in India. Some of them totally changed the course of Indian history. A few of them are enumerated below:

1. *First battle of Tarain: The first battle of Tarain was fought between Muhammad of Ghor and Prithviraj Chauhan of Delhi in 1191 A.D. In this war, Muhammad was defeated, and his plan of Indian conquest was put on hold.*
2. *Second battle of Tarain: The second battle of Tarain was fought between Muhammad of Ghor and Prithviraj Chauhan of Delhi in 1192 A.D. In this battle, Muhammad was victorious. With this victory, he could establish the Turkish Empire in India.*
3. *First battle of Panipat: The first battle of Panipat was fought in 1526 A.D. It was fought between Ibrahim Lodi of Delhi and Babur of Kabul. In this war, Babur defeated Ibrahim Lodi and founded the Mughal Empire in India.*
4. *Battle of Kanwa: The battle of Kanwa was fought in 1527 A.D. It was fought between Mughal emperor Babur and Rana Sang Ramsingh of Mewar. In this war Babur was the victor. This victory established the Mughal supremacy over the Rajputs.*
5. *Battle of Gogra: The battle of Gogra was fought in 1529 A.D. It was fought between Babur and Nasrat Shah of Bengal. It resulted in the elimination of Afghan threat to the Turkish power in India for the time being.*
6. *Battle of Chausa: The battle of Chausa was fought in 1539 A.D. between Mughal emperor Humayun and Sher Khan.*

In this battle, Humayun was defeated. It facilitated Sher Khan to march on to Delhi and Agra.

7. *Battle of Bilgram: The battle of Bilgram or Kanauj was fought between Humayun and Sher Khan. Sher Khan defeated Humayun in this battle in 1540 A.D., removed the Mughal Empire from India and established the Sur Empire in its place.*
8. *Second battle of Panipat: The second battle of Panipat was fought in 1556 A.D. It was fought between Akbar and Hemu. In this war, Akbar defeated Hemu and re-established Mughal rule in India.*
9. *Battle of Haldighati: The battle of Haldighati took place in 1574 A.D. between Akbar and Rana Pratap Singh. The defeat of Rana in this war gave supremacy over Rajasthan to Akbar.*
10. *Third battle of Panipat: The third battle of Panipat was fought between Ahmad Shah Abdali of Afghanistan and the Marathas in 1761 A.D. In this war, the Marathas were routed. This war facilitated the rise of British power in India.*

Tactics and Strategy of War

Shivaji does not figure in any great battle. He waged no great battle but he was a master of guerrilla warfare.

The Spartans of 500 B.C. were the precursors to the Templer Knights 1000 A.D..

Sparta was a military state and emphasis on military fitness began virtually at birth. Shortly after birth, a mother would bathe her male child in wine to see whether the child was strong. If the child survived, the father brought it before the Gerousia. If they considered the child to be puny or deformed, it was thrown into a chasm. Even in death, marked head stones were granted only to soldiers who died in combat.

The Templer Knights were the most skilled and committed to the Christian military orders of the Middle Ages. The Templer Knights with their distinctive white mantles and red cross were the officially-endorsed fighting unit of the Catholic Church.

It was these Templer Knights who fought with the Muslim Hashasins under Saladin during the Crusades and reached a stalemate. The Hashasins were trained in combat, linguistics and strategies under '*furusiya*' the Islamic warrior code. After being drugged, they were taken to a paradise-like garden filled with attractive young maidens and beautiful plants in which these *fidais* would awaken. There they were told by an old man that they were witnessing their place in paradise and should they wish to return to this paradise, they should serve the Hashasin cause.

The tactics and strategy of war learned by the Muslims during the Crusades were further improved by the Mongols, like Chenghis Khan. The Mongol army was trained, organised and equipped for mobility and speed. Each Mongol warrior would travel with multiple mares, allowing him to quickly switch to a fresh mount as needed. The Mongols could eat, sleep and shoot arrows while riding. They usually rode mares whose milk they drank, when food was low. But, in a real crisis, they also slit a vein in the neck of the horse and drank its blood. The invention of the stirrup allowed them to turn and shoot arrows or throw spears backwards. They had learned to time the release of their arrows when all four of the horse's hoofs were on the ground. These Mongols were the ancestors of the Mughals.

It is these Mughals combined with the Rajputs whom Shivaji defeated time and again with his meagre resources.

What is further surprising is that a recent programme on History Channel ranked the Rajputs above the Centurions in combat. Yet Shivaji and his comparatively untrained Marathas were able to defeat the combined Mughal-Rajput armies consistently The reason was that Shivaji resorted to guerrilla warfare.

Guerrilla Warfare

For example, as we saw above, Afzal Khan came with an army of 10,000, but Shivaji engaged him in a man-to-man contact. He drew him into his lair where a trap was laid for him and disembowelled him. His army of 10,000 with cannons and elephants came to a naught against the mountainous terrain of Javali. We have an incisive commando raid.

After the debacle of the Adilshahi at Javali under Afzal Khan on 10th November, 1659 and again at Panhala on 13th July, 1660 under Siddi Jauhar, Aurangzeb ordered Shaista Khan to attack Shivaji as per the Mughal-Adilshahi accord.

Amir ul Umra Nawab Bahadur Mirza Abutalib aka Shaista Khan, with his better equipped and provisioned army of 1,00,000 that was many times the size of the Maratha forces, seized Pune on 9th May, 1660. Shaista Khan was almost thirty years older than Shivaji.

Shaista Khan

Cosmo de Garde describes Shaista Khan's camp:

"This proud Khan had with him two sets of field tents each carried by three hundred elephants. When he set out from the first, the other was fitted in the place where he would stop that day. Each set of tents contained houses for him. The tent in which he used to give an audience was sixty feet in length and thirty feet in breadth, and its covering was supported by ropes of iron, fifteen feet in height. This was followed by bed chambers, private rooms, gardens full of flowers, conveyed in millions of vases and so delicious that one who saw them would doubt whether they were natural." CS/VD/359

He had set up his residence at Lal Mahal, Shivaji's palace, in the city of Pune, amidst tight security. Shivaji planned an attack on Shaista Khan during the month of Ramzan when Muslims fast during the day, abstaining from food and drink from sunrise to sunset. But after sunset, they indulge in a heavy meal which results in a deep slumber.

An Incisive Commando Raid

Shivaji planned a raid on Shaista Khan on 5th April, 1663. It was the anniversary of the coronation of Badshah Aurangzeb. The celebrations on that day were bound to be on a grander scale. Drums were beaten at 6.00 a.m., 9.00 a.m., 12.00 noon, 3.00 p.m., 6.00 p.m. 12.00 midnight, and 3.00 a.m. Shivaji, along with 2,000 of his trusted men, started from Pune region. He distributed about 1,600 mavles in two groups under Peshwa Moropant Pingle and Sarnobat Netaji Palkar, along the way from Katraz to Kariyat Maval. Baji Sarjerao had horses ready for Shivaji's escape.

Shivaji infiltrated the Mughal camp in Pune with 400 men using a wedding party as cover. Some of the intruders included the brothers Chimnaji and Babaji, Koyaji Bandal and Chandji Bandal. Since the Mughal army also consisted of Maratha soldiers, it was difficult for someone to distinguish between Shivaji's Maratha soldiers and the Maratha soldiers of the Mughal army.

After overpowering and slaying the palace guards, 25 Marathas broke into the mansion by breaching an outer wall. They approached Shaista Khan's quarters. The cooks, who were preparing the pre-dawn meal, heard the noise and reported it to Shaista Khan, but he brushed aside their suspicions with words 'must be a mouse'. But one of his maid-servants proved alert enough to extinguish the lamps. Chimnaji, whom Shivaji had taken along for his excellent night vision, identified Shaista Khan. Shivaji then personally confronted Shaista Khan in a face-to-face attack and severed three of his fingers with his sword (in the darkness) as he fled through an open window. This scuffle was in the dark and for the first time resulted in Shivaji's mavles hacking and killing women. So ferocious was the attack that one guard was chopped into so many parts that he had to be buried in a basket. By now the guards were alerted. Shivaji and his mavles came out shouting, "*Gamin, gamin*", i.e. enemy, enemy, creating utter confusion. Some came out and berated the guards: "Is this the way you perform your duty?" Still others came out and told the drummers that Shaista Khan had ordered them to play the drums louder.

Chaos

In the general chaos, Shivaji escaped towards Sinhgad. But to confuse the pursuers, he had tied flaming torches to the horns of bulls and herded them towards Katraz Ghat, misleading the enemy once again.

Shaista Khan narrowly escaped death and lost his three fingers as a brief letter from Phillip Giford, dated 12th April 1663, reads.

"Yesterday a letter arrived from the Raja to Raoji Somnath giving an account of how he himself had with choice 400 men gone to Shaista Khan camp. There upon some pretence (which he did not insert in his letter), he got into the tent to salaam *and presently slew all the watch, killed Shaista Khan's eldest son Abdul Fath, his son-in-law, twelve of his chief women, 40 great persons attending him, the general Shaista Khan (whom he thought dead, but since years he lives), wounded six more of his wives, two more of his sons and after all this, returns, losing but six men and forty wounded."* Mehen/256

An angered Aurangzeb, who learnt of this news on his way from Lahore to Kashmir, transferred Shaista Khan to distant Bengal '...a hell, well stocked with bread.'

The *Alamgir Nama* has a brief entry on the 5th of May, 1663:

"Amir-ul-Umra, i.e. Shaista Khan, Raja Jaswant Singh and others had been appointed to extirpate the accursed Shivaji. Now he with the audacity and malignity made a night attack on the Amir-ul-Umra's camp. As this incident occurred due to the negligence of that grandee, it became the cause of the Emperor's displeasure and he decided to dismiss Amir ul Umra from the subhedari of the Deccan." mhn/256.

Shaista Khan came with a force of one lakh, but Shivaji engaged him with only 400 men. Another 500 waited outside the camp. So, instead of a great battle, we have an incisive commando raid.

The Strategy and Tactics a Guerrilla

Guerrilla warfare is a form of irregular warfare and refers to conflicts in which a small group of combatants including, but not limited to, armed civilians (or 'irregulars') use military tactics, such as ambushes, sabotage, raids, the element of surprise, and extraordinary mobility to harass a larger and less-mobile traditional army, or strike a vulnerable target and withdraw almost immediately.

The strategy and tactics of guerrilla warfare tend to focus around the use of a small, mobile force competing against a larger, more unwieldy one. The guerrilla focusses on organising in small units, depending on the support of the local population, as well as taking advantage of terrain more accommodating of small units.

Tactically, the guerrilla army would avoid any confrontation with large units of enemy troops, but seek and eliminate small groups of soldiers to minimise losses and exhaust the opposing force. Not limiting their targets to personnel, enemy resources are also preferred targets, all of which is to weaken the enemy's strength; to cause them eventually to be unable to continue the war any longer, and to force them to withdraw.

"Why does the guerrilla fighter fight? We must come to the inevitable conclusion that the guerrilla fighter is a social reformer, that he takes up arms responding to the angry protests of the people against their oppressors, and that he fights in order to change the social system that keeps all his unarmed brothers in ignominy and misery."

—Che Guevara

Cosmo de Guarda describes Shivaji's strategy as follows:

"Shaista Khan was surprised that Shivaji never suffered any loss; and this was due to the execution of the order that they should never (permit themselves to) be caught but should do what they could without risk and having done so, should immediately leave with all the booty, for Shivaji said that he prized the lives of his solders above all the interests of the world. They delivered an assault, robbed and killed whom they met and by the time the Mughals were mounted, not a single enemy was seen and they stood stupefied, listening only to the complaints of the wounded, robbed and despoiled." mhn/248

The *Chitnis Chronicle* describes the strategy further:

"The Mughal army should be immobilised by capturing its supplies, grass, wood and provisions. Why should we go out and

seek battles? We should cut off his supplies and exhaust him. We should (lure and) destroy him in some difficult place. We should let him besiege some fortress and then beat him there. Thus, by several cunning means, we should wear him out." mhn/248

San Tzu

As San Tzu put it pithily:

'All warfare is based on deception. The army should not only be physically strong, it should also be mentally strong, i.e. esprit de corps. When able to attack, we must seem unable; when using our forces, we must seem inactive; when we are near, we must make the enemy believe we are far; when we are far, we must make him believe we are near. Hold out baits to entice the enemy, feign disorder and crush him. The good tactician plays with his adversary as a cat plays with a mouse.'

Most kings and generals did not take part in the actual battle preferring to direct it from a nearby hillock. If they did take part they did so astride an elephant. Shivaji was the only king who led from the front astride a horse and with a sword in hand. The attacks on Afzal Khan and Shaista Khan which made the whole of Hindustan look at him in awe saw him put his own life in peril.

Spies are the Eyes and Ears of a Kingdom

Much of the credit of Shivaji's escapades goes to the spies. Chanakya says, "Spies are the eyes and ears of a kingdom."

San Tzu says:

"Spies should be paid well for everyday costs in time, money and lives. So, neglecting the use of spies is nothing less than a crime against humanity. Spies are recruited from worthy men who have been degraded from office, criminals who have undergone punishment, favourite concubines who are greedy for gold, men who are aggrieved at being in subordinate positions or have been passed over in promotions. Such men should be approached with rich presents. They should never be known to anybody nor should anybody know them."

Chhatrapati Shivaji used spies to carry out espionage for raids on Surat, Burhanpur, Jalna and from the escape from Agra. Notable among them were Bahirji Naik, who carried out espionage for Shivaji and commanded a force of 3,000, but besides Bahirji, not a single name is known. The spies were made up of wandering communities, like Ramoshis, Dhangars, Bhils, Lamans, Vanzara, Pardhi, Mahadeo Koli and Masan Jogis. Shivaji also used his spy network to find a way out of tricky situations like Panalgad.

When he sacked Surat, he knew from his spies how much wealth each merchant had and where it was stored. He also knew who were the philanthropists and who were the cut-throat businessmen. Shivaji paid all his men well, but the spies were paid the highest rate. The spies came from the wandering gypsy-like communities and were looked down upon, but Shivaji gave them the title of Naik.

Guerrilla Warfare in the 20th Century

The tactics of guerrilla warfare were used successfully in the 20th century by—among others—Mao Zedong and the People's Liberation Army in the second Sino-Japanese War and Chinese civil war; Fidel Castro, Che Guevara and the 26th of July movement in the Cuban revolution; Ho Chi Minh, Vo Nguyen Giap, Viet Cong and select members of the Green Berets in the Vietnam war; the Liberation Tigers of Tamil Eelam in the Sri Lankan Civil War; the Afghan Mujahideen in the Soviet war in Afghanistan; George Grivas and Nikos Sampson's Greek guerrilla group EOKA in Cyprus; Paul Emil von Lettow-Vorbeck and the German Schutztruppe in World War I; Josip Broz Tito and the Yugoslav Partisans in World War II; and the antifrancoist guerrilla in Spain during the Franco dictatorship; the Kosovo Liberation Army in the Kosovo war; and the Irish Republican Army during the Irish War of Independence. Most factions of the Taliban, Iraqi insurgency, Colombia's FARC, and the Communist Party of India (Maoist) are said to be engaged in some form of guerrilla warfare, as was, until recently the Communist Party of Nepal (Maoist).

On 10th May, 1978, the then Minister of state for Planning and Urban Development, Mohan Dharia is known to have said that in his interactions with Ho Chin Minh of Vietnam, the latter had confirmed that in their prolonged struggle against the mighty American army, the people of Vietnam had studied the war tactics of Shivaji and not only were they inspired by it, they had successfully put it to good use. (*Maharashtra Times*)

□

Shivaji and the Sack of Surat

Nadir Shah's Invasion in 1739

The great Iranian warrior Nadir Shah invaded India in 1739. Despite superiority in number, the Mughal forces were easily defeated by the Persians. Nadir entered Delhi with Mohommad Shah as his hostage on March 11. When a rumour broke out that Nadir had been assassinated, some of the Indians attacked and killed the Persian troops. Nadir reacted by ordering his soldiers to plunder the city. During the course of one day (March 22), 20,000 to 30,000 Indians were killed by the Persian troops, forcing Mohammad Shah to beg for mercy, Nadir Shah agreed to withdraw, but Mohammad Shah was forced to hand over the keys of his royal treasury and surrender the Peacock Throne to the Persian emperor.

The Peacock Throne thereafter served as a symbol of Persian imperial might. Among a trove of other fabulous jewels, Nadir also gained the Koh-i-Noor and Darya-ye-Noor diamonds (Koh-i-Noor means 'Mountain of Light' in Persian, Darya-ye-Noor means 'Sea of Light').

Persian troops left Delhi at the beginning of May 1739. Nadir's soldiers also took with them thousands of elephants, horses and camels, loaded with the booty they had collected.

The plunder seized from India was so rich that Nadir stopped taxation in Iran for a period of three years following his return.

The Sack of Surat

It is pertinent to compare the maturity shown by Shivaji

during the sack of Surat with the general massacre by Nadir Shah.

The raid on Surat is known for strategic movement of cavalry by Shivaji through enemy's terrain covering almost a distance of 300 km.

As Shaista Khan was in Maharashtra for more than three years, the financial condition of the state was dire. So, to improve his finances, Shivaji planned to attack Surat.

Surat was 'the greatest emporium of the Orient and the richest jewel of the Mogol'. It was situated about 20 kms from the mouth of the Tapi river. It was a key Mughal power centre, and a wealthy port town which generated a million rupees in taxes. In the centre of the town was a fort which had only four towers and inside there were mere wooden platforms for guns. In short, it was neither protected by art nor nature. Virji Vora, a Hindu, was worth eight million and was considered to be the richest merchant in the world. Similarly, Haji Zahid Beg-a-Muslim was not very far behind. The defences of the city were poor, as the local commander Inayat Khan appointed by Aurangzeb was corrupt and instead of the stipulated force of nearly 5,000 soldiers, he had appointed only 1,000 and pocketed the rest of the money himself.

Besides the local Hindus and Muslims, the city was inhabited by Dutch, English, Portuguese, Turks, Armenians, Persians, Arabs, Parsees and Jews.

In keeping with his usual cunningness, Bernier states that 'Shivaji pretended during the march that he was a Raja going to the Mughal court'.

On the night of 5th January, 1663, Shivaji arrived and camped 8 kilometres from Surat. Guarda says:

"At the break of dawn, he divided his men into four parties and ordered them to attack on all sides shouting his name which was the most formidable battery. He was not mistaken for it was heard with the same terror, as is excited when a furious tiger enters a herd of cows. But no one was in the peril of life, for it was the strict order of *Sevagy* that unless resistance was offered, no one should be killed, and as none resisted, none perished.' (STGM/ HS SARDESAI, p. no. 420)

The Loot

Thevenot believed that:

'This Raja carried away in jewels, gold and silver to the value of thirty French millions.'

Carre going into great detail about this incident, averred:

'Seva-jy coolly gave his orders even as he liked, as if it were a town that had already recognised his authority and none came forward to oppose him. The sack lasted for three days and three nights. Sevagy then left Surate as easily as he had entered it having found in a single city all the wealth of the east and securing such war funds as would not fail him for a long time.' (STGM/HS SARDESAI, p. no. 420)

Francois Valentine says:

'Everything of beauty existing in Surat was that day reduced to ashes and many considerable merchants lost all that the enemy had not plundered through this terrible fire narrowly escaping with their lives.' (STGM/HS SARDESAI, p. no. 420)

Bernier asserted:

"He rushed into the place, sword in hand and remained nearly three days, torturing the population to compel a discovery of their concealed riches. Burning what he could not take away, Sevagy returned without the least opposition, laden with gold and silver to the amount of several millions." (STGM/HS SARDESAI, p. no. 420)

"...Surat was under sack for nearly three days, in which the Maratha army looted all possible wealth from Mughal and Portuguese trading centres. However, there was an attempt on the life of Shivaji by the emissary sent by the Mughal *sardar*. Shivaji had to complete the sacking of Surat before the Mughal Empire at Delhi was alerted and could not afford to waste much time in attacking the British..."

Justification of the Loot

During those days, it was customary for the Mughal soldiers to appropriate four-fifth of the booty for their own use: remitting only one-fifth of the rest to the Khalifa. According to the Mohammedan law, there cannot be peace between a Mohammedan king and infidel states, and it is the Muslim king's duty to slay and plunder in them. So, in India, it had been the practice of Mohammedan sovereigns to mercilessly squeeze the people wherever they invaded. Thus, looting became an integral part of the war strategy. Shivaji justified his spoiliation by saying, as he did to the Mughal governor of Surat, "Your emperor has forced me to keep an army for the defence of my people and country. That army must be paid by his subject." (STGM/HS SARDESAI, p. no. 443)

All this loot was successfully transported to Maharashtra before the Mughal Empire at Delhi could get the news of the sacking of Surat. This wealth later was used for building Sindhudurg, a sea-port which Shivaji built from scratch.

It is possible to stun the world around you by doing something extraordinary. If the Afzal Khan episode gave Shivaji a pan-Indian popularity, his bravado of looting Surat made him an international celebrity where he was discussed in all the Muslim and a substantial part of the Christian world. With this act the son of a *jahgirdar* formally declared war on the Mughal Emperor Aurangzeb.

The Assassination Attempt

During the sack of Surat, a young man came under the pretext of paying obeisance to Shivaji and then suddenly, whipping out a concealed dagger, he tried to stab Shivaji in the chest. A Maratha bodyguard, that stood before the Rajah with a drawn sword, struck off the assassin's hand with one swipe. With a second blow, he cracked the assassin's skull. But so great was the force of the assailant's momentum that he was not stopped. His mutilated and bleeding body banged into Shivaji and the two fell on the ground together. Seeing the blood on Shivaji, his followers thought that he had been killed, and the cry ran through the camp for a general massacre. But Shivaji rose up from the ground and forbade any massacre.

He was not indiscriminate in his plunderer is proved by a statement of Bernier: *'I forgot to mention that during the pillage of Sourate, Seva-Gi, the holy Seva-Gi respected the inhabitation of the Reverend Father Ambrose, the Capuchin missionary. 'The Frankish Padrys are good men', he said, 'and shall not be molested.' He spared the house of a Delale or Gentile broker of the Dutch, because he assured that he had been very charitable while alive. The dwellings of the English and Dutch likewise escaped his visits.'*

Shivaji and the Great Escape

The World's Great Escapes

Throughout history, prisoners of all sorts have gone to unheard of lengths to free themselves from confinement, whether it be a house arrest of Shivaji or a life sentence in Alcatraz. Most have failed, but a significant minority has tasted freedom through patience, skill, and in, many cases, sheer luck.

Some of the world's great escapes have been described herewith.

A-Single Person Escapes

1. *Mary Queen of Scots (1561) escaped from Lochveleen Castle).*
2. *Rev. John Gerard (1597) and the Earl of Nithsdale (17150) escaped from the Tower of London.*
3. *Gionomo Casinova (1755) escaped from Venice.*
4. *Henry Brown, a slave (1816), escaped in a box 3×3 feet from North Carolina.*
5. *Buffalo Bill aka William Cody (1860) escaped from the American Indians.*

B-Group Escapes

1. *Dalai Lama (1959) escaped when China attacked Tibet.*
2. *Frak Morris with the brothers Clarence and John Angling escaped from Alcatraz, 1962.*
3. *Numerous escaped across the Berlin Wall till, 1989.*

4. *Daring resque of 255 hijacked hostages from Entebbe. (1976).*
5. *The Great Escape (Germany)*

War Camp Stalag Luft III

The Great Escape, as it came to be known, was a mass escape attempt from the prisoner-of-war camp Stalag Luft III located near the Polish town of Zagan.

The purpose-built camp was opened in April 1942 and the Germans considered it to be practically escape-proof. Prisoners were fairly well treated and the Geneva Convention of 1929 regarding treatment of prisoners-of-war was followed.

The camp housed mainly British and American airmen whose planes had crashed on Axis territory. The Germans generally captured prisoners with the words 'For you, the war is over.' However, it was the sworn duty of all captured military personnel to continue to fight the enemy by surviving, communicating information and escaping. Many of the prisoners at Sagan were re-captured escapees. The Germans believed that security at the new camp was so tight that it would be impossible for anyone to escape.

Escape Committee

It was realised early on that for any escape attempt to succeed, it had to be well planned and organised. The Prisoners at Zagan, therefore, established an escape committee. Chief escape officer was Squadron Leader Roger Bushell, a former escapee who had been recaptured several times. He was known as 'Big X'.

The committee decided to build three tunnels and the plan was to effect the escape of at least 200 prisoners. The tunnels were given the code names 'Tom', 'Dick' and 'Harry'. There were two main problems to be considered—How to get rid of the dirt that was dug away and how to prevent the tunnels from collapsing.

In order to prevent the tunnels from collapsing, they had to be shored up with wood. The prisoners used bed-boards for this task and as the tunnels grew longer and more wood was needed, many prisoners found themselves sleeping uncomfortably on beds with little support. Some even converted their beds to hammocks.

Getting rid of the dirt from the tunnels was problematic because the earth removed was a different colour to the earth around the camp. One method used was to construct long bags which could be filled with earth then hidden in the trouser legs. A cord around the neck would open the bags, thus releasing the earth on a patch of ground that was being dug or cultivated by another prisoner. Those dispersing the dirt in this way were known as 'Penguins'. More than 100 tons of earth was disposed of in this way. Another method involved filling empty Red Cross boxes, placing the boxes in the middle of a group of men who would then gradually bury the earth.

Other important members of the escape committee were the forgers who made maps and forged papers and the tailors who made civilian clothes out of blankets and other materials that were scrounged and altered uniforms.

The Escape

The discovery of the tunnel 'Tom' was a major blow to the escape committee and all tunneling had to be suspended for a time to avoid further detection. Eventually, 'Harry' was completed and the night of the Great Escape was planned for 24th March, 1944, a moonless night. Lots were drawn for the 200 places and maps, papers and disguises were completed.

On the night itself, all allotted escapees took up positions in hut 104. It was planned that the escapees would leave the camp in stages. Everyone was very nervous and tense, a situation that was made worse by the discovery that the tunnel was around 10 feet short of the woods. This meant that the tunnel exit was on the path of a perimeter guard. By the time that a decision was made on how to signal when the coast was clear, it was around 10 p.m. Further delays were caused by some men panicking in the tunnel.

By 4 a.m., it was clear that it would be impossible for all 200 men to escape and the decision was made to close the tunnel at 5 a.m. At around 4.45 a.m., a shot was heard at the tunnel exit. The tunnel had been discovered.

76 men had escaped through the tunnel. Of the remainder, those that were found waiting their turn in hut 104 were sent to the cooler—the camp name for the solitary confinement cells.

The Outcome

Of the 76 men who escaped, three made it home to the UK, 23 were recaptured and sent back to Sagan. Hitler personally ordered the execution of the other 50 men.

The commandant of Stalag Luft III, Lindeiner, was court-martialed by the Gestapo for not preventing the escape.

Morale among the prisoners was low when the executions became common knowledge and few were keen to attempt further escape attempts.

Although only three men managed to reach safety and 50 men were murdered, the escape caused havoc among the Germans. Thousands of police, Hitler youth members and soldiers were diverted from wartime duties to search for the escapees.

Urns containing the ashes of the 50 who were executed were brought to the camp. British airmen constructed the memorial to commemorate their deaths.

Mirza Raje Jaisingh

The failure of Shaista Khan and the sack of Surat had made a mockery of the Mughal Empire. Aurangzeb decided to send his best Hindu and Muslim generals to the Deccan and subjugate Shiva.

On 3rd March, 1665, Mirza Raje Jaisingh reached Pune with a force of 4,00,000 cavalry. There were 500 elephants, 3 million camels, 10 million oxen of burden."

He had three large cannons called Abdulla Khan, Fatah Lashkar and Haleli. Each cannon was dawn by 40 yokes of oxen. Niccoli Manucci, an Italian, was in charge of the artillery. (stgm / sar /345)

Under him were deputed Diler Khan, Daud Khan, Raja

Raisingh Sisodia, Raja Sujan Singh Bundala, Kirat Singh, Mulla Yahia Navayat, etc.

On reaching the Deccan, he formed a coalition of all the enemies of Shivaji, namely the Portuguese, Raja of Jawahar, Baji Chandra Rao, Ambaji More of Jawli, Mankoji Dhangar, Afzal Khan's son Fazl Khan, Atmaji and Kahar Koli, the Raja of Chanda, etc.

The Seige of Purander Fort

On 30th March, he reached Purander which was 4 kms south of Saswad and rose 800 m above its base and 1,500 m above sea level. It was a double fort with a sibling in the east, called Vajragad. They were separated by the Bhairav Khind. Purander Fort has a *machi* or ledge running round it at an height of 700 m, i.e. the citadel or Balle Killa was 100 m above the *machi*. On the west of the Bhairav Khind were the two towers (*buruj*). the *kala buruj* and the *safed buruj*. The commander of the fort was Murar Baji.

The accompanying figure shows how Jaising's forces had surrounded Purander-Vajragad. Jaisingh decided to take Vajragad first. Diler Khan was put in command and directed all his efforts to dragging the monstrous guns to the top of the steep and difficult hill. It took three days to raise the cannon Abdulla Khan and mount it opposite Vajragad. In another three and a half days a second cannon Fateh Lashkar was taken there. So too the cannon Haleli.

On 13th April, Diler Khan 's division stormed the tower and drove the Marathas into an enclosure behind it. Next day the victorious Mughals pushed on to the inner enclosure and tried to capture it. The garrison oppressed by their fire capitulated in the evening.

Jaisingh disarmed those who were captured but wisely allowed them to return home in order to tempt the garrison at Purander—by this leniency, to surrender instead of fighting to the last. They were also chivalrously given robes of honour. In Jaisingh's words, "Vajragad was the key that would unlock Purander." During this time, Netaji Palkar with his flying columns was trying to break the siege. To put in Khafi Khan's words, "The surprises of the enemy, their gallant successes, attacks on dark nights, blocking of roads and difficult passes, burning of jungles, made it very hard for the imperialist to move about. The Mughals lost many men and beasts."

Vajragad—the Key that Would Unlock Purander

After the capture of Vajragad on 16th April, Diler Khan sat down before Purander like grim death, 'doing in one day what could not be achieved elsewhere in one month'.

May came and the Maratha garrison began to throw down lighted naptha oil, leather bags full of gunpowder bombs and heavy stones, which effectively stopped the adavance of the Mughals.

The Mughals now decided to build a tower of wooden logs (*damdama*). This was complete by 30th May and cannons were mounted on it. Once these cannons started firing from a superior height, the Maratha garrison evacuated the *Kala Buruj* and retired to the trenches behind it. Thus, five towers and one stockade of the lower fort fell into the hands of the Mughals.

A few days later, Murar Baji took 700 men and attacked Diler Khan who was trying to climb the hill with 5,000 Afghani troops. There was severe fighting at close quarters. Murar Baji and his *Mavles* had already killed about 500 Pathans when he spied Diler Khan. Along with 60 desperate *Mavles*, he made a beeline towards Diler. The Khan was shocked at this suicidal and maniac charge. In admiration of Murar Baji's matchless courage and loyalty, he asked him to yield and promised him his life and a high post under him. Murar indignantly refused and was going to strike at Diler when the latter shot him down with an arrow. Three hundred *Mavles* fell with him and the rest retreated to the fort, preparing to fight another day. Undismayed by their leader's fall, they continued their struggle saying:

"What though one Murar Baji is dead? We are all as brave as he, and we shall fight with the same courage."

The Fall of Purander

But now the fall of Purander was imminent. However, Shivaji

with his usual foresight had started negotiations much earlier.

The first letter that Raghunath Pandit took to Jaisingh stated:

"It would be better for the Mughal army to invade Bijapur rather than suffer hardships in this hilly region."

To which Jaisingh answered:

"Do no faith in your hills. God willing, they will be trodden flat under the hoofs of the imperial army. If you want to save your life, place in your ear the ring of servitude to the imperial court."

On 9th June, Raghunath Pandit secured an assurance from Jaisingh that:

'Shivaji may come for to visit Jaisingh, and may return back safely, regardless of the outcome of the visit.'

On 10th June, news came that Shivaji was approaching Purander. Jaisingh sent his secretaries Ugrasen and Udairaj to warn Shivaji that *'he should come if and only if he was willing to surrender all his forts'.*

On hearing this, Shivaji said:

"I have entered imperial service.

My forts will be added to the imperial domains."

Jaisingh himself writes:

"The fire of fighting could be seen from my place. Shiva(ji) immediately on arriving offered to surrender Purander. I answered 'This fort has already been conquered through the exertions and valour of the Imperial forces In an hour, in a minute, the garrison of the fort would be put to the swords. If you want to make a present to the Emperor, you have many other forts for the purpose. He (Shivaji), begged for the lives of the besieged garrison. So, I sent Gazi Beg with a servant of Shivaji to Diler Khan and my son to take possession of the fort and let off its inmates."

The Treaty of Purander

The terms of the treaty agreed to were:

1. That twenty-three of Shivaji's forts, large and small, of which the revenue was four lakh hons (about twenty lakh rupees) should be annexed to the empire.

2. Twelve forts belonging to Shivaji, one of which was Rajgad and the standard revenue of which was one lakh of hon, should be held by Shivaji on condition of service and loyalty to the imperial government.
3. His son Sambhaji, however, would be created a *mansabdar* of five thousand. He would serve under the Emperor or the Viceroy of the Deccan. The words used by Shivaji were, "I have not the face to wait on the Emperor. I shall send my son as His Majesty's servant and slave, and he will be honoured with the rank of a commander of five thousand horses, the same number of troopers, each man with two horses. Wherever the high *Diwan's* office assigns him a *jagir* on condition of payment for six months, it will be accepted by me. He will constantly attend on duty."
4. As for himself, Shivaji requested, "Exempt me from *mansab* and service... wherever in your Deccan wars, I am appointed to any duty, I shall, without delay, perform it."
5. Shivaji's request with regard to Bijapur territory. If out of Bijapuri territory of which Bijapuri tal Konkan yielding four lakhs of hons is in my possession, some *mahals* of Balaghat, of which the total revenue is nine lakhs of hons, be granted to me and an imperial *farman* be issued to the effect that if at any time, the imperial command is sent for the conquest of Bijapur, the above *taluqs* would be left to me, then I agree to pay a tribute of forty lakhs of hons to the emperor, by instalments of three lakhs every year." (SMP, p.g.150)

Shivaji Agrees to Go to Agra

In the treaty of Purander, Shivaji had expressly stipulated that he was not to be called upon to enter Mughal military service (*mansab*) nor to attend the imperial court. Yet, Jaisingh could convince Shivaji to go to Agra to meet Emperor Aurangzeb for his fiftieth birthday in June 1666.

The reasons perhaps were as follows:

1. Manucci, who was in Jaisingh's camp at that time (January 1666), states: "Diler Khan, being habituated to treachery, wished several times to kill Shivaji and to this intent, solicited Raja Jaisingh to take his life or at least give him leave to do so. He would assume all responsibility and see that the Raja was held blameless. He said that the Emperor would rejoice at such a result." SMP/156
2. Jaisingh plied him with hopes of high reward and used a thousand devices (as he wrote in his letters) to induce him to go to Agra. The *Maratha Chronicles* assert that Jaisingh gave Shivaji hopes that after his visit to the Emperor, he was likely to be sent back as the Viceroy of Mughal Deccan with sufficient men and money for the conquest of Bijapur and Golconda. Because all generals so far from Aurangzeb to Jaisingh had failed, only a born general and renowned conquerer like Shivaji ccould be expected to succeed. Maybe Jaisingh even promised to request that the Emperor should order the Siddi, now an imperial servant, to cede the Janjira fort to him.
3. The third reason, though far-fetched, was that perhaps Shivaji thought he could form a grand all-India alliance of the Hindus and Rajputs to take on the might of the Mughals.

Shivaji's Entourage

Shivaji's visit to Agra and escape is well described in the Rajasthani letter No. 21, Parkaldas to Kalyandas Diwan, Tuesday, 29 May, 1666.

"You have asked me to let you have details regarding Shivaji's visit here. Well, he has come alone with only one hundred retainers and his escort numbers from two hundred to about five hundred and fifty men in all. Among the latter, one hundred are mounted on their own horses and the rest are bargirs *of the Paga (that is, mounted on horses supplied by their master).*

When Shiva(ji) rides out in a palki, *many foot men wearing costumes like the Turks, big like Khadauts go before him. His flag is orange and vermillion coloured, with golden decorations stamped on it. In his train the camels are few and are only meant for carrying luggage, so they are very heavily loaded. The Banjaras are hundred (each with a pair of pack-oxen). All his high officers have* palkis *to ride in and, therefore, he carries many* Palkis *with him.*

At sight, Shivaji's body looks lean and short. His appearance is wonderfully fair in complexion and even without finding out that he is, one does feel instinctively that he is a ruler of men. His spirit and manliness are apparent. He is a very brave, high-souled man and wears a beard. His son is nine-years old and very marvellously handsome in appearance and fair in complexion.

Shivaji has come with a rather small contingent, but with great splendour of equipment. A large elephant goes before him carrying his flag. An advance guard of troopers also precedes him. The horses have gold and silver trappings. The Deccani infantry too marches before him. In this manner, he comes to Agra, with the whole of his contingent moving with great care and pomp. He has two female elephants saddled with Haudas *which follow him. A* Sukhpal *(a sort of* Palki *with a dome-shaped top) is also carried before Shiva(ji). Its poles are covered with silver. His* Palki *is completely covered with silver plates, but its legs and pegs are covered with gold plates. With this splendour, he has come."*

Shivaji Arrives in Agra

The Rajasthani letters written by the officers of Kumar Ramsingh, during the visit of Shivaji to Agra are our best source of information on this episode. Shivaji was to have arrived in Agra on the 11th of May.

"A letter written by Kumar Ramsingh to Shiva(ji) has been sent, saying that he should arrive here (Agra) on 11th May and have his audience of the Emperor.

"The Emperor has ordered that the Kumar and Fidai Khan should go out on one day's march from Agra and welcome Shiva(ji) in advance and conduct him (to the capital). So, he will be presented at the court on 11th May."

Actually, Shivaji arrived at Malukchand's *Sarai* on 11th May, Kumar Ramsingh sent Girdharilal to receive him.

Ramsingh and Shivaji Meet

On 12th May, Shivaji rode out towards Agra. But due to Ramsingh being on guard duty, Shivaji was received neither by high officials who should have been deputed to do so, nor with marks of ceremony and respect due to Shivaji's status. The Rajasthani letter dated 15th May, 1666 states: "On 12 May, it was Ramsingh's turn for guard duty (round the royal palace). Hence, he rode out directly from there to welcome Shiva(ji) by advancing (towards his camp) and sent Girdharlal Munshi ahead, to go, mount Shiva(ji) and conduct him towards Agra. The Munshi went, mounted Shiva(ji) and brought him by the route of the Daharara garden. The Kumar and Mukhlis Khan, however, went by the path of the eunuch Firoza's garden where the Kumar's camp was situated. When Kumar learnt that Shiva(ji) was coming by the path of the Daharara, he deputed Dungarwal Chudhari and Ramdas Rajput to conduct Shiva(ji) to the other path (of Firoza's garden). These two went and guided Shiva(ji) to the Kumar's encampment through the marketplace. Further on was the Nurgani garden where the two met each other."

The Historic Interview

The Rajasthani records should be considered as most authentic for a version of Shivaji's interview with Aurangzeb. The records state: "The Kumar and Mukhils Khan were conducting Shivaji (to the court). In the meanwhile, the Emperor had left the Diwa-i-Am (public audience hall) and was sitting in the select audience hall (Diwan-i-Khas popularly known as ghusat khana). Shiva(ji) went to the latter place. The Emperor ordered Asad Khan Bakhshi to bring Shiva(ji) forward and present him for audience. Asad Khan conducted him to the Emperor. Shivaji presented one thousand *mohars* and rupees two thousand as *nazar* and rupees five thousand as *nisar* (propitiatory alms). Sambhaji, the son of Shivaji, was then presented to the Emperor and he offered five hundred *mohars* and rupees one thousand as *nazar* and rupees two thousand as *nisar*. Shivaji was made to stand in the place of

Tahir Khan, in front of Rajal Rai Singh. The Emperor neither talked with him nor addressed any word to him.

It was the Emperor's birthday and the betel leaves (pan of the ceremony) were distributed to the princes and the nobles and, hence, Shiva(ji) too got one. Next, the *khilats* (robes) for the occasion were presented to the princes, Jafar Khan and Raja Jaswant Singh. At this, Shiva(ji) became sad and fretful; he flew in to a rage and his eyes were filled with tears. The Emperor noticed it and told the Kumar, *"Ask Shiva(ji) what ails him."*

Then the Kumar came to Shiva(ji)'s side and the latter said, *"You are seeing, your father has seen, your* padishah *has seen what a man I am, and yet you have deliberately kept me standing so long. I cast off your* mansab. *If you wanted me stand, you should have done so according to the right order of precedence."*

He then and there turned his back and began to walk away violently from his place in the line of noblemen. Then the Kumar seized his hand, but Shiva(ji) wrenched it away, came to one side and sat down. The Kumar followed him to that place and again tried to persuade him, but he would not listen, and cried out, *"My death day has arrived. Either you will slay me or I shall kill myself. Cut off my head and take it there if you like, but I am not going (back) to the Emperor's presence."*

"As Shiva(ji) would not be persuaded, the Kumar went up to the Emperor and reported (the case) to him. The Emperor ordered Multafat Khan, Aquil Khan and Mukhlis Khan to go, console Shiva(ji), invest him with a *khilat* and then bring him to the throne. The three nobles came and asked Shiva(ji) to wear the *khilat* but he replied, *"I refuse to accept a* khilat. *The Emperor has purposely made me stand below Jaswant Singh. I am such a man and yet I am deliberately kept standing. I decline the Emeror's* mansab. *I will not be his servant. Kill me. Imprison me if you like, but I will not wear the* khilat." So, they returned and reported all this to the Emperor, who ordered the Kumar to take Shiva(ji) with himself to his own residence and persuade him. The Kumar took Shivaji along with himself to his residence, seated him in a private chamber and reasoned with him, but he would not listen. After keeping him for about half an hour with himself, the Kumar dismissed Shiva(ji) to his own camp."

People's Reaction

The news of Shivaji's daring behaviour spread rapidly. It sent a thrill of admiration among the common people. The Rajasthani letter dated 29th May, 1666 says: "*The people had been praising Shivaji's high spirit and courage before. Now that after coming to the Emperor's presence, he has shown such audacity and returned such harsh and strong replies, the public extols him for his bravery all the more.*" After Shivaji returned to his camp, the nobles expressed their disapproval of Shivaji's conduct to the Emperor. According to Rajasthani records, they said "*Shivaji committed such a gross breach of etiquette and yet Your Majesty overl*ooks." On the same day, Kumar Ramsingh spoke persuasively to Shivaji, Shivaji said, "*Very well, I shall send my son with my brother (Ramsingh). Let him take up service and he will serve the Emperor. I too shall go after two days or so.*"

On the 13th of May, when Kumar Ramsingh went to the court, he was asked by the Emperor about Shivaji. He replied, "*He has fever, so he will not come today.*" The same day Ramsingh took Sambhaji, the son of Shivaji with him. The Emperor gave Sambhaji one *saropa*, one jewelled dagger and one pearl necklace.

The letter of the 15th of May, quoted above, further says, "*Shivaji has not attended the Emperor's audience since then until today (15th May). Raja Jaswant Singh, Jafar Khan, Begum (Jahanara) and the other nobles of the hostile party told the Emperor, "Shiva(ji) displayed such rudeness and contumacy and yet Your Majesty overlooks it. The report of it will spread from country to country. So, for some days, he (Shivaji) was not taken to the court.*"

Aurangzeb's Designs against Shivaji

The continued representations made by the nobles to the Emperor against Shivaji were now having their effect. According to the letter of 16th May, Begum Jahanara, the minister Jafar Khan and Rajah Jaswant Singh, again spoke to the Emperor. They said, *"Who is this Shiva(ji) that in your royal presence he committed such contumacious and insolent acts, and yet Your Majesty passes over them? In this way, many* Bhumias *(land-holders) will come here and act rudely. Then how will administration continue? The news will reach every country that such a Hindu audaciously did every kind of rudeness and all will act similarly."*

Raja Jaswant Singh said, *"He is a mere* Bhumia, *and he came here and displayed such violence and discourtesy, and Your Majesty overlooks it. It is Your Majesty's concern, but he ought to be punished."* The Begum Saheb too, urged strongly, *"He has looted Surat, carried away Shaistaa Khan's daughter and done such rudeness in the royal presence. How far is it proper to wink at it?"*

"Then it came into the Emperor's heart or the policy was discussed (opinion was formed after discussion) whether to kill Shiva(ji), to confine him in some fortress or to keep him in prison. He (Emperor) ordered Siddi Fulad to take Sivaji(ji) to Radandaz Khan's house."

Shivaji in Real Danger

Shivaji was now in real danger. It was Ramsingh who took immediate action to ward off the danger by standing security for Shivaji. The letter of 16th May referred to above, states, "The news of it (Emperor's design against Shivaji) reached Kumar Ramsingh. He, therefore, went to Muhammad Amin Khan's house (The *Bakshi* or the Paymaster General) and argued with him, saying, *"The Emperor has decided to slay Shiva(ji) but he has come here under a guarantee of safety from my father. So, it is proper that the Emperor should first kill me, call up my son and kill him too, and only after slaying us put Shiva(ji) to death or do what he likes to him."* So, Muhammad Amin Khan reported Ramsingh's exact words to the Emperor, who replied, *"Ask the Kumar if he will stand security for Shiva(ji), that if he escapes or does any mischief, he will be responsible for the loss, and whether he will sign a security bond."*

Shivaji's Offer

The Rajasthani letter of 29th May, 1666 states:

"Shivaji has written a petition to the Emperor and submitted it through Muhammad Amin Khan as his mediator, in which he states, '*If Your Majesty restores to me all my forts taken by you, I shall pay you two crores of rupees. Give me leave to depart. I shall leave my son here in your service. I shall take every oath that Your Majesty may ask for. I have come here in firm faith in Your Majesty's (promise). My devotion is strong. Wherever you plan a campaign, summon me and I shall attend before you. Your Majesty is now engaged in a war with Bijapur. Let me go there, fight and die, and thus serve Your Majesty.*"

Aurangzeb's Reaction

The Emperor replied, *"He (Shivaji) has gone off his head because of my leniency towards him. How can he be given leave to depart for home? Tell him firmly that he must not visit anybody."* Hence, strong patrols have been posted round Shiva(ji)'s residence.

In the first week of June, Shivaji was once again in danger of losing his life. The Rajasthani letter of 7th June states: "The Emperor first sent a message to Shiva(ji). *"Hand over all your forts to me. I will restore your mansab. Call your nephew too. I will give mansab to him also."* Shivaji's reply was "I do not want any mansab. I have no control over the forts." The Emperor was very much displeased over this reply and asked Fulad Khan and the artillery "Go and kill Shiva(ji)." Message was sent to Kumar Ramsingh. "It is learnt that men are coming from your place and, thus, you are collecting force." Kumar submitted in reply, "I was ordered to proceed to Kabul, hence, I had called them. But now as the orders for going to Kabul have been cancelled, I have sent instructions accordingly. No one is now coming from there. I am a hereditary servant of the empire.... Shivaji too is a servant of the throne. If Your Majesty wishes so, you may imprison him or kill him." The Begum Saheb too urged, "Mirza Raja is your noted servant and on his assurance (*qaul*) Shiva(ji) has come here. He is also your servant.... If you will kill him, no one will have any faith in your (*qaul*)." So, that day, due to the Begum Saheb's intervention, the Emperor let the matter rest. Jafar Khan, Muhammad Amin Khan and the Begum were favourable to Shiva(ji). While Jaswant Singh was instigating the Emperor against Shiva(ji). The Emperor is demanding the forts, but Shiva(ji) is not ready to do so and says, "The forts are not in my control..."

It is said that one day Shiva(ji) came to Kumar Ramsingh and told him, "I had thought that your word carried much weight in the empire, but here you are requesting so much to the Emperor for me and he is not accepting anything. Hence, you should tell the emperor, 'Here is Shiva(ji). He is no longer under my care. If you so wish, you may kill him.' Then Kumar replied, 'I will not leave you like that.'

Two days ago, the Kumar ordered our men to be on guard only with Shiva(ji) and so they also are there now.

The above letter records the wild rumours which began to circulate in Agra about Shivaji's prowess. It was rumoured that Shivaji used to fly in the air about fourteen or fifteen arms distance from the ground. Shaista Khan was said to have written to the Emperor that if Shivaji were not put to death, he (Shaista Kahn) would turn *faqir* (mendicant). It was also rumoured that when Aurangzeb went for prayers to the mosque, police patrols were posted at various places and strictest possible security measures were undertaken. Of course, these were all rumours. But it shows the reaction of the population of Agra to the presence of Shivaji in their midst.

9th June, 1666

The Kumar's men too are keeping watch over Shivaji. The Kumar is saying. "The Emperor has put him under my control too. If he escapes or kills himself, I shall have to answer for it." So, the Kumar goes and personally keeps a watch on Shivaji's bed, while Tejsingh and his Rajput retainers, Arjunji, Sukh Singh Nathawat and other Rajput Thakurs patrol on all sides of him.

Shiva(ji) has sent word to the Kumar, "You have given the Emperor a bond of security for me. You now take it back. Let the Emperor do what he likes with me." The Kumar is trying to reassure and reason with Shiva(ji) but the latter would not listen. The Kumar further said to him, "A letter has been written to Maharaja (Jaisingh). You be patient and see what he has to say in reply (about you)."

On Friday, 7th June, Shivaji sent away all his servants, saying, "Go away. Let none remain with me here. I shall stay here alone. Let me be killed if they wish to kill me." His men struck their tents and loaded them for departure and then sent word to Kumar, "We are going away." But Ramsingh has reassured his (Shivaji's) servants, telling them, "Do not stay there, but come away thence and live in the garden behind my camp." In this way, Shiva(ji)'s muddle is going on and nothing has yet been settled.

"Shiva(ji) has directly sent word to the Emperor through Siddi Fulad Khan "I have given congee to my troops, I beg that they may be given passports to go away."

Evidently, the Mughal government feared that Shivaji might escape from Agra. Otherwise, the following letter of 12th June, 1666 would not have become necessary.

"Orders have been received. If ever Shiva(ji) were to escape from Agra and to Manjabad Paragana, he is detained." Instructions have accordingly been issued in all the villages.

Rajputs Praise Shivaji

In the same letter is recorded a conversation among the Rajputs about Shivaji. It is as follows: "One day when Ballu Shah, Tejsingh and Ramsingh were sitting together, Mahasingh Shekhawat said, "Shivaji is very clever; he speaks the right word, after which nobody need say anything more on the subject. He is a good Rajput and we have found him just what he was reported to be. He tells us such appropriate things marked by the characteristic qualities (or spirit) of a Rajput that if they are borne in mind, they will prove useful some day." Then addressing

Tejsingh, Mahasingh said thus, "It is sheer destiny that has brought him here. But when there were four good men of high rank like you round Mirza Raja, why did you not speak to him (against sending him into Aurangzeb's claws)? You should have reasoned with and dissuaded the Maharaja." Tejsingh replied, "The Maharaja listens to only one man, his secretary Uderaj. Who else would venture to counsel him?"

Kavindra Kavishwar

Obviously, he was Kavindra Paramanand whose biographical poem on Shivaji known as *Surya Vamsha Puran* or *Shiva Bharat* is one of the early sources for the life of Shivaji. He seems to have accompanied Shivaji to Agra. The Rajasthani letter of 22nd July, 1666 states: "*Shivaji has a poet entitled Kavindra Kavishwar to whom he gave a male elephant, a female elephant, one thousand rupees in cash, a horse and a full suit. He has promised to give one more elephant to the poet, and he is going to give it. Shivaji is saying, 'The Emperor does not grant me a passport, or I might have gone out of Agra, as I had entered it, on horseback, I will now give my horses and elephants and will sit down here as a mere* faqir.'

Shivaji's Escape

Parkaldas writing to Kalyandas, states, "Since four days prior to the flight of Shiva(ji) there was much strictness about guards. Once again the Emperor ordered that Shivaji be killed, but soon after he changed to keeping him in the *haveli* (house) of Raja Vithaldas. Shivaji used to know all about these orders (of the Emperor). Hence, to ascertain facts, Shivaji came to Kumar's camp. Kumar, however, did not meet him. Hence, after waiting there for some time, Shiva(ji) went away. Later Kumar said, "Tell the imperial guards not to let Shiva(ji) come to my residence. Let them tell him that the Emperor has forbidden even to his coming to my place." The Kumar forbade Shiva from coming to him. Then Shiva(ji) realised that evil (day) is near, so he escaped.

"*On the inner patrol were Ram Krishan Brahmin, Jiva Joshi, Srikishan Upadhyaya and Purohit Balram, all four from Kumar's staff. Outside the* deorhi *(gate), there was the guard of musketeers. All around the place were Minas on guard duty. There were imperial troopers on duty. Finally, there were the military men posted there by Fulad Khan. There were also Rajput Thakurs (posted by Kumar) all around there. But that he escaped in spite of all these guards is a matter of real astonishment."*

Parkaldas to Gegeraj, Monday 3rd September, 1666

"When the day was four Gharis *old, the news came that Shiva(ji) had escaped... Even when a thousand men were on the* chauki. *On that day, none could ascertain at what time he had fled, in what manner and during whose period of watch. Later, after some guessing, it was concluded that he had escaped by crouching in the baskets slung from poles which used to come in and go out. The news of Kumar's reduction of* mansab *and prohibition to the audience and the fort reached us later in the afternoon."*

It could only mean that Aurangzeb either did not believe in the story of baskets or did not desire that the collusion or the negligence of the officials guarding Shivaji be exposed. It must also be noted that while Ramsingh's *mansab* was reduced, no action was taken against Fulad Khan whose men too were responsible for keeping watch on Shivaji.

One need not suppose that Shivaji allowed himself to get into the basket. He was not a man to allow him to be bottled up and rendered helpless. Sambhaji, a lad of nine, must have been seated in the basket while Shivaji might have accompanied the bearers disguised as a servant.

After leaving Agra, Shivaji moved with his son rapidly to Mathura. Leaving Sambhaji in charge of a Brahmin family of Mathura, Shivaji left Mathura. According to *sabhasad*, Shivaji went to Benares and then moving through Gondwana, and the Golconda territory, arrived at Rajgad. The contemporary historian Bhimsen Saksena states that Shivaji's return route lay through Allahabad, Benares, Gaya, Jagannath Puri and the territory of Golconda.

According to Sir Jadunath, Shivaji's route must have been

Mathura, Allahabad, Bundelkhand, Gondwana and Golconda. (however, no historian can still be sure.)

The escape of Shivaji caused a life-long regret to Aurangzeb, *"See how the flight of the wretched Shiva, which was due to carelessness, has involved me in all this distracting campaign to the end of my days."*

A = The failure of the great escape of Stalag luft III shows that it is perhaps easy to escape from a prison but difficult to reach your destination of safety.

B = Shivaji arrived in Agra as a guest with pomp and glory of about 1,500 retainers. He planned an escape leaving almost nobody behind. Shivaji was a prisoner with his son and planned the escape himself.

C = After the escape, he covered a minimum distance of 1,600 miles in 40 days. This was during August when the monsoon is at its height and the rivers are flooded.

D = He had obtained travel papers for his men. Assuming he used them himself, the start he had was only of about 14 hours.

E = His disguise was so perfect that when he reached Rajgad, no one could recognise him.

F = His master stroke was in leaving his son Sambhaji behind in Mathura and declaring him to be dead.

□

Shivaji and Troy

Helen

The Trojan Horse is a tale from the Trojan War, as told in Virgil's Latin epic poem The Aeneid. *The events in this story from the Bronze Age took place after Homer's* Iliad, *and before his* Odyssey. *It was the stratagem that allowed the Greeks finally to enter the city of Troy and end the conflict.*

The cause of the Trojan War can be traced all the way back to the courtship of Helen. Helen was stunningly beautiful. Many Greek princes courted her for marriage. Her step father feared that trouble from rejected suitors would follow Helen and her groom. To insure Helen's safety, her stepfather made all the men who wanted to be her husband, swear an oath to protect Helen and her chosen groom. Helen chose King Menelaus of Sparta.

When Paris abducted Helen to Troy, all the Greek princes were bound by the oath they had taken when they were courting her. Since it was their duty to help Menelaus recover Helen, the Greeks sent one thousand ships to Troy to recover Helen; hence the saying, 'A face that could launch a thousand ships.'

Agamemnon and Menelaus

Agamemnon, brother to Menelaus, led the Greek forces. The fleet of one thousand ships was delayed off the Greek coast. The winds continued to blow west, the opposite direction the Greeks needed to sail to Troy. Agamemnon consulted an oracle which told him to sacrifice his daughter to Artemis and the winds would turn.

He complied with the oracle, an act for which his wife never forgave him. After the sacrifice, the Greek ships headed east for Troy.

For the first nine years of the war, the Greeks attacked the surrounding cities and outlying areas to cut off the food supply from Troy. The city of Troy itself had huge walls which were built with the help of the gods. It was not until the tenth year that the Greeks attacked the city of Troy itself.

The war was not going well for the Greeks at this point.

The Greeks learned from a captive Trojan prophet that four things had to happen if they were to conquer Troy.

1. *Achilles' son Neoptolemus, who the Greeks had abandoned on an island several years earlier, had to join the fight.*
2. *The Greeks had to use the bow and arrow of Hercules.*
3. *Bones of Agamemnon's grandfather had to be brought to Troy.*
4. *A wooden statue of Athena had to be stolen from the Trojan citadel.*

The Greeks, through the great energy and cunningness of leaders like Odysseus, were able to accomplish all four of the tasks.

Odysseus

Odysseus came up with a plan to get into the city. With Athena's help, the Greeks built a large horse out of the wood from their ships. They hid their warriors on the inside of the horse and waited for the Trojans. The Greeks pretended to sail away. When the Trojans approached the horse, a Greek solider named Sinon met them. He claimed the Greeks had attempted to sacrifice him, but he escaped. He claimed the horse was an offering to Athena and that they should take the horse into their city to get Athena's protection, the Trojans pulled the horse into their city as a victory trophy. That night the Greek force crept out of the horse and opened the gates for the rest of the Greek army, which had sailed back under cover of night. The Greek army entered and destroyed the city of Troy, decisively ending the war.

Trojan Horse

Metaphorically a 'Trojan Horse' has come to mean any trick or stratagem that causes a target to invite a foe into a securely protected bastion or space.

The Trojan priest Laocoön guesses the plot and warns the Trojans, in Virgil's famous line 'Timeo Danaos et dona ferentes' (I fear Greeks even those bearing gifts). which became known as 'beware of Greeks bearing gifts'. Helen of Troy also guesses the plot and tries to trick and uncover the Greek men inside the horse by imitating the voices of their wives

Inside the horse, Anticlus would have answered, but Odysseus shut his mouth with his hand. King Priam's daughter Cassandra, the soothsayer of Troy, insists that the horse would be the downfall of the city and its royal family. She too is ignored, hence their doom and loss of the war.

We shall compare this ten-year siege with a typical commando raid by Shivaji.

Kondana

As we shall see later by the treaty of Purander on June 1665, Shivaji had conceded twenty-three forts to Raja Jai Singh. One of them was Kondana.

After he escaped from Agra on 19 August, 1666, Shivaji was not eager for war with the Mughals. He wanted peace for some time to organise his government, make a revenue settlement of his lands, repair and provision his forts and consolidate and extend his power on the western coast at the expense of Bijapur and the Siddis.

Legend says that one day Jijamata while at Rajgad was staring far away in the distance when she saw the outlines of Kondana Fort as perhaps she had seen every day. But that day she called for her son Shivaji and demanded that he conquer Kondana and make it a part of *swarajya*.

Shivaji was a keen judge of human nature and always could pick the right man for the right job. This time he picked Tanaji Malusare.

Tanaji Malusare

Tanaji was one of Shivaji's closest friends; the two had known each other since childhood. It is said that Tanaji at that time was busy preparing for his son Raiba's wedding ceremony. He came to invite Shivaji and Jijamata along with his family to come to the marriage ceremony and bless the couple. Naturally, Shivaji had to think of someone else for the attack on Kondana. But Tanaji came to know of the proposed raid on Kondana. He went up to Shivaji and demanded that he be put in charge of the Kondana raid. Shivaji reminded him that his son's marriage ceremony was a month away. It was then that Tanaji said the now-famous words:

"First let's celebrate the wedding of Kondana and then we will celebrate Raiba's wedding."

Kondana is situated 20 kms south-west of Pune. It is 1320 m above sea level. The fort is shaped like the blade of an axe and is three kms along the perimeter. There are two convoluted and steep paths which lead to two fortified gateways—the Pune darwaza in the north-west and the Kalian *darwaza* in the south-east. The only side that was comparatively less heavily guarded was the west side of the hill but it was sheer cliff. The fort was manned by 1,200 Rajputs under the command of Udaybhan Rathod.

Monitor Lizard (Ghorpad)

The *mavles* started from Rajgad but must have split on the way and converged at the foot of Kondana. There Tanaji must have taken the locals, like Ramoshis, Dhangars, Bhils, Lamans, Vanzara, Pardhi, Mahadeo Koli, and Masan Jogis in confidence and probed various possibilities of scaling the cliff. They must have suggested the west-side cliff.

Tanaji had about six hundred men with him. He divided them into two teams. The first team led by his brother Suryaji approached the fort through the gate. The second team led by Tanaji himself would scale the west-side cliff with the help of a monitor lizard (*ghorpad* in Marathi).

Tanaji reached the fort first, but his presence was detected. A fierce combat took place between Tanaji and Udaybhan. Udaybhan managed to rid Tanaji of his shield; still Tanaji fought Udaybhan. by tying a cloth over one of his hands and using it to ward off the sword attacks. Tanaji managed to bitterly fight Udaybhan for some time. However, Tanaji lost his life in the battle. But he also managed to kill Udaybhan. However, Suryaji reached the fort by the... and threw himself in the conflict. He also cut the ropes so that none of the *mavles* could retreat from the skirmish. Almost five hundred Rajputs were killed but the Marathas also lost about fifty *mavles*. The Marathas were victorious. As planned before-hand, Suryaji lit the hay stacks from the stable, signalling victory. Shivaji renamed the fort from Kondana to Sinhagad in his honour. His words after hearing about the demise of Tanaji were, "*Gad ala pan Sinha gela*" (Meaning although the fort was captured, a lion was lost in the battle).

The ten-year siege of Troy and the lightning raid by Tanaji bring forth the basic tenet of Ts'ao Kung and San Tzu.

"He who wishes to fight must first count the cost."

A siege means that vicory will be long in coming. Then the soldiers' weapons will grow dull, their ardour will be dampened, treasure will be spent and the army grows old. A long siege means a massive supply chain. That, in turn, means broken chariots and exhausted horses and oxen. Therefore, for a successful siege, no supply wagon should be loaded more than twice.

In war, let your objective be victory, not lengthy campaigns. The value of time, i.e. being ahead of your opponent, i.e. surprise counts more than numerical superiority.

□

Shivaji's Forts and the Great Wall of China

The Great Wall of China (*wanli changcheng)*

During the reign of Emperor Wen Di of the Han dynasty, Chao Cuo (220-154 B.C.) presented a memorial to the emperor on building beacon towers to guard against the Hu (Xiougnu) in which he said: "The Hu people wandered about where there was water and grass, different from the people who settled down in the Central Plain areas and engaged in agricultural production. Nowadays, the Hu people graze their sheep and cattle in several places and hunt around the frontier areas. From the former domain of the state of Yan in the east to Gansu in the west, the whole of north China is frequently plundered and harassed by the Hu people. If Your Majesty does not go to the rescue, the people will despair, but if you send soldiers to save people, there is still the problem of how many soldiers to send—if too few, they won't be able to defeat the Hu; if too many, troop movements will be slow and the Hu people will run away. So, the best way to deal with these nomads is to build high walls and deep moats and station soldiers at the fortresses; to build a long wall, set up passes in easily defended terrains and build castles."

1. *The Great Wall of China (wanli changcheng) is the longest man-made structure in the world. The wall with branches and spurs runs over mountains, across valleys and through desserts.*

2. *The length of all Chinese defence walls built over the last 2,000 years is approximately 31,070 miles (50,000 kms). Earth's circumference is 24,854 miles (40,000 kms).*
3. *During its construction, the Great Wall was called 'the longest cemetery on earth' because so many people died building it. Reportedly, it cost the lives of more than one million people.*
4. *Many people denounce the buiding of the walls, in particular, Qin Shi Huang's Great Wall, saying he was a tyrant who wasted the country's wealth and worked people, to death building the Great Wall.*
5. *Commenting on the hard and bitter labour, a Han writer Chen Lin (217 A.D.) wrote in one of his poems "Never give birth to boys, but feed girls with meat for don't you see the white bones that hold the great wall from underneath."*
6. *Because the Great Wall was discontinuous, Mongol invaders led by Genghis Khan ('universal ruler') had no problem going around the wall and they subsequently conquered most of northern China between A.D. 1211 and 1223.* They ruled all of China until 1368 when the Ming defeated the Mongols.
7. *It is common to hear that the mortar used to bind the stones was made from human bones or that men are buried within the Great Wall to make it stronger. Wu Longham said in his poem*

   "The wall is so tall because it is stuffed with the bones of soldiers.

   The wall is so deep because it is watered with the soldier's blood."

   Popular legend about the Great Wall is the story of Meng Jiang Nu, a wife of a farmer who was forced to work on the wall during the Qin dynasty. When she heard her husband had died while working on the wall, she wept until the wall collapsed, revealing his bones so she could bury them.
8. *At one time, family members of those who died working on the Great Wall would carry a coffin on top of which was a caged white rooster. The rooster's crowing was supposed*

to keep the spirit of the dead person awake until they crossed the wall; otherwise, the family feared the spirit would escape and wander forever along the wall.

9. *During the Chinese Cultural Revolution (1966-78), the Great Wall was seen as a sign of despotism, and people were encouraged to take bricks from it to use in their farms or homes.*
10. *During the Ming dynasty, nearly one million soldiers were said to defend the Great Wall from 'barbarians' and non-Chinese.*
11. *The manpower to build the Great Wall came from frontier guards, peasants, unemployed intellectuals, disgraced noblemen, and convicts. In fact, there existed a special penalty during the Qin and Han dynasties under which convicted criminals were made to work on the wall.*
12. *In an age when swords, spears, knives axes, bows and arrows were the major weapons, walls served to block cavalry, organise defence forces and light signals—all effective measures. But after gunpowder was invented in the Tang dynasty, it was used very extensively in the strong 'thunder gun' and 'iron gun'. In the Yuan dynasty, there were guns that could tear openings in the wall where soldiers could enter.*
13. *When Chenghis Khan looked at the wall and sighed in frustration, an officer named Ja Bal suggested, "From here north, there is a narrow path in the dark forests that allows only one horse with one man on it. I have gone over that pass once. Chenghis Khan took this path and encircled the Kin capital i.e. present-day China."*

Forts of Shivaji

Let us now compare the wall of the forts that Shivaji built. His letter dated 22nd September, 1677 to Sir W.M. Langhorne tells us of the efforts that he put into them:

"Since my arrival in Karnatak, I have conquered several forts and I intend to fortify them. You are likely to have with you men adept at blowing mines and building cartridges for guns. When I

enquired at Goa and Vengurla for such men, I was told that they have gone with you to Chinnapattan and Pullicat. Please send me 20-25 such men. Rest assured, I shall give them enough work and pay them well. I shall be thankful if Your Worship does this kindness towards us. Once again, I request you to send as many such workmen as you can."

Before the Ming dynasty, the wall was built with rammed earth, adobe, and stone. About 70 percent is made from rammed earth and adobe. Bricks were used after the Ming dynasty.

It is interesting to compare the Great Wall of China with the forts of Shivaji as a defence mechanism.

Captain Graham in his famous report on Kolhapur says about the forts:

"A strong hold on every hill as if inviting the inhabitants to depend on themselves instead of the sovereign's support and encouraging in each petty chieftain that spirit of independence which is so striking a character of the natives of the Maratha country." (Stgm/hss/559)

The Background

As we saw earlier, Shivaji as a young boy had realised the importance of forts. Shivaji militarised almost the entire society, including all classes, with the entire peasant population of settlements and villages near forts actively involved in their defence.

Shrikrishna is known to have said '*With the help of a fort, even women can defend the land.*'

Sambhaji (Shivaji's son) in his treatise *Buddhabhushan* wrote that "*one warrior can fight against a hundred of the enemy and a hundred can battle against a thousand.*"

Douglas has aptly said that:

- *"Shivaji's dwelling was among the rocks and his strength lay in everlasting hills. He was a man of the forts. Born in a fort, the forts made him what he became and he made the forts what they were. The terror of the Mughals, the cradle of his nation, the steps of his ambition, the basis of his conquest, his home and his joy. He built many of them but strengthened all of them."*

- P.K. Ghanekar/*Athato Durg Jignyasa* /57/37

Confidence

A confident Shivaji wrote to the imperial officers:

"For the last three years, you have been under orders from Aurangzeb to seize my country and forts. Ye are reminded that even the steed of imaginable exertion is too weak to gallop over this hard country and that its conquest is difficult. My home is unlike the forts of Kalyani and Bidar and is not situated on spacious plain. It has lofty mountain ranges, 200 leagues in length and forty leagues in depth. Everywhere there are 'nalas' *difficult to ford and sixty forts of rare strength have been built. Afzal Khan came against and perished ...Amir-ul-Umra Shaista Khan was sent against these sky-kissing ranges and abysmal valleys ...at last as all false men deserve, he encountered a terrible disaster and went away in disgrace. It is my duty to guard my land."*

"The wise should beware this river of blood,

No man can ford in safety, its terrible flood." (Stgm/hs sardesai/360)

- Towards the end of his career, he had a control of 360 forts to secure his growing kingdom. His ministers more than once pointed out to him that he spent too much on forts. Shivaji is known to have said:

  "Even if each fort holds against the enemy, Swarajya will remain for 360 years."
- Henry Oxyden along with Robinson and Michell arrived at Raigad on 22 May for Shivaji's coronation. He noted: *"We arrived at the top of that strong mountain which is fortified more by nature than art, being of very different access and but one avenue to it, which is guarded by two narrow gates and fortified with a strong high wall and bastions thereto, all the other parts of the mountain is a direct precipice so that it's impregnable except the treachery of some in it betrays it."*

- In his *Ajnyapatra*, Amatya declared, *"The essence of the whole kingdom, 'is forts'. If there are no forts, during a foreign invasion, the open country becomes supportless and is easily desolated, and the people are routed and broken up. If the whole country is thus devastated, what else remains of the kingdom? Shivaji built this kingdom on the strength of forts. He also built forts along the seashore. With great exertion, place suitable for forts should be captured in any new country which is to be conquered. The condition of a country without forts is like a land protected only by passing clouds. Therefore, those who want to create a kingdom should maintain forts in an efficient condition, realising that forts and stronghold alone mean the kingdom, the treasury, the strength of the army, the prosperity of the kingdom, our places of residence and resting places, nay, our very security of life.'*

'A great foe like Aurangzeb came and conquered the great states of Bijapur and Bhaganagar. He struggled very hard against this kingdom for thirty to thirty-two years. What was the result of his efforts? A portion of this kingdom remained unconquered because there were forts in the country. Later, an opportunity came to regain the former glory of the kingdom.' Amatya further says, *'A king without forts is like a cobra without poison fangs or an elephant without rut.'* CS/SMP/35

Sonopant, while speaking on the importance of forts, advised Shivaji:

"Wise men say, the king is the forhead (of the kingdom) , the minister is the mouth, the army are the arms, the rest of the body is the general population, friends are the joints and forts are the bones."

Three Lines of Defence

- Shivaji himself constructed about 15-20 totally new forts (including key sea-forts like Sindhudurg), but he also rebuilt or repaired many strategically placed forts to create a chain of 300 or more, stretched over a thousand kilometres across the rugged crest of the

Western Ghats. Each were placed under three officers of equal status lest a single traitor should be bribed or tempted to deliver it to the enemy. The officers (sabnis, havaldar, sarnobhat) acted jointly and provided mutual checks and balance.

- The forts of Shivaji could be divided into three lines of defence. The first line was the forts along the north and north-west of *Swarajya*. The northern-most fort was Sudhagad while Rajgad and Torna lay to the south. The sea-forts of Jaigad, Vijaydurg and Sindhudurg formed the second line of defence. The forts from Daulatabad in Karnataka to Jinji in Tamil Nadu were the third line of defence. Shivaji's aim was to take into possession most of the important strongholds in the south so that in times of stress and difficulty, the government of Maharashtra could move into them. Jinji, Gingree or Chenjee, in South Arcot (Tamil Nadu) was one such powerful fort.

Shivaji's foresight in building a second Maratha capital deep in the south was of inestimable value to the national cause after his death. The capture and murder of his eldest son, Sambhaji, by Aurangzeb in March 1689 and the defeat of the Maratha forces in all theatres of war, in contrast to their resounding successes against their enemies during his life-time, threatened to annihilate his hard-won realm. But the fugitive Rajaram, his second son, saved it from falling into tearful ruins by seeking the asylum in Jinji. Zulikar Khan put a siege on Jinji for nine years starting 1890 but he could get Jinji only after he reached an understanding with Rajaram in 1897. (Stgm/hss/686)

While discussing the efficacy of a mechanism of defence, it is clear that in the case of a wall, even if one part is breached, the whole wall is rendered useless. This is exactly what Chenghis Khan did. After all, just as a chain is only as strong as its weakest link, so also a wall is only as strong as its weakest part. On the other hand, even if one fort is lost, the garrison can escape to another fort and live to fight another day.

And, most importantly, as Shivaji said, "even if one fort fights for one year, we have 350 years. Our *swarajya* will remain (alive) for 350 years."

The above treatise proves beyond doubt that the great wall built over 2,000 years with slave labour was not as efficient for defence as the 350 forts built/repaired by Shivaji over hardly 30 years.

Shivaji and his forts so epitomised freedom and *swarajya* that the Shivaji Festival started by Lokmanya Tilak, at Raigad in 1896, was the first salvo of our freedom struggle fired against the British government.

Shivaji's Navy

The East India Company

The East India Company was formed in 1600. The navy began to develop and eventually it would become the most powerful in the world. It would rely on foreign trade by English merchants for its finance. And, in return, the navy would provide the English merchant class with access to foreign markets through war and coercion, whenever needed. It is clear that the British Navy played a crucial role in establishing Great Britain as the foremost, military, economic and imperial power in the world by the end of the Napoleonic wars.

Around 1600, the now Protestant island nation began to rely on its navy as the source of their wealth and defence. Between 1646 and 1659, the navy grew by an outstanding 217 vessels: 111 were captured and 106 were built. After Cromwell's death and the restoration of the Stuart dynasty in 1660, the navy built another 25 battleships of the first, second and third classes. But the development of the navy did not guarantee immediate success, especially considering that the Dutch remained the foremost naval power in the Atlantic. After 1649, England fought three wars with the foremost naval power in Europe at the time of the United Provinces (The Netherlands). England's main objective was to destroy Dutch trade and shipping and replace the Dutch as the leading maritime trading power. The first two wars, which lasted between 1652-4 and 1665-7, produced relatively little progress on the trading front. The last war in 1672-4 was hardly decisive and ended with only modest gain for the English. Under Charles II, who was instated as king in 1660, the 'blue water' policy, as it is known was officially made a policy. Under this policy, commercial wealth and naval power came to be seen as 'mutually sustaining'. No wonder it was said 'the sun did not set on the British empire'. Flourishing trading that was fuelled by the English navy would provide funds in the form of customs revenue, as well as manpower would guard existing overseas markets, as well as under the expectation that this would lead to new markets. This policy made much sense, since Great Britain was an island; a strong navy would almost surely secure them from attack by a continental power.

Francis Drake has rightly put it: *"He who is powerful on the sea can decide whether to fight or not to fight. He can disembark his troops wherever he wants and if the enemy is too strong, he can embark his troops and move away to safety."*

Navy in Medieval India

The Mughals were the one of the richest empires of the world. Even when Akbar conquered Gujarat and with it Surat, he never thought of setting up a navy. In his landward expansion of power, profit by sea-borne trade was beyond his grasp. The trot of a horse attracted him more than the dull flutter of the ship's canvas. All the Mughal emperors depended on the Siddis of Janjira for their naval needs.

The seafaring communities were mostly illiterate and, therefore, devoid of any theoretical knowledge about their own calling. In effect, the intellectual castes were divorced from the seafaring communities, stunting the progress of the navy. The Brahmins of that time imposed excommunication eventually loss of caste which was more dreadful than death, and costly *prayaschitta* (penance) for persons travelling the sea. The Indian Ocean was, therefore, under the domination of the Portuguese in Goa and the British in Surat. (*A History of the Maratha Navy and Merchant Ships* /BK Apte xxi)

The Birth of Shivaji's Navy

A Portuguese letter dated 6th August, 1659 says,

"A son of Shahaji, rebelled against Adilshah, has captured the areas near Bassein (Vasai) & Chaul. He has grown strong. He has constructed some fighting vessels in the Bhiwandi, Kalyan and Panvel ports of the Bassein region. We are, therefore, forced to remain alert. We have ordered the Portuguese captain not to allow these vessels to come out of the ports and see that they do not move out on the seas."

This was the beginning of Shivaji's navy and now Shivaji was threat to all his foreign enemies also.

'Uniting ships with forts, the Raje saddled the navy.'

He was in full control of Kalyan which began to hum with navy-building activities by 1657-58.

Shivaji built his first twenty armed ships with the help of two Portuguese artisans, Roe Leitao Viegas and his brother Fernao Leitao Viegas. Shivaji had declared that these ships were built to meet the menace of the Siddi of Janjira.

When master of such a long coastal strip, he deemed it necessary to undertake the construction of a navy. Immediately after 1657, and sometime before 1659, Shivaji had set afloat the keel of his first ship in the creek of Kalyan. This was the early beginning of the Maratha navy.

In response to a letter dated 19th June, 1659, from the captain of Vasai, the governors in Goa wrote:

"A letter should be written to Antonio de mellow de Castro that he is not to permit Shivaji's mentioned sanguices to sail down the river or make an exit from Vasai creek. If Shivaji makes an attempt to do so, all necessary resistance should be offered to defeat such an attempt. If he asks for a permit, even that should be diplomatically refused. Since it is necessary to prevent the sanguices, some duly manned galiots should be kept ready.. The expenses incurred should be given from the Portuguese royal treasury."

On 19th July1659, a letter from Shivaji was received and dicussed in Goa.

"He (Shivaji) has hostile relations with the Siddis of Danda Rajapuri. When he attacked them, the Portuguese captains of Chaul and Vasai gave them all possible help (provisions and ammunition). The Abyssinians are, therefore, living there without any worry. This is detrimental to the friendship that the Portuguese enjoy with Shivaji. He (Shivaji) is aware that the governors at Goa do not know that the captains are acting against him. The governors ought to write to the captains that they should maintain good relations with Shivaji and stop helping the Siddis."

The matter was discussed and the following action decided upon.

"The captains, Antonio de Mellow de Castro and Dom Francisco de Castel Branco of Vasai and Chaul, respectively should be sent letters according to Shivaji's request. It is necessary to maintain amiable relations with him. Because he is powerful, has control over Kalian, Bhivandi and the entire Konkan region and can cause immense harm to Portuguese interests.

"A second letter should be sent instructing the captains to ostensibly stop giving help to the Abyssisinians of Danda, but permitting them at their discretion to continue doing so, but so secretly that no one should get a wind of it, nor make Shivaji aware of it."

On 16th August, 1659 the governors of Goa wrote a letter to their king. The relevant portion reads:

"One of the sons of the Adilshahi has captured territory in the vicinity of Vasai and Chaul. He has built many warships at Kalyan and Panvel areas of Vasai region. We have ordered the captains of Vasai to prohibit their exit to the sea."

However, the Portuguese decided to strike off the very roots of the infant navy.

There is evidence that the Portuguese Viceroy had by a proclamation made on 19th May, 1668, ordered all Portuguese nationals in the service of the Delhi, Bijapur and Shivaji armies to return to Portugal. Antonio de Melo de Castro made a frantic effort to withdraw all the Portuguese from Shivaji's service even before his warships had been completed because they would have been a source of trouble not only to the Siddi, but to the Portuguese also. As a result of this, one day, all Portuguese in Shivaji's service quit their jobs and fled. (*Portuguese-Mahratta Relations* by Pissurlenkar p. 36)

Rui Leitao Viegas

Shivaji had been building the sanguices relying on the proficiency of Rui Leitao Viegas and his son Fernao Veigas and the three hundred Portuguese and topaz workmen under him. The captain of Vasai sent Joao de Salazar de Vasconcelos (30th September, 1659) to induce the Portuguese to leave the gentoo's service.

Rui Vegas fled Shivaji and wrote a letter on 7th October, 1659, the gist of which is reproduced below:

"I, Rui Veigas was in the service of Shivaji along with many white and black Christians under me who had deserted Portuguese service.

"Vasconcelos came and convinced me to leave Shivaji's service and return to the Portuguese king's service.

"I have now come to Bombay port to resist the Dutch enemy."

In February 1663, the English at Surat report that he was fitting out two ships of considerable tonnage for trading with Mocha (in western Arabia) and loading them at Jaitapur, two miles up the Rajapur river, with 'goods of considerable value which were by storms or foul weather driven upon his coast'. Two years later (12th March, 1665), they write that from each of the eight or nine 'most considerable ports in the Deccan' that he had seized, he used to 'set out 2 or 3 or more trading vessels yearly to Persia, Basra, Mocha, andc.' Again, we learn that in April 1669, a great storm on the Karwar coast destroyed several of his ships and rice-boats, 'one of the ships being very richly laden'. (F.R. Surat, Vol.2, 86,105)

After the sack of Surat, Shivaji seriously decided to become a naval power. The Surat council's letter dated 26th June, 1664 to Karwar speaks of him having built about sixty frigates.

A letter from Goa dated 25th August, 1664 instructs the captain at Chaul not to resist Shivaji, but to adopt a policy of conciliation in view of his overall strength. A letter from the Dutch at Surat to Amsterdam on 6th June, 1664 says that Shivaji was fitting a large number of frigates in all his sea ports with the intention of capturing His Majesty's ships coming from Mocha so that the commerce may be diverted to his.

Coastal Forts

As the Konkan came increasingly under possession, Shivaji started building a number of coastal fortresses, such as Padmadurg, Vijaydurg, Suvarnadurg, Sindhudurg and Khanderi-Underi to give protection to his coastal navy and to watch and curb the activities of the Portuguese to Bombay and Bassien.

Mughals and Vijapur were land-based powers. They always neglected building up a navy. Their pilgrim and merchant ships depended on Europeans in the sea. Under such circumstances, Shivaji's stress on naval activities reveals his far-sightedness; his naval conquest of Basnoor and Gokarna in 1665 are of immense importance while trying to grasp the personality of this man.

Shivaji Armada, 1

The foreigners would refer to the Maratha fleet as Shivaji Armada, 1 in their official correspondence. *(stgm = p. 607-17 hs sardesai)*

The successful encounter against Basrur had far-reaching consequences. As Sabhasad records, "This is the unique example in medieval history, where a king was personally leading the Armada. This personal experience taught Shivaji not only the importance of navy as a limb of the state, but also the technique of naval warfare."A merchant fleet is also the nursery of a national fighting navy. It is quite clear from the references in the East India Company's records that Shivaji had established commercial relations with Mocha (western Arabia), Persia, Bussera, Aden, Muscat, etc."

He had built six types of ships like Gurabs, Galbats, Sibars

Tarandes, Tarus and Pagars... in this manner, seven hundred ships were equipped in the sea. It is difficult to get the numerical strength of Shivaji's navy, though we find some stray references to his 'Armada' in the English records. Sabhasad says that the Maratha navy was formed into two squadrons of 200 vessels each and commanded by two admirals, Darya Sarang and Mai Nayak.

English report, 1673 says, *"His fleet consisting only of small grabs and slight and inconsiderable boats, very ill fitted, and his men totally inexperienced to the sea."* *However, they were scared of "the deeper designs for his Armada. But his designs are so well laid and secretly carried on that no judgement can be made of them till they are executed."*

'*Ajnyapatra*' or 'Royal Edict'

Shivaji's naval policy has been epitomised by his contemporary Ramachandrapant Amatya in one of the sections in his treatise on Maratha polity titled *Ajnyapatra* or 'Royal Edict' written before 1717. Jadunath Sarkar says, "Nothing proves Shivaji's genius as a born statesman more clearly than his creation of a navy and naval base. While pointing out the importance of navy, Amatya, the author of *Anjyapatra*, says, *"Navy is an independent limb of the state. Just as a king's fame for success on land is in proportion to the strength of his cavalry, so the mastery of the sea is in the hands of him who possesses the sea. Therefore, a navy should necessary be built."*

The English, of course, describe the Maratha vessels as *pitiful things (mosquito craft), so that one good English ship would destroy a hundred of them without running herself in danger.* (Saht/js/208)

Yet the first encounter between the English and the Maratha vessels took place on 19th September, 1679 outside the bay of Khanderi when Lt. Francis Thorpe along with John Bradbury, George Cole, and Henry Welch of the *Ocean Queen* were either imprisoned or wounded. (orme MSS116)

The second battle between the English and the Maratha took place on 18 October, 1679, north of Chaul. The Marathas attacked the shibbar 'Dover 'under sergeant Mauleverer and carried it off.

James Douglas writes: *"It was a great mercy that Shivaji was not a seaman. Otherwise, he might have swept the sea as he did the land ...He liked the sea but the sea did not like him."*

The Siddis of Janjira

The Siddhis of Janjira were a small naval aristrocracy originally from Abyssinia. Their constitution provided for the rule of the fittest and not heredity. Their central place of activity was at Janjira, an island fort. The rulers of this house owed allegiance to the Shahs of Ahmadnagar, Bijapur and the Mughals as it suited their interest. Their policy was always to back the winning horse. But due credit must be given to their excellent seamanship and sturdiness by virtue of which they survived those days of great turmoil. In the seventeenth century, the Siddis of Janjira attained eminence as a naval power. The Siddis with their stronghold at Janjira were a constant source of nuisance to the Marathas. On the sea, they were a deadly enemy. Despite their immense resources and repeated attacks, the Marathas were never able to subdue this small maritime principality. (*A History of the Maratha Navy and merchant ships*/BK Apte)

Shivaji had captured the eastern part of the Kolaba district adjoining the Siddi's territory, but the latter still held Danda-Rajapuri and much of the neighbouring land. The Siddi had too small an army to defy the regular Maratha forces on land, and he seems to have confined himself to making raids by surprise and doing petty acts of mischief to Shivaji's villages in that region as is clear from the Maratha chronicler's description of the Siddi as "an enemy like the mice in a house,"*(Sabh.66.)

Any treaty between Shivaji and the Siddi could not possibly last long. To the Siddi, the loss of the Kolaba territory meant starvation, and, on the other hand, it was Shivaji's 'lifelong ambition to capture Janjira' and make his hold on the west coast absolutely secure. The Maratha gains on the Kolaba coast were now organised into a province, and placed under an able

Viceroy, Vyankaji Datto, with a permanent contingent of the 5 to 7 thousand men (sabh.66). At this, the Siddis, in order to 'fill their stomachs', had to direct their district, which had now come under Shiva's way. The Maratha chief, therefore, realised that he must create a formidable navy and set up fortified bases along the coast, if he was to ensure the protection of his seaside districts and the conquest of Janjira, which would continue as a thorn in his side if left in enemy hands. (Sabh.67)

Siddi Qasim

In 1669, Shivaji's attack upon Janjira was renewed with great vigour. The contest came to a crisis next year (1670). Shivaji staked all his resources on the capture of Janjira. Fath Khan, worn out by the incessant struggle, impoverished by the ruin of his subjects, and hopeless of aid from his suzerain at Bijapur, resolved to accept Shiva's offer of a large sum and a rich *jagir* as the price of giving up Janjira. But his three Abyssinian slaves roused their clansmen on the island against this surrender to an infidel, imprisoned Fath Khan, seized the government, and applied to *Adil Shah and Mughal* viceroy of the Deccan for aid.

The Mughals readily agreed, and the Siddi fleet was transferred from the overlordship of Bijapur to that of Delhi, and Siddi Sambal, one of the leaders of the revolution, was created imperial admiral with a *mansab* and a *jagir* yielding 3 lakhs of rupees. "The other Siddi captains preserved the distinct command over their own crews and dependents, and an aristocratical council determined the general welfare of this singular republic." (Orme's Frag.57; K.K.ii.224.)

Siddi Qasim, the new governor of Janjira, 'was distinguished among his tribesmen for bravery, care of the peasantry, capacity, and cunning. He busied himself in increasing his fleet and war-material, strengthening the defences of his forts and cruising at sea. He used to remain day and night clad in armour, and repeatedly seized enemy ships, cut off the heads of many Marathas and sent them to Surat. (K.K., ii.225). His crowning achievement was the recovery of Danda from Shivaji's men. One night, in February 1671, when the Maratha garrisons of that fort were absorbed in drinking and celebrating the spring carnival (Holi), Qasim secretly arrived at the pier with 40 ships, while Siddi Khairiyat with 500 men made a noisy feint on the land-side. The full strength of the garrison rushed in the latter direction to repel Khairiyat, and Qasim seized the opportunity to scale the sea-wall. Some of his brave followers were hurled into the sea and some slain, but the rest forced their way into the fort. Just then the powder-magazine exploded, killing the Maratha commandant and several of his men, with a dozen of the assailants. Qasim promptly raised his battle-cry *Khassu! Khassu*! and shouting "*My braves, be composed; I am alive and safe*," he advanced, slaying and binding to the centre of the fort, where he joined hands with Khairiyat's party, and the entire place was conquered.

Shiva had been planning the capture of Janjira, and now he had failed to hold even Danda! It is said that during the night of the surprise, the moment the powder-magazine blew up, Shiva, who was 40 miles away, started from his sleep and exclaimed that some calamity must have befallen Danda!

To the end of his life, hostilities continued between the Marathas and Siddis, intermittently, indecisively, but with great bitterness and fury. Gross cruelty and wanton injury were practised by each side on the captive soldiers and innocent peasantry of the other, and the country became desolate. The economic loss was more keenly felt by the small and poor state of the Abyssinians than by the Marathas, and the Siddis at times begged for peace, but did not succeed, as they were not prepared to accept Shiva's terms of ceding their all to him.

In September 1671, Shivaji sent an ambassador to Bombay to secure the aid of the English in an attack on Danda. But the president and council of Surat advised the Bombay factors "not to positively promise him the grenades, mortar-pieces, and ammunition he desires, nor to absolutely deny him, in regard, we do not think it convenient to help him against Danda, which place, if it were in his possession would prove a great annoyance to the port of Bombay." (F.R.Surat, 87.)

Towards the end of 1672, the foreign traders who had very wisely maintained their neutrality, though it was a 'ticklish game'. In the following August, however, the ship *Soleil d' Orient* of the new French East India Company founded by Colbert, arrived at Rajapur and secretly sold 80 guns (mostly small pieces) and 2,000 maunds of lead to Shiva's fleet. The French gave similar help in November 1697 when they sold him 40 guns for the defence of Panhala. (O.C.3722; 3734.F.R.Surat to Co., 12 Jan. 1674; Vol.108, *Rajapur to Surat*, 30 Dec. 1679.)

In February 1674, we learn from an English letter, *"the war betwixt the Siddi and Shivaji is carried on but slowly, they being both weary,"* and the president of Surat was requested by the Siddi *"to mediate a peace between them."* (O.C.3939.)

Grand Assault on Janjira, 1675-1676

In September 1675, we read of Shivaji making preparations for taking that fort by a land and sea attack. That island had been besieged by Shiva with a great force some months earlier. The neighbouring coast was dotted with his outposts and redoubts, and he also built some floating batteries and made an attempt to throw a mole across the sea from the mainland to the island of Janjira.

- They felled all the wood around to make floating platforms with breastworks, from which the walls were to be assaulted.

But the attempt failed. Siddi Qasim arrived with the Abyssinian fleet, broke the line of investment, infused life into the defence, made counter-attacks, burnt the floating batteries and forced the Marathas to raise the siege (end of December 1676.)

War with the English for Khanderi Island, 1679

The difficulty of capturing Janjira set Shiva thinking of some other island in the neighbourhood which would afford him a naval base. His choice fell on Khanderi ('Kennery'), a small rocky island, one and a half miles by half a mile, situated 11 miles south of

Bombay and 30 miles north of Janjira. As early as April 1672, the people of Surat learnt of his intention to build a fort on the island. The English president at once decided to prevent it as affecting the interests of Bombay even more than those of Surat, because no ship could enter or issue from Bombay harbour without being seen from Khanderi. (F.R. Surat 87, *Surat to Bombay*.22 April; Vol.106, 1 May, 1672.)

At the end of August 1679, Shiva allocated one lakh of hun from the revenues of Kalian and Chaul to be spent on the work. On 15th September, we find 150 men of Shiva with four small guns under breast-works of earth and stone all around it. A request from the Deputy Governor of Bombay 'to quit the place as it belonged to the island of Bombay', was declined by the Marathas in the absence of orders from Shivaji to that effect. The English, therefore, resolved that if the occupation of the island was persisted in and the Maratha fleet under Daulat Khan came there to protect the fortifications, they would 'repel them with force as an open and public enemy.' (Orme MSS. 116.F.R. Surat, 4, Consult. 4 and 15 Sep.,1679.)

The first encounter between the English and the Marathas at sea took place on 19th September and ended in a reverse for the sons of the *Ocean Queen*. The larger English ships were still outside the Bay of Khanderi, because the soundings had not yet been taken and they could not be brought closer to the island. Lieutenant Francis Thorpe, with some *shibars,* made a rash attempt to land on the island, 'positively against orders'. The Englishmen were assailed with great and small shots from the shore works. The rash drunken young officer was killed with two other men (John Bradbury and Henry Welch), several others were wounded, and George Cole and many other Englishmen were left prisoners on the island. The lieutenant's *shibar* was captured by the enemy, while two other *shibars* escaped to the fleet in the open sea. Next day, the Marathas carried off another English *shibar*. Sergeant Giles timidly offering no resistance. (Orme MSS.116.)

Early, in October, the Maratha fleet was got ready to go to the succor of Khanderi. The second battle with the English was fought on 18th October, 1679.

"At daybreak the entire Maratha fleet of more than 60 vessels under Daulat Khan suddenly bore down upon the small English squadron consisting of the Revenge frigate, 2 *ghurabs* of two masts each, 3 *shibars* and 2 *manchwas*—eight vessels in all, with 200 European soldiers on board, in addition to the *lascars* and white sailors. The Marathas advanced from the shore a little north of Chaul, firing from their prows and moving so fast that the English *ghurabs*, having Sergeant Mauleverer and some English soldiers on board, with great cowardice struck its colours and was carried off by the Marathas. The other *ghurab* kept aloof, and the five smaller vessels ran away, leaving the *revenge* alone in the midst of the enemy. But she fought gallantly and sank five of the Maratha gallivants, at which their whole fleet fled to the bar of Nagothna, pursued by the *revenge*. Two days afterwards the Maratha fleet issued from the creek, but on the English vessels advancing, they fled back. Such is the inefficiency of 'mosquito craft' in naval battles fought with artillery that even fifty slender and open Indian ships were no match for a single large and strongly built English vessel. At the end of November, the Siddi fleet of 34 ships joined the English off Khanderi and kept up a daily battery of the island. (Orme, 81-84.)

But the cost of these operations was heavily felt by the English merchants, who also realised that they could not recruit white soldiers to replace any lost in fight, and, therefore, could not 'long oppose him (Shiva), lest they should imprudently so weaken themselves as not to be able to defend Bombay itself, if he should be exasperated to draw down his army that way.' Moreover, during the monsoon storms, the English would be forced to withdraw their naval patrol from Khanderi, and then Shiva would 'take his opportunity to fortify and store the island, maugre all our designs'. So, the Surat council wisely resolved (25th October), that the English should 'honourably withdraw themselves in time', and either settle this difference with Shivaji by means of a friendly mediator, or else throw the burden of opposing him on the Portuguese governor of Bassein or on the Siddi, and thus 'ease the Hon'ble company of this great charge'. The Surat factory itself was in danger and could spare no European soldier for succouring Bombay. (F.R. Surat4, Consult. 25 and 31 Oct. 3, 8 and 12 Dec. 1679.)

The dreaded reprisal by Shivaji against Bombay almost came to pass. 'Highly exasperated by the defeat of his fleet before Khanderi', he sent 4,000 men to Kalian-Bhivandi with the intention to land in Bombay by way to Thane. The Poruguese governor of Bassein having refused to allow them to pass through his country, the invaders marched to Panvel (a port in their own territory) opposite Trombay island, intending to embark there on seven *shibars* (end of October 1679). The inhabitants of Bombay were terribly alarmed. The Deputy Governor breathed fire, but the President and Council of Surat decided to climb down. On receiving a courteous letter from Shivaji sent by way of Rajapur, they wrote: 'a civil answer, demonstrating our trouble for the occasion his fortifying so insignificant a rock as Khanderi, which is not in the least becoming of a prince of his eminence and qualifications; and though we have a right to that place, yet to show the candour of our proceedings, we are willing to forget what is past, and therefore have given instructions to the Deputy Governor of Bombay to treat with such persons as he shall appoint about the present differences'. The Deputy Governor was 'very much dissatisfied' with this pacific tone and held that a vigorous policy of aggression against Shiva's country and fleet would 'give a speedy conclusion to this dispute to the Hon'ble Company's advantage'. But the higher authorities at Surat only repeated their former order that Bombay should avoid a war with Shiva and 'frustrate his designs of fortifying Khanderi either by treaty or by the Siddi's fleet assisting us to oppose him thereon'. The two English captains consulted each other and took the same view. At the end of December, the Marathas dragged several large guns to Thal (on the mainland) and began to fire them at the small English craft lying under Underi for stress of weather. (Orme MSS. 116.)

Sindhudurg Fort

For a long time, Shivaji felt the need of sea-fort of the calibre of Janjira fort which was the nucleus of the Siddi sea-faring activities. During the invasion of Basrur, Shivaji camped at Malvan. At that time, he chanced to see an island off the coast of Malvan. When he asked its name, he was told it was called 'Kurte' island. Shivaji futher inspected it along with the local fishermen, like Tasaji, Gomaji and Savji Koli and his advisors like Krishna Savant and Bhanji Prabhudesai. After considering all aspects, Shivaji decided that the island was an ideal site for a sea-fort. Accordingly he gave instructions to his trusted builder-architect Hiroji Indulkar to study the feasibility of building a sea-fort on the island.

Hiroji Indulkar gave his report in favour of building the sea-fort.

"Among eighty-four docks (that I visited), there is no better site to build a fort. It is shear rock. The site is excellent."

The island was surrounded on all sides by sea and the only way to approach it was by a serpentine route from the mainland. It was surrounded by rocks which would make it impossible for the large frigates of the *toppikars* to come close enough to mount an attack. At the same time, it would be a safe haven for the smaller *shibars* and *gurabs* of the fledgeling Maratha navy. Also Malvan was situated midway between Devgad and Vengurla.

While this seaport was coming into existence, Shivaji was busy with his campaigns and raids. But he had designated an army of five thousand *mavles* to keep it secure from his many enemies. However, he always had this seaport on his mind. In a letter to Hiroji Indulkar, he wrote:

*"Bear in mind that I am always thinking of Sindhudurg. The construction should be perfect and sturdy. The workers are new at this job. (This was the first seaport that was built from scratch) Do treat them with understanding and consideration but get the best out of them. The foundation of each wall should be very broad. It (foundation) should be about a metre (two hand length) from the edge of the rock. The rampart (*tat*) may be broad in some places*

and a little narrow in some. Do whatever is appropriate. We have dispatched lead for pouring to bind the foundation stones. Inspect the quality and measure the quantity before accepting it. The Toppikar *merchants are a cunning tribe. They will steal the* Kajal *from your eyes (if you are not vigilant) and you will not even know about it. They may return and even charge you again for the same job/materials. (Luckily) we have a good amount of sweet water on the island. Collect all the sand for building near the sweet-water tanks. Rinse the sand in the sweet water three to four times. This will wash away the saltiness. Use only saltfree sand. We are sending you* chunam *(calcium carbonate) rock from the* ghats. *Inspect it properly. There will be no adulteration. Yet it is better to be vigilant. Pay the labourers their daily wages promptly.*

There should be no cause for question (complaint on that account)."

Shivaji was invited as a guest of the Emperor to Agra to take part in his fiftieth birthday celebration which fell on 12th June, 1666. However, instead of the hospitality promised, Shivaji was under virtual captivity and the threat of death loomed large on him. On 19th August, 1666, Shivaji escaped from Agra and by a circuitous route (yet unconfirmed) reached Rajgad on 12th September, 1666.

During this period of crisis, the construction of Sindhudurg fort proceeded steadily and surely under the supervision of Govind Vishwanath Prabhu. Shivaji's chief architect Hiroji Indulkar kept himself abreast of all activities. The construction of the fort was complete on March 1667...ghn

Chitragupta Bakhar says:

"Among eighty-four docks, this was the best sea-fort,

Despite the opposition of eighteen foriegners, this unconquerable Shiv Lanka was constructed,

Like a heavenly star on earth,

Like a tulsi *Vrindavan in front of a temple,*

A jewel of the kingdom '

Shivaji was gifted the fifteenth gem among the..."

The Bakharkars have eloquently described Sindhudurg as *'a diamond in the necklace of forts worn on the neck of his swatantralaxmi.'*

Kublai Khan's Navy

Kublai (or Khubilai) Khan (23 September, 1215 – 18 February, 1294) was the fifth Great Khan of the Mongol Empire from 1260 to 1294 and the founder of the Yuan Dynasty in East Asia.

Like Shivaji, he tried to start a navy but with disastrous results. Kublai Khan twice attempted to invade Japan. Both times it is believed that bad weather, or a flaw in the design of ships that were based on river boats without keels, destroyed his fleets. The first attempt took place in 1274 with a fleet of 900 ships. The second invasion occurred in 1281. The Mongols sent two separate forces this time; an impressive force of 900 ships containing 40,000 Korean, Chinese, and Mongol troops set out from Masan, while an even larger force of 1,00,000 sailed from southern China in 3,500 ships, each close to 240 feet (73 m) long. The fleet was hastily assembled and ill-equipped to handle the sea.

Dr. Kenzo Hayashida, a marine archaeologist, headed the investigation that discovered the wreckage of the second invasion fleet off the western coast of Takashima. His team's findings strongly indicate that Kublai Khan rushed to invade Japan and attempted to construct his enormous fleet in only one year (a task that should have taken up to 5 forced years). This forced the Chinese to use any available ships, including river boats, which did not have a curved keel to prevent capsising in order to achieve readiness. Most importantly, the Chinese, then under Kublai's control, were forced to build many ships quickly in order to contribute to the fleet in both the invasions. Hayashida theorises that had Kublai used standard, well-constructed ocean-going ships, which have a curved keel to prevent capsising, his navy might have survived the journey to and from Japan and might have conquered it as intended.

David Nicolle writes in *The Mongol Warlords* that *"huge losses had also been suffered in terms of casualties and sheer expense, while the myth of Mongol invincibility had been shattered throughout eastern Asia."* He also wrote that Kublai Khan was determined to mount a third invasion, despite the horrendous cost to the economy and to his and Mongol prestige of the first two defeats, and only his death and the unanimous agreement of his advisers not to invade prevented such a third attempt.

The disastrous failure of Kublai Khan to start a navy more than underlines the success of Shivaji's attempt to start one. It is significant that Shivaji found an apt successor in Kanhoji Angre and his family who raised the navy which made the English, Portuguese, Dutch and French buy their permits. It is equally sad that the Peshwa took the help of the English to scuttle the Angria navy a century after its inception.

□

Coronation

Mansabdari Raja

Before the time of Shivaji, though Adil-Shahi and Vijaynagar were independent kingdoms, all the foreign powers equated the Mughal empire with the government of Hindustan. When signing any international treaty or understanding, they addressed the Mughals as the Great Mughal or the Emperor of India.

By this time, the position of the Rajputs had degraded tremendously. They had retained their titles of Raja by giving their daughters to the *janankhanas* of the Mughals. But this title was given and taken at the pleasure of Mughals. It was not hereditary and expired with the expiry of the incumbent. The Rajput would call himself a Raja and perhaps the Mughals also addressed him as 'Raja', but, in essence, they were employed as commanders of the Mughal *durbar* and were accordingly ranked not by the area or population they 'ruled', but by the strength of the cavalry/infantry they commanded i.e. *mansabdari* of *panchhazri* or *saathazari*. As if this was not enough to show them their rightful place, they were posted away from their land and people in distant places, for example, Jaisingh in Maharashtra and Mansingh in Orissa and Bengal.

On their being appointed as a 'Raja', the Rajputs had celebrations and a throne ceremony, but there was no Hindu coronation, i.e., the ritual bathing or *rajyabhishek*.

The word 'king' meant a Mughal, so much so that even in

their heyday the subjects and officers of the Bahamani, Adilshahi, Nizamshahi kingdoms thought that their kings were subservient to the Mughal Badshah who, in turn, was subservient to the Shah of Iran, who was the *Khalifa*.

At the beginning of the 17th century the senior Maratha families owed their allegiance to the Adilshahi. To them Shivaji was a recent upstart. For example, the More of Javali was a long time *sardar* of Bijapur. He had also been conferred with the title of 'Chandrarao'.

'How dare You call Yourself a King?'

When Shivaji started his *efforts towards establishing swarajya*, he invited Chandrarao More to join him. When the invitation was spurned, Shivaji then sent a letter threatening to invade him. In this letter he had refered to himself as Shivajiraja. At this, a belligerent More sent back a message

"How dare you call yourself a king? If you get this letter while dining, come to wash your hands in Javali. We are ready for a fight."

Another incident that can be quoted is the Ranza affair wherein the Patil of Ranza had raped a Kunbi (serf) girl. When he was brought in chains to Shivaji, his constant complaint was "*by what authority do you judge me*?" What the Patil was trying to say was that punishments could be metted out only by superior authorities, like a king, or a person of a higher caste, a Brahmin or a panchayat.

And Shivaji by no means was a king. Not yet. So, going strictly by the laws present then, the Patil was right.

To the Mughal Emperor, Shivaji was a mere *zamindar* (*bhumiya*), and to Adil Shah, he was the rebellious son of a vassal *jagirdar*. He could not claim equality of political status with any king.

Then again, so long as he was a mere private subject, he could not, with all his real power, claim the loyalty and devotion of the people over whom he ruled. His promises could not have the sanctity and continuity of the public engagements of the head of a state. He could sign no treaty, grant no land with legal validity or an assurance of permanence. The territories conquered by his sword could not become his lawful property, however undisturbed his possession over them might be in practice. The people living under his sway or serving under his banners could not renounce their allegiance to the former sovereign of the land, nor be sure that they were exempt from the charge of treason for their obedience to Shivaji. The permanence of his political creation required that it should be validated as the work of a sovereign.

The Hindrances

Even the mighty Hindu Vijaynagar Empire did not have a king that was coronated according to Vedic tradition. This very ancient ritual of *rajyabhishek* had disappeared from India after 1000 A.D.. People knew of this ritual only from stories in the *Ramayana* and *Mahabharata*. Every Hindu in the Deccan longed for *swarajya* and that implied a *chhatrapati*.

But the first hindrance to the realisation of this ideal was that according to the Hindu scriptures, only a Kshatriya could be crowned the king. Now the Bhosles had been mere tillers of the land three generations ago, i.e. at the time of Babaji. Malloji (Shivaji's grandfather) became a *sardar* only after finding a pot of gold. Till then, even Jijabai's father Lakhoji Jadhav felt that the Bhosles were lower than him in status and had at first refused the proposal of Jijabai's marriage to Shahaji. He, of course relented and the marriage did take place, but only after the mediation by the Nizam under whom both the Bhosles and the Jadhavs were *sardars*.

Shivaji got around this obstacle by sending Balaji Avji to Rajasthan, who traced his pedigree to the purest breed, descended in unbroken line from the Maharanas of Udaipur, the sole representatives of the solar line of the mythical hero, God Ramchandra.

The second hindrance was that Shivaji had not undergone the thread ceremony which was by rule a part of the rituals of the

Kshatriyas on attaining puberty. Shivaji in 1674 was 44-years old and had seven wives. There was no way by which he could have a thread ceremony at this age.

The third and the greatest hindrance was that in the time of Akbar, a Brahmin Krishna Narsingh Shesh, put forth a treatise named *Shudrachar Shiromani* in which he postulated that Parshuram had killed all the Kshatriyas of the world. As a result there were only two castes left in Hindustan, i.e. the Brahmins and the Shudras. This idea had percolated down quite deeply in the common man. So, even if Shivaji had proved his warriorness, i.e. Kshatriyatwa, the public at large and especially the Brahmins refused to accept him as king. The corollary to this malignant idea was that since there were no more Kshatriyas, there could be no Hindu ruler and only Muslims had the right to rule. The Hindus had to be satisfied as their subservient slaves. This idea had become so deep-rooted because for five hundred years before the advent of Shivaji, there had been no Hindu *rajyabhishek*.

Shivaji had to fight against this mind, both of his subjects and more importantly, the haughty Brahmins.

Gagabhat

He had to find a Brahmin who could help him negotiate a way out of this maze. He found one in Kashi and his name was Gagabhat.

First, Gagabhat accepted Shivaji's pedigree.

Then he wrote a treatise 'Kayastha Dharmapradip' in which he squashed all the arguments that Krishna Narsingh Shesh had enumerated in *Shudrachar Shiromani*.

Thirdly, Gagabhat resurrected the *rajyabhishek* ritual again after studying Vedic literature and coronated Shivaji.

This was a revolutionary event, considering the rigid religious society existing at the time. On one hand, Shivaji was relating himself with Rama, Yudhishthira and Vikramaditya. On the other hand, he was appealing to emotions of all Hindus in India, stating that they have a formal Hindu Empire in India, which was fighting for the cause of Hindus. According to Hindu *Puranas*, the lineage of Kshatriya kings was lost in *kaliyuga*. By performing this ritual, Shivaji was symbolically stating that *kaliyuga* was over and *satyayuga* had begun. He was making a statement that a new age had begun.

The Coronation

The coronation took place on the 6th of May.

The essentials of a Hindu king's coronation are abhishek—the ritual bathing and *chatra dharan*—holding the royal umbrella over the head of the monarch.

At the auspicious time chosen by Gagabhat, Shivaji walked to the place he was going to be given the ritual bath. He was dressed in a pure white *dhoti*. Round his neck were garlands of flowers. He sat on a gold *chaurang*—two-foot square stool, usually two feet high. On his left sat his senior queen Soyra Bai. The *palav* of her *Paithani* sari was knotted to Shivaji's garment, in sign of her being his *ardhangini* or equal partner in this world and the next.

The heir-apparent Sambhaji sat behind him. At the appointed time, Gagabhat and his Brahmins started chanting the *shastras* to the tune of the *dhol* and *shehnai*. The eight ministers stood at the eight directions of the compass. Gagabhat officially presided over the ceremony, and had a gold vessel filled with the sacred waters of the Rivers Yamuna, Sindhu, Ganga, Godavari, Krishna and Kaveri. He held the vessel over Shivaji's head and chanted the coronation *mantras*, as the water kept dripping from the several tiny holes in the vessel on Shivaji, his queen and the prince. Next, sixteen Brahmin *savashni* a woman whose husband was alive performed *pancharti*, an *arti* with five lamps on a tray.

After the ritual bath, Shivaji changed his dress from pristine white to royal scarlet, richly embroidered with gold. He put on gold jewellery studded with precious stones. His turban was dripping with pearls and gems. He worshipped his arms and armaments, his Bhavani sword which had won him many a combat, and his shield which had brought him safe from all his battles.

At the appointed time, Shivaji entered the Coronation Hall.

Everywhere saffron flags were visible. Saffron was a colour that Shivaji had adopted long before. In fact, when he went to Agra, his flag was saffron and gold.

In the centre was a gold throne made of solid gold and weighing 32 maunds. The basal platform was made of planks of banyan and fig trees as prescribed for coronations.

The base was decorated with a gold plate engraved with ferocious beasts on four sides—the lion, the tiger, the cat and the hyena. The throne had eight pillars, each supporting a lion in gold. The pillars were embossed with flowers, leaves, creepers and nymphs. The cushion consisted first of deer skin and then tiger skin with a layer of gold between them. On top of this was a velvet cushion embroidered in gold. On the right side of the throne stood two large fish heads of gold with very big teeth. This signified his mastery on the seas.

On the left side were several horses' tails. This was an insignia of the Turks and signified royalty. There was also a pair of golden evenly balanced scales on a lance head and signified justice.

The Prime Minister Moropandit poured 8,000 gold hons on Shivaji's head as the beginning of the 'golden bath'. Nilo Pandit, the chief accountant showered 7,000 golden hons and so it continued.

As Shivaji mounted the throne, small flowers made of gold were showered on him. Sixteen *sawasins* (married Brahmin women) performed his *pancharti* (the circular waving of trays containing five lamps). The Brahmins lifted their voices, chanting the holy hymns. The drum beats grew louder. *Gagabhat* advanced to the throne and held the royal parasol made of woven gold and fringed with pearls over Shivaji's head. He hailed him as 'Shivaji Chhatrapati'.

And the crowd roared, 'Victory to Shivraj'.

As planned, all the cannons from the ramparts of Raigad were fired and this was taken up fort to fort along the *ghats,* so that if at all there was a soul who did not know that Shivaji had become Chhatrapati, he would now know.

It is interesting to know what Aurangzeb felt and did when he came to know of the coronation.

He is said to have got down from his throne and did not eat or drink for two days. He said, "*Khuda* has taken away the throne from the Muslim emperor and given it to the Marathas (*Kafir*). This is the limit."

Why Chhatrapati

It speaks volumes for Shivaji's statesmanship to have conceived of all the implications of an *abhisikta raja* and the significance of the unique title of *chhatrapati*. No Hindu or Indian prince, or for that matter, any ruler whatsoever had borne the significant name of *chhatrapati* symbolising the 'protective umbrella' instead of the truculent bird of prey, the eagle of the Caesars (or Kaisers), or the lion or 'king of beasts', or the dragon of the celestial emperors, or even the *suvarna garuda-dhwajya* of the ancient Yadava rulers of Maharashtra.

A very good illustration of the manner in which the Chhatrapati discharged his trust as leader and protector of Hindu Dharma and civilisation is to be found in an interesting document which, if it is authentic, might be considered as the magna carta (see below) of Maratha *swarajya*. STGM/HSS/377>>

It is dated 28th January, 1677 and recounts the circumstances of Shivaji's coronation in accordance with ascertained sacred laws for the protection of all Hindu rcligious and social traditions.

'It promises to render the most speedy and impartial justice to all who should invoke Shivaji's dispensation following established traditions, scriptures and public opinion; and calls upon people of all communities to act with one accord and cooperate with the government in defeating the yavanas *coming from the north. This done, it concludes the rulers and subjects will be alike blessed by God.'*

It reveals the spirit of Shivaji's administration. It shows that he was not a mere empire-builder adding territory to territory. It proves that Shivaji was a man with a mission who drew his inspirations from history, from the classics, from the society and culture around him, from Ramdas and the saints of Maharashtra and, more constantly, from his mother Jijabai as an embodiment of all these. She had nursed his body and spirit and lived just long enough to witness his coronation. Then she said her *Nunc Dimittis*. Stgm/hss/377

Magna Carta

Magna Carta is an English charter, originally issued in the year 1215 and reissued later in the 13th century in modified versions, which included the most direct challenges to the monarch's authority to date. The charter first passed into law in 1225. The 1297 version, with the long title (originally in Latin) The Great Charter of the Liberties of England, and of the Liberties of the Forest, *still remains on the statute books of England and Wales.*

The 1215 Charter required King John of England to proclaim certain liberties, and accept that his will was not arbitrary, for example, by explicitly accepting that no 'freeman' (in the sense of non-serf) could be punished except through the law of the land, a right which is still in existence today.

Magna Carta was the first document forced on to an English king by a group of his subjects, the feudal barons, in an attempt to limit his powers by law and protect their privileges. It was preceded and directly influenced by the Charter of Liberties in 1100, in which King Henry I had specified particular areas wherein his powers would be limited.

Despite its recognised importance, by the second half of the 19th century, nearly all of its clauses had been repealed in their original form. Three clauses remain part of the law of England and Wales, however, and it is generally considered part of the uncodified constitution. Lord Denning described it as 'the greatest constitutional document of all times—the foundation of the freedom of the individual against the arbitrary authority of the despot'. In a 2005 speech, Lord Woolf described it as 'first of a series of instruments that now are recognised as having a special constitutional status', the others being the Habeas Corpus Act, the Petition of Right, the Bill of Rights, and the Act of Settlement.

The charter was an important part of the extensive historical process that led to the rule of constitutional law in the English-speaking world, although it was 'far from unique, either in content or form'. In practice, Magna Carta in the medieval period did not, in general, limit the power of kings, but by the time of the English Civil War, it had become an important symbol for those who wished to show that the king was bound by the law. It influenced the early settlers in New England and inspired later constitutional documents, including the United States Constitution.

It is important to note that though King John of England was forced to sign the Magna Carta, Shivaji did this voluntarily.

□

Shivaji and Geneva Conventions

The Geneva Conventions

The Geneva Conventions comprise four treaties and three additional protocols that set the standards in international law for humanitarian treatment of the victims of war. The singular term 'Geneva Convention' refers to the agreements of 1949, negotiated in the aftermath of World War II, updating the terms of the first three treaties and adding a fourth treaty. The language is extensive, with articles defining the basic rights of those captured during a military conflict, establishing protections for the wounded, and addressing protections for civilians in and around a war zone. The treaties of 1949 have been ratified, in whole or with reservations, by 194 countries.

Protected persons are entitled, in all circumstances, to respect for their persons, their honour, their family rights, their religious convictions and practices, and their manners and customs. They shall, at all times, be humanely treated, and shall be protected, especially against all acts of violence or threats thereof and against insults and public curiosity. Women shall be especially protected against any attack on their honour, in particular against rape, enforced prostitution, or any form of indecent assault. Without prejudice to the provisions relating to their state of health, age and sex, all protected persons shall be treated with the same consideration by the party to the conflict in whose power they are, without any adverse distinction based, in particular, on race, religion or political opinion. However, the parties to the conflict may take such measures of control and security in regard to protected persons as may be necessary as a result of the war.

—Article 27, Fourth Geneva Convention

In diplomacy, the term 'convention' does not have its common meaning as an assembly of people. Rather, it is used in diplomacy to mean an international agreement or treaty. The first three Geneva Conventions were revised and expanded in 1949, and the fourth was added at that time.

- *First Geneva Convention for the Amelioration of the Condition of the Wounded and Sick in Armed Forces in the Field, 1864.*
- *Second Geneva Convention for the Amelioration of the Condition of Wounded, Sick and Shipwrecked Members of Armed Forces at Sea, 1906.*
- *Third Geneva Convention relative to the Treatment of Prisoners of War, 1929.*
- *Fourth Geneva Convention relative to the Protection of Civilian Persons in Time of War, 1949.*

The whole set is referred to as the 'Geneva Conventions of 1949' or simply the 'Geneva Convention'.

A Disciplined Army

On the day of Dashera, the army would set out from camp for the country selected by the Rajah. At the time of departure, a list was made of all the property of every man, high or low, carried for himself. The troops were to subsist in foreign parts for eight months. No woman or female slave or dancing girl was allowed to accompany the army. A soldier keeping any of these was beheaded. No woman or child was to be taken captive, only men. Cows were exempt from seizure, but bullocks may be taken for transport only. Brahmins and Mullahs were not to be molested. No soldier should misconduct himself. On their return, the whole army was searched and the property found was compared with the old list and the excess found was deducted from their salary.

The generals would deliver their booty in gold, silver, jewels and costly clothes to the Rajah, present their accounts and take their dues from the treasury. The officers and men were to be promoted or punished according to their conduct during the campaign (*Shivaji and His Times*, Jadunath Sarkar, p. 286)

The French traveller Francois Bernier wrote in his *Travels in Mughal India*:

"I forgot to mention that during pillage of Sourate, Seva-ji, the Holy Seva-ji! Respected the habitation of the reverend father Ambrose, the Capuchin missionary. 'The Frankish padres are good men', he said 'and shall not be attacked.' He spared also the house of a deceased Delale or Gentile broker, of the Dutch, when assured that he had been very charitable while alive."

A Maratha folklore tells of an event when Shivaji was presented a beautiful Muslim princess (daughter of Amir of Kalyan, Maharashtra) as a trophy by one of his captains. Shivaji was reported to have told this lady that if his mother was as strikingly beautiful as she was, perhaps he would have been handsome as well. He wished her well and allowed her to return to her family unharmed and under his protection.

In the medieval period, people were harassed by the soldiers stationed in a region or marching through a village. Shivaji was a strict disciplinarian who would not allow his army to misbehave.

Shivaji's Circular to Army Officers

Shivaji's circular letter dated 9th May, 1674 to his army fully illustrates his anxiety for the welfare of his people and the good name of his soldiery. It runs:

"To *jumledars, havaldars* and *karkuns* (i.e. accounting officers) in charge of the army stationed at the village of Havarn in the district of Chiplun of Dabhol division.

"His Highness (i.e. Shivaji) has made arrangements for the cavalry at Chiplun and there is no intention to return to the upcountry hereafter. Owing to the stay of the army at Chiplun, all the grain and other necessaries, that were stored for the rainy season in the Dabhol division, have been almost exhausted, entailing hardships upon the people of the district for the army's requirements of fodder and other necessaries. The cavalry had to remain inactive for twenty days in the hot season of Vaishakh (e.g. about April-May). As it was necessary, corn has been supplied to the cavalry from various forts. Now, you will ask for any amount of rations of grain and grass, feed recklessly while supplies are available and when they are exhausted will get nothing in the height of the rainy season. Then you will starve and the horses will start dying, which will mean that you yourselves have killed them.

"Then you will start molesting the people. Some of you would go and bring the grains from the peasants, some others would bring bread, some grass, some firewood, and some vegetables. If you behave in this fashion, the poor peasants who are somehow eking out a bare livelihood will start leaving. Many of them will start dying of starvation. This would mean that you are worse than the Mughals. Such would be the curse of the peasants. Then you will be blamed for the plight of the people and the horses. So, troopers and footmen, bear this in mind and behave properly. Some of you may be staying in cavalry cantonments or different villages. You have no business to molest the people in any way or to step outside your residence. His Highness has given you your salaries from the treasury. Whatever one wants, whether it be grain, or grass for cattle that you might be keeping, or fuel or vegetables, he should buy it in the market or when it comes round for sale. You must not quarrel with or oppress anybody.

"Authorities will issue ration in such a way that the supplies assigned for the cavalry should last for the whole season. You must take these accordingly, so that you will not starve and will have your food every day and the horses will also gain strength. There is no need to argue with the authorities for nothing or to say 'Give me this' or 'Give me that' or to break into store-rooms and plunder the stores.

"Troopers are living in barracks. Some of them will light a fire, some will make hearths at wrong places, some will take light for smoking tobacco without noticing that hay is lying about or the wind is blowing, Then suddenly there will occur an accident.

When one barrack catches fire, all others shall also be burnt down. Then even if some peasants are beheaded (as scapegoats) or the authorities are censured, not a piece of timber would become available for constructing (new) barracks and not a single one can be built. This is to be understood by all. Therefore, let due warning be taken by all. Officers should always make rounds to see that there is no danger from fires or hearths. If you keep the lamps burning at night, mice might carry away the lighted wick and cause mischief. This must not happen. Precautions should be taken against fires and everything should be done to safeguard barracks and grass. Then the horses will outlive the season. Otherwise, there will be no need to stable the horses nor to feed them because that will be the end of cavalry! Then you will be free from all care! Therefore, it is that I have written to you in so much detail.

"All *jumledars, havaldars and karkuns* should hear this letter being read to them and remain vigilant. Often and often, day after day, you should keep yourself informed and give strict instructions. And whoever will fail to act according to this order, whoever will be guilty of this offence, whoever will be found to blame, that Maratha will not be spared of his honour, not to mention service. Soldiers! Bear this in mind. You will not be spared if you commit excesses. Therefore, bear this in mind and behave properly." p. 390 to 391 (Shivaji—His Life & Times).

Shivaji's Version of the Geneva Code

The above passage is Shivaji's version of the Geneva Code. It is important to note that the Geneva Code came into being after a lot of deleberation between nations and in stages over a hundred years. The first Geneva convention was held in 1864 and the fourth was held in 1969. What is, however, unique is that the concept of the Geneva convention struck Shivaji, an individual and that too in the medieval ages.

It must be emphasised that Shivaji was aware of all the atrocities committed by the Muslim invaders right from the first raid of Mohammed Ghazni, who sacked the Somnath Mandir to the demolition of the Keshavrai Mandir in Mathura by Aurangzeb. Yet it is creditable that even under the greatest provocation, Shivaji never allowed power to corrupt him.

It is pertinent to note that not only did Shivaji not demolish any mosque, but he did not touch even one mosque which was built in the place of a destroyed *mandir*.

In fact, under the gravest of provocation, when he was under personal attack in Surat, he did not order a general massacre.

The following chapters on 'Shivaji and Justice', 'Shivaji and Religion' and 'Shivaji and Slavery' bring out these noble facets of his character all the more explicitly.

□

Shivaji and Religion

Kafi Khan

Even Kafi Khan, a hostile writer, conceded that "*whenever Shivaji's army went on military expeditions, no harm came to mosques, the book of God or women of anyone. Whenever a copy of the Quran came into his hands, he treated it with respect and gave it to some of his Musalman followers. When the women of any Hindu or Muslim were taken prisoners by his men and they had no friend to protect them, he watched over them until they were restored to their relations. Such restrained behaviour on the part of a conquerer and such a high sense of virtue and morality are rare at all times. Shivaji's self-discipline and generosity towards his foes were a characteristic of his nature which, to quote Justice Ranade, 'stands out in marked contrasts with the looseness and ferocity of those times.'*

This behaviour was so shocking for those times that were they written by a Hindu, perhaps we would not have believed in them. Today, we believe in them only because it is written by a hostile source.

Muslims in Shivaji's Service

There were many Muslims amongst Shivaji's forces like Siddi Hillal (cavalry head), Siddi Wahawaha (cavalry); both died with Baji Prabhu at Ghod Khind, Noorkhan Baig (first *sarnobat*), Madari Mehtar (bodyguard, especially during Shivaji's Agra visit), Kazi Haider (secretary in charge of Urdu/Persian correspondence), Shama Khan (*sardar*), Siddi Ambar Wahad, Hussain Faan Miyan (officer), Darya Sarang/Ibrahim Khan/Siddi Sambal (who was previously a part of the Siddis of Janjira but later shifted loyalties to Shivaji/Siddi Misri (the nephew of Siddi sambal)/Sultan Khan/ Daud Khan (naval officer), Daulat Khan (admiral), seven cavalry regiments, 700 Pathans, besides many Muslims in the Maratha navy, Mohamed Sais in charge of Shivaji's stables. Shivaji's only portrait was painted by Mir Mohammed which was later printed in the book *Storia de Mongor*, by Mannuci, an Italian. He was a follower of Baba Yakub of Kelshi. This should prove that Shivaji wasn't just a leader of Hindus only, but had followers from all religions and regions (including Abyssinians, like the Siddis, the Portuguese and the English).

In fact, today we know what Shivaji looked entirely due to the portrait of Shivaji painted by a Muslim artist, Mir Mohammed. This painting was printed in the book '*Storia de Mogor*' by the Italian adventurer, Mannucci.

He took the momentous step of recruiting 700 Pathans to his infantry, in response to the earnest plea of Gomaji Naik, an old retainer of his maternal grandfather, Jadhavrao of Sindkhed. The Pathan contingent which had been the employee of the Bijapure *durbar* was now placed under a Brahim commander, Raghunath Ballal, the man who had played a leading role in the destruction of the Mores of Javali.

Religious Bigotry of Aurangzeb

The religious bigotry of Aurangzeb is well brought out in the following passage:

The Maasir-Alamgiri enthusiastically appreciative of this observes: '*On the 17th Zil-kada 1079 H. (18th April 1669), it reached the ears of His Majesty, the protector of the of the faith, that in the provinces of Thatta, Multan and Benares, but especially in the latter, foolish Brahmins were in the habit of expounding frivolous books in their schools, and that students and learners, Musalmans as well as Hindus, went there, even from long distances, led by a desire to become acquainted with the wicked sciences they taught. The director of the faith, consequently, issued orders to all the governors of provinces to destroy with a willing hand the schools and temples of the infidels; and they were strictly enjoined to put an entire stop to the teaching and practising of idolatrous forms of worship. On the 15th Rabiu-l ahar, it was reported to His Religious Majesty that, in obedience to orders, the government officers had destroyed the temple of Bishvanath at Benares. In the month of Ramazan 1080H (December 1669), in the 13th year of the reign, this justice-loving monarch, the constant enemy of tyrants, commanded the destruction of the Hindu temples of Mathura known by the name of Dehra Kesu Rai, and soon that stronghold of falsehood was levelled with the ground. On the same spot was laid, at great expense, the foundation of a great mosque. The den of inequity was thus destroyed. 333 lakhs were expended on this work. Glory be to God who has given us the Faith of Islam that, in the reign of the destroyer of false gods, an undertaking so difficult of accomplishment has been brought to a successful termination. This vigorous support given to the true faith was a severe blow to the arrogance of the Rajas... The richly jewelled idols taken from the pagan temples were transferred to Agra and there placed beneath the steps leading to the Nawab Begum Sahib's mosque, in order that they might ever be pressed under foot by the true believers. Mathura changed its name into Islamabad.'*

Shivaji, a Humanitarian

In contrast, Shivaji's sentiments of inclusivity and tolerance of other religions can be seen in an admonishing letter to Aurangzeb, in which he wrote:

"In Your Majesty's reign, many of the forts and provinces have gone out of your possession, and the rest will soon do so too because there will be no slackness on my part in ruining and devastating them. Your peasants are downtrodden; the yield of every village has declined,—in the place of one lakh (of rupees) only one thousand, and in the place of a thousand, only ten are collected, and that too with difficulty. When poverty and beggary have made their homes in the palaces of the Emperor and the princes, the condition of the

grandees and officers can be easily imagined. It is a reign in which the army is in a ferment, the merchants complain, the Muslims cry, the Hindus are grilled, most men lack bread at night and in the day, inflame their own cheeks by slapping them (in anguish). How can the royal spirit permit you to add the hardship of the jaziya *to this grievous state of things? The infamy will quickly spread from west to east and become recorded in books of history that the Emperor of Hindustan, coveting the beggars' bowls, takes* jaziya *from Brahmins and Jain monks, yogis, sannyasis, bairagis, paupers, mendicants, ruined wretches, and the famine-stricken, that his valour is shown by attacks on the wallets of beggars, that he dashes down to the ground the name and honour of the Timurids.*

"May it please Your Majesty, if you believe in the true divine book and word of God (i.e. the Quran), you will find there (that God is styled) Rabb-ul-Alamin, the lord of all men, and not Rabb-ul-Musalmin, the lord of the Muhammadans only. Verily, Islam and Hinduism are terms of contrast. They are (diverse pigments) used by the true divine painter for blending the colours and filling in the outlines (of his picture of the entire human species); if it be a temple, the bell is rung in yearning for him only. To show bigotry for any man's own creed and practice is equivalent to altering the words of the holy book. To draw new lines on a picture is equivalent to finding fault with the painter...

"In strict justice, the jaziya *is not at all lawful. From the political point of view, it can be allowable only if a beautiful woman wearing gold ornaments can pass from one province to another without fear or molestation. (But) in these days, even the cities are being plundered, what shall I say of the open country? Apart from its injustice, this imposition of the* jaziya *is an innovation in India and inexpedient.*

"If you imagine piety to consist in oppressing the people and terrorising the Hindus, you ought first to levy the Jaziya *from Rana Raj Singh, who is the head of the Hindus. Then it will not be so very difficult to collect it from me, as I am at your service. But to oppress ants and flies is far from displaying valour and spirit.*

"I wonder at the strange fidelity of your officers that they neglect to tell you of the true state of things, but cover a blazing fire with straw; may the sun of your royalty continue to shine above the horizon of greatness. hss Page 253

This celebrated letter to Aurangzeb protesting against the imposition of *Jaiziya* marks him out not as a provincial but as a national figure in history.

In thus issuing a strident call for toleration of all religions, not only because such a spirit was necessary for the well-being of the state, but because intolerance was an insult to divinity, Shivaji emerges not only as a great leader of Indians, but also as a humanitarian.

Shivaji as a Saviour of Hinduism

As pointed out earlier:

'The Hindus were often defeated even before the battle started. The Muslims destroyed the temples and amassed great wealth from them. The Hindus humanised their idols; their gods ate and drank. and even otherwise behaved like people. If the Muslims could destroy their living gods, how could the Hindus dare to fight with them?'

Aurangzeb's frenzy continued for several years. Cart-loads of idols were taken also from Jodhpur to the capital.

'To be trodden upon by the faithful. The Jaziya was reimposed Hindu fairs and festivals were prohibited. Hindus were forbidden to wear arms and fine dresses, and to ride well-bred horses, elephants, and to go in palanquins, According to the law, 21/2$_{p.c.}$ should be taken from Musalmans and 5$_{p.c.}$ from Hindus (customs duty).'

Jadunath Sarkar, whose 1928 biography of Aurangzeb in four volumes, suggested that Aurangzeb intended nothing less than to establish an Islamic state in India, an objective that could not be fulfilled without '*the conversion of the entire population to Islam and the extinction of every form of dissent*'; and to render this scenario more complete, he proposed that the *jaziya* (poll-tax) on non-Muslims, which Aurangzeb had re-instituted in 1679, was aimed at forcibly converting Hindus to Islam.

If you can't fight them, join them. The carrot, if not the stick worked for everyone, i.e. *mansabs* for the Kshatriyas (Rajputs), *dakshina* for the Brahmins (*see darshanias* of Akbar), lower taxes for the Baniyas, and equality and respect for *Shudras* and *Chandalas*. 20 per cent of the population converted while Aurangzeb was in Agra.

The last 30-35 years of his life he devoted to fighting Shivaji and the Marathas and, therefore, he could not afford to have a religious rebellion on his hands. So, conversions were put on hold.

No wonder Kavi Bhushan says, "*Were it not for Shiva, the whole of Hindustan would be circumcised.*"

The Battle of Tours

October 10, 732 A.D. marks the conclusion of the Battle of Tours, arguably one of the most decisive battles in all of history.

A Moslem army, in a crusading search for land and the end of Christianity, after the conquest of Syria, Egypt and North Africa, began to invade Western Europe under the leadership of Abd-er-Rahman, governor of Spain. Abd-er Rahman led an infantry of 60,000 to 4,00,000 soldiers across the Western Pyrenees and towards the Loire river, but they were met just outside the city of Tours by Charles Martel, known as the Hammer, and the Frankish army.

Martel gathered his forces directly in the path of the oncoming Moslem army and prepared to defend themselves by using a phalanx style of combat. The invading Moslems rushed forward, relying on the slashing tactics and overwhelming number of horsemen that had brought them victories in the past. However, the French army, composed of foot-soldiers armed only with swords, shields, axes, javelins and daggers, was well trained. Despite the effectiveness of the Moslem army in previous battles, the terrain caused them a disadvantage. Their strength lay within their cavalry, armed with large swords and lances, which along with their baggage mules, limited their mobility. The French army displayed great ardency in withstanding the ferocious attack. It was one of the rare times in the Middle Ages when infantry held its ground against a mounted attack. The exact length of the battle is undetermined. Arab sources claim that it was a two-day battle, whereas Christian sources hold that the fighting clamoured on for seven days. In either case, the battle ended when the French captured and killed Abd-er-Rahman. The Moslem army withdrew peacefully overnight and even though Martel expected a surprise retaliation, there was none. For the Moslems, the death of their leader caused a sharp setback and they had no choice, but to retreat back across the Pyrenees, never to return again.

Not only did this prove to be an extremely decisive battle for the Christians, but the Battle of Tours is considered the high water-mark of the Moslem invasion of Western Europe.

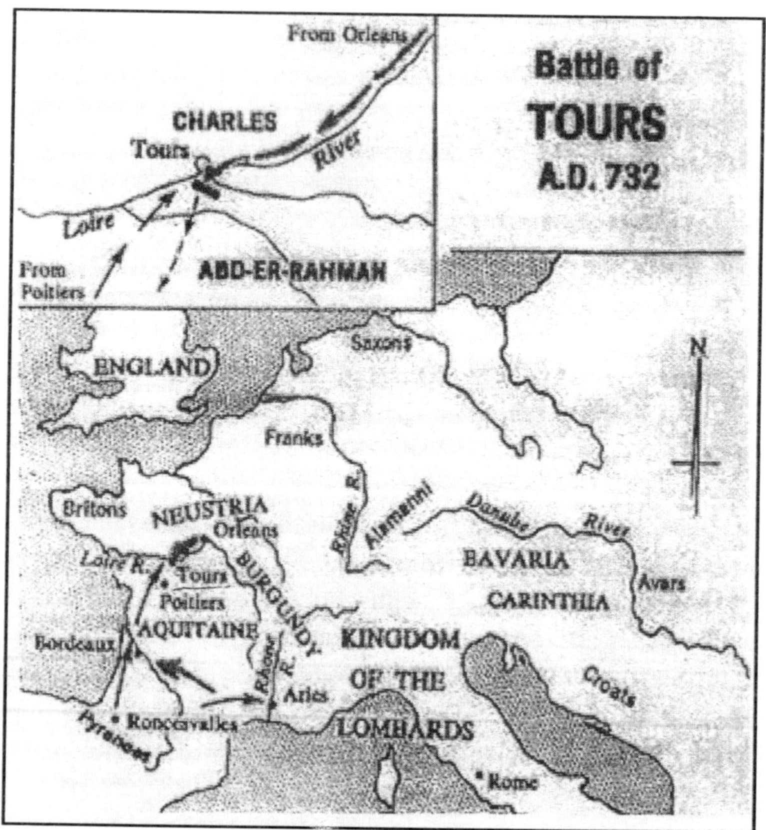

Gibbon best puts everything in the right perspective when he talks about the significance of the Battle of Tours:

"A victorious line of march had been prolonged above a thousand miles from the rock of Gibraltar to the banks of the Loire; the repetition of an equal space would have carried the Saracens to the confines of Poland and the highlands of Scotland; the Rhine is not impassable than the Nile or Euphrates and the Arabian fleet might have sailed without a naval combat into the mouth of the Whales. Perhaps the interpretation of the Quran would now be taught in the schools of Oxford, and her pulpits might demonstrate to a circumcised people the sanctity and truth of Mahomet." Mehendale in Shivaji—His Life and Times, pg 640.

□

Shivaji's Diplomacy

The previous discussions have shown without doubt that Shivaji used his brains rather than his brawn.

In 1646, Shivaji took his first fort, Torna from its Bijapuri commander by some cunning device without fighting. He found a treasure amounting to two lakhs of hons.

In 1648, he took advantage of a family feud of Nilkanth Rao and got the control of Purander Fort.

When Afzal Khan came, he flattered him so much that Afzal Khan was convinced to come all the way to Javali which proved to be a veritable trap.

Raja Jaisingh came with a force of 4,00,000. When during the siege of Purander, the Marathas lost Murar Baji, Shivaji knew that defeat was eminent. He sued for peace and lost 23 forts and only 12 remained for himself. But if you peruse the treaty minutely, one realises that though on paper he gave 23 forts, he actually gave away only 20. Also there was no mention of the sack of Surat from where he walked away with one crore rupees. Thirdly, he got himself exempted from imperial service, allowing instead his son Sambhaji to be appointed a *panch hazari*. He saw the efforts of 20 years go down the drain in a matter of four months. But he was confident that he could win them back. He knew than it was a time for diplomacy. The life of his men was more important that glory of war. Like the phoenix, he rose from ashes and fought on to create an empire and be coronated.

His ultimate aim was to win, for which he would not mind a tactical retreat. So, he surrendered to the Mughal representative

Raja Jai Singh as a tactical retreat and bounced back when times changed and turned out a winner in the end. He followed the principles of Chanakya of '*sama dama danda bheda*' to ensure victory for the Hindavi *swarajya*.

Diplomacy in Agra

But his real flair for diplomacy was seen in Agra.

When Shivaji walked out of Aurangzeb's *durbar*, all the *sardars* were aghast and we have already seen how they bayed for his blood. Jahanara resented the mild attitude taken by the Emperor against the imprudence of Shivaji in the court because she was directly affected by the plunder of Surat from where she received certain privileges...

Yet when Aurangzeb started planning to kill Shivaji, she started pleading his case before the Emperor. She told the Emperor, "If you kill him, no one will have faith in your assurances." This was because Shivaji had displayed a high degree of humility and generosity, so that within a short time, besides Jahanara, Shivaji had also won over Jaffer Khan and Mohammed Amin Khan Bakshi. The only person who remained hostile was Jaswant Singh.

Shivaji could successfully gain the sympathy of almost all the influential officers of Agra, alleging that 'the Emperor had invited him for his birthday celebrations and then suddenly changed colours and for no fault of his, thrown him in prison.'

Needless to say, a lot of credit for this change of heart of the courtiers had to go to the liberal presents that Shivaji sent them.

Shivaji and Zinnat-un-Nissa

Zinnat-un-Nissa was Aurangzeb's second daughter from his wife Udaypuri Begum. She was born in 1643. Both of them were Aurangzeb's favourites. As with most people in Agra Zinnat-un-Nissa was also impressed by the courage, nobility and courteousness of Shivaji. The daredevilry of Afzal Khan's assassination, the escape from Panhalgad, the raid on Shaista Khan, the sacking of Surat must have awed her. But what must have really made a mark on her was the chivalry that Shivaji showed with respect to the prisoner-maid of Kalian. Comparing a woman prisoner to his mother, instead of raping her must have shocked her and surely warmed the cockles of her heart.

When Shivaji went to Agra, he was 36 and she was 23, i.e. both of them were undoubtedly in the prime of their youth. Of course, she did not meet him in the *haveli* in which he was imprisioned. Neither did she declare her undying love for him, but it may be true that she had deep in her heart a profound respect for the man, the likes of which she had neither met or heard of before. So, whether it was a platonic relationship, one does not really know.

There are two circumstantial evidences for that.

The first being that Zinnat-un-Nissa did not marry during her whole lifetime. As a daughter of the Emperor, she surely must have had many proposals which she must have declined for some reason or the other.

Zinnat-un-Nissa was her father Aurangzeb's favourite daughter. She was well versed in diplomacy and politics. Whether she had some role to play in changing Aurangzeb's descision to kill Shivaji is unknown. But what is known is that after the death of Shivaji, Aurangzeb came down to the Deccan. He first cruelly killed Sambhaji and later captured Sambhaji's family—his wives Yesubai and Durgabai, his son Shahu, his elder sister Renuakka and his daughter Kamalja. Though Aurangzeb mercilessly killed Sambhaji, he surprisingly did not harm any of his imprisoned family. During the 27 frustrating years that Aurangzeb spent in the Deccan and knowing his cruel nature, it is surprising he did not harm the descendants of Shivaji. It is suggested by many historians that they were safe only because of the good offices of Zinnat-un-Nissa.

Diplomacy after Agra

Shivaji during his life-time signed many treaties. He also broke most treaties that he signed when he found it in his interest to do so. He broke treaties he had signed with the English, the Portuguese and the Mughals. But he was diplomatic enough never to break treaties that he made with the Adilshahi and the

Kutubshahi. As far as possible, Shivaji never fought with two strong enemies at the same time. That was the essence of diplomacy. All historians are sure that two of the greatest warriors of modern times, Napoleon and Hitler were winning their war against Britain and her allies until they invaded Russia. Opening up a second front has always been a sure recipe for defeat.

But perhaps the most shocking piece of diplomacy that Shivaji showed was after his escape from Agra. Rather than gloat about it, he wrote a letter dripping in humility and perhaps sarcasm.

3rd October, 1667 (from Persian *Akhbarat*): The Emperor received a letter from Prince Muhammad Muazzam (the new Viceroy of the Deccan) to this effect: Shivaji has written a letter to me saying, "I am a hereditary slave of the Imperial court and my son Sambhaji has been created a commander of five thousand (with 5,000 trooper rank) but has received no *jagir* as *Tankha* (or subsistence allowance). I now beg that His Majesty would pardon the offences of this servant, restore the *mansab* of my son and assign a *jagir* to him. I am ready to render service in person wherever I am ordered."

To understand this letter better, one should bear in mind that Aurangzeb had asked Shivaji to return the one lakh rupees he had given to him as his travel expenses from Rajgad to Agra.

□

Shivaji and Crisis

Survival of the Fittest

The true test of a living organism is its capacity to survive a crisis. The Maratha state created by Shivaji in the course of three decades proved its vitality during the thirty years that followed his death on 4th April, 1680. Indeed, if the Darwinian test of survival is to be applied to both, the Mughal empire and the Marath kingdom, not by the same principle of 'live and let live' but by the militant method of exterminating the rival—the Marathas proved their fitness to survive by the external and immutable law of evolution. While the grandiose structure of the Mughal imperial system was tottering to its fall, the Maratha power was advancing to a crescendo of staggering success.

Here is somebody who, from the start, never had the might to defeat his rivals in a frontal battle; who after the Purander treaty saw the efforts of 20 years go down the drain in a matter of four months, but still fought on to create an empire with 29 years of constant struggle and enterprise. (Shivaji: the Great Maratha, p. 935 H.S. Sardesai)

Orme, the well-known English historian, gives Shivaji the highest tribute by holding that in courage, resourcefulness and quickness of action, he had few equals in his time. "*No general ever traversed as much ground as he did at the head of armies.*" "*He met,*" *writes the historian,* "*every emergency of peril, however sudden and extreme with instant discernment and unshaken fortitude. The ablest of his officers acquiesced to the imminent superiority of his genius and the boast of the soldier was to have seen Shivaji charging sword in hand."*

Shivaji the 'Immortal'

Shivaji in his short life-time faced crisis after crisis—the duel with Afzal Khan, the escape from Panhalgad, the raid on Shaista Khan, the loss of 23 forts after the Pratapgad treaty and most important the escape from Agra. But Shivaji seemed to lead a charmed life. The English wrote in 1680. "Indeed Sevagy hath died so often that some begin to think him immortal."

In the ensuing treaty of Purander, signed between Shivaji and Jai Singh on 11th June, 1665, Shivaji agreed to give up 23 of his forts and pay compensation of 4,00,000 rupees to the Mughals. He also agreed to let his son Sambhaji become a Mughal *sardar*, serve the Mughal court of Aurangzeb and fight with Mughals against Bijapur. He actually fought alongside Raja Jai Singh's Mughal forces against Bijapur's forces for a few months. His commander, Netaji Palkar, joined Mughals, was rewarded very well for his bravery, converted to Islam, changed his name to Quli Mohammed Khan in 1666 and was sent to the Afghan frontier to fight the restive tribes.

Justice Ranade writes: '*Throughout his career of thirty-four years, Shivaji did not on a single occasion suffer defeat where he led his armies in person; and when his affairs were at their worst, he seemed to gather new courage and resource from the inspiration of the dangers around him.*

During the siege of Ramsej, seven miles north of Nasik, the Marathas revealed their resourcefulness to Aurangzeb. 'If we believe Kafi Khan who was present at the siege' writes Sir Jadunath Sarkar, 'the fort had no iron cannon, but the garrison hollowed out trunks of trees and fired leather missiles from them, which did the work of ten pieces of artillery.' The Marathas never faltered in a crisis because they were fighting for a higher goal, namely *swarajya* or freedom. (Shivaji: the Great Maratha, p. 950)

□

Shivaji and Liberty, Equality, Fraternity

Liberté, égalité, fraternité

Liberté, égalité, fraternité, French for 'liberty, equality, fraternity (brotherhood)', is the national motto of France, and is a typical example of a tripartite motto.

The Declaration of the Rights of Man and of the Citizen of 1789, defined Liberty in Article 4 as follows:

"Liberty consists of being able to do anything that does not harm others; thus, the exercise of the natural rights of every man or woman has no bounds other than those that guarantee other members of society the enjoyment of these same rights."

Equality, on the other hand, was defined by the 1789 Declaration as Judicial Equality (Art. 6).

"The law must be the same for all, whether it protects or punishes. All citizens, being equal in its eyes, shall be equally eligible to all high offices, public positions and employments, according to their ability, and without other distinctions than that of their virtues and talents."

"The third term, 'fraternité', was the most problematic to insert in the triad, as it belonged to another sphere—that of moral obligations rather than rights, links rather than statutes, harmony rather than contract, and community rather than individuality." The word preaches brotherhood (bhaichara)

Take the case of America. Although American society does

not overtly recognise or extol fraternity, this is not to say that fraternity has not played a major role in the development of American society. In fact, fraternity, albeit under different names, has played a vital role in the growth of the American nation. As a country peopled by many different nationalities, races and religions, the 'great melting pot', it could only function smoothly if these different groups learned to live together in harmony, and some measure of success has been achieved in the US in blending so many different races together under one flag—more, some say, than any other nation in history.

They may begin at fraternity, and from there spread to equality and to liberty. When people are disunited, when they have no fraternity, they live in suspicion and fear of each other, and start thinking, 'They can do it, why can't I?'; "They have it, why don't I?" Lack of equality and liberty (that is, liberties are not equal) naturally follow.

Liberty

We have already discussed that the caste that a person was born in decided the work and status of an adult. Whereas Islam preached equality and unity in work and prayer, merit rather than birth decided status in life and even a child could become a ruler and establish a dynasty. On the other hand, if a Hindu was a natural swordsman, but was born in a potter family, there was no way he would be allowed to fight, for that was the prerogative of the Kshatriyas. On the other hand, if a Kshatriya was blessed with good literary skills and had an aptitude for mathematics, he was obviously well suited for studying the *Vedas* and astronomy. But he was forced only to fight even if he had no stomach for it, because the study of *Vedas* and astronomy was the absolute realm of the Brahmins.

Shivaji changed all that. He asked for each family to provide him with one son for the cause of *swarajya*.

"His readiness to recognise merit, no matter in whom it existed and to reward it generously, drew towards him a large band of

brave, intelligent, resourceful men who stood steadfast by his state long after his death."

The best example is that of Jiva Mahala, a barber by caste but a skilled exponent of the *dand-patta* (long sword). Shivaji is known to have hand-picked him at a wedding procession where he was exhibiting his skills. In any other time and place, that is what he would have remained—a performer. It was under the tutelage of Shivaji that he became a warrior embedded in history.

Equality

If Shivaji's readiness to recognise merit was legendary, so was his swiftness of punishment.

The following passage best brings out Shivaji's concept of equality:

Cosme da Guarda says in '*Life of the Celebrated Shivaji*': "*Such was the good treatment Shivaji accorded to people and such was the honesty with which he observed the capitulations that none looked upon him without a feeling of love and confidence. By his people, he was exceedingly loved. Both in matters of reward and punishment, he was so impartial that while he lived, he made no exception for any person; no merit was left unrewarded, no offence went unpunished; and this he did with so much care and attention that he specially charged his governors to inform him in writing of the conduct of his soldiers, mentioning in particular those who had distinguished themselves, and he would at once order their promotion, either in rank or in pay, according to their merit. He was naturally loved by all men of valour and good conduct."*

Shivaji had his advisors, his council of eight ministers, the *ashtapradhan mandal*. But they were not a coterie. Each of them except Panditrao (who was in charge of religious decisions) were expected to perform military duties. But he was accessible to each and every one of his subjects.

Shivaji advised Sambhaji, *"It is the duty of a ruler to listen not only to the great, but also to the humble. Because he himself had often received better and sounder council from the latter. Moreover, it was the work of a man rather than his worth (caste) that determined his real importance to society.*

"What I should most recommend to you is that in no case should you have a favourite if you are to spare your subjects from jealousy." He added that "by strictly adhering to this principle a ruler could count on the support of all sections of his people in a period of real crisis"

The Khandoji Khopde Episode

When Afzal Khan came with his army, Khandoji Khopde, sure of the Khan's success, was one of the first Maratha *sardars* to join him in return for the *deshmukhi* of Utroli. Contrary to his expectations, Shivaji disembowelled the Khan. Khandoji Khopde knew that soon Shivaji would come after him. He requested his father-in-law, Haibatrao Shilimkar, a staunch supporter of Shivaji, to request Kanhoji Jedhe to secure a pardon from Shivaji. Kanhoji Jedhe was one of the first *jagirdars* to join Shivaji along with his five sons. (I pour water over my *jagir.*)

Shivaji could not refuse Kanhoji Jedhe and he pardoned Khandoji Khopde. But every time he saw the traitor, he was consumed with anger. And one day he gave orders to cut Khandoji Khopde's right hand and left leg. When Kanhoji Jedhe naturally asked Shivaji why he went back on his word, Shivaji replied, "I cut off the hand that raised a sword against *swarajya* and the leg that took him to the enemy. But as per my promise, I pardoned his life."

Rewards and Punishments

As Shivaji's *swarajya* grew, the job opportunities grew, those who showed exemplary courage or performed a particularly daunting task were assured promotions and rewards. They were not only free from any sort of exploitation, but were provided the means to develop confidence, guts, intelligence and imbibe it all in their very village. They did not have to go to the capital or town; it was all available at their doorstep.

Just as Shivaji was quick with his praise, he was equally just and prompt with his punishments. Shivaji was unique because he felt that every person had a role to play in the building of *swarajya*. He often said:

"Just as every alphabet is part of a mantra, *just as every plant had some medicinal value, so also every man has his use."* For Shivaji, it was only a matter of finding his aptitude and attitude, assessing his strengths and weaknesses then and fitting him in the right job. Once done, such a man is willing to take up the most dangerous assignment.

Shivaji evaluated his officers and men very stringently. Maligners and shirkers were taken to task. Shivaji did not tolerate any weak links in his chain (of command). Such officers were unceremoniously sacked, however high be their status or position. It is pertinent to point out at this juncture that Shamraj Nilkanth, the first Peshwa, was summarily sacked when his leadership was found grossly wanting during the siege of Janjira in... Narhari Anandrao was appointed in his place and then again, he too was removed shortly within one year in... and Moropant was appointed in his place.

□

Shivaji and Sanskrit/ Marathi Language

Promotion of Sanskrit/Marathi

The house of Shivaji was one of the Indian royal families who were well acquainted with Sanskrit and promoted it. The root can be traced from Shahaji who supported Jayram Pindye and many like him. Shivaji Maharaj's seal was prepared by him. Shivaji continued this trait and developed it further. He got *Rajya Vyavahar Kosh* (a political treatise) prepared in which he compiled Sanskrit equivalents of Persian, Arabic, Turkish and Deccani Urdu. He named his forts as Sindhudurg, Prachandgarh, Suvarndurg, etc. He named the *Ashta Pradhan* (council of ministers) as per Sanskrit nomenclature, viz. *Nyayadhish, Senapati*, etc. His Rajpurohit Keshav Pandit was himself a Sanskrit scholar and poet. After his death, Sambhaji, who was himself a Sanskrit scholar (his verse, *Budhbhushanam*), continued it. Serfoji II from the Thanjavur branch of the Bhosale continued the tradition of printing by modern methods, first book in Marathi Devnagari.

Shivaji was well educated as per the dictates of the times. We have already seen previously that Shivaji was well educated as per the standards of the times.

Language Reform

Shivaji desired to shake off what he perhaps perceived as enforced affectation. His desire to do so became apparent as early as 1646. The earliest of his letters which have survived is dated 28th January, 1646, and it bears his seal in Sanskrit for which there was no precedent for several centuries before him. Later, he ordered the completion of a lexicon to remove the influence of the 'language of Muslims' (e.g. the Persian language) by replacing Persian words that had crept into the indigenous lexicon by ones in Sanskrit. At his behest, Raghunathpant Hanmate and Dhundhiraj Lakshman Vyas executed this work· this lexicon, called the *Raja-vyavahara-kosha*, seems to have been compiled in 1677. Even before that, since his coronation, Shivaji had already begun using in his deeds of grant Sanskrit words in place of Persian. He had renamed several designations in his government to that end at the time of his coronation. The result was, thus, summarised by V.K. Rajwade, the doyen of Maratha historians:

Date of Letter	Persian Words	Marathi Words	Total	Percentage of Marathi Words
1628	202	34	236	14.4
1677	51	84	135	62.2
1728	8	119	127	93.7

(MHN pg-372)

Literary Works Commissioned

Some of the literary works commissioned or supported by Shivaji are as ennuemerated below:

Lekhan Prashasti (writing skills) by Balaji Awaji

Afzal Khan Vadh Powada (The Ballad of the Slaying of Afzal Khan) by Shahir Adyan Das

Rajvyavarkosh (Administrative Terminology) by Raghunath Pandit and Dhundiraj Vyas

Karnakousthub by Bal Sangmeshwarkar

Ganimi Kawa (guerilla war) by Pandit Sankarsh Sakalkale

Shivkaryodaya (Unification of Hindus) Gagabhatt

Shenvi ani Kayastha Prabhu, a religious judgement by Gagabhatt

□

Shivaji and Socio-religious Reforms

Prevention of *Sati*

It is said by some authorities that the practice was more common among the higher castes, and among those who considered themselves to be rising in social status. It was little known or unknown in most of the population of India and the tribal groups, and known in the lowest castes. According to at least one source, it was very rare for anyone in the later Mughal empire, except royal wives to be burnt.

Jijabai wanted to commit *sati* after the death of her husband Shahaji, but was prevented from doing so by Shivaji, thus setting an example to his subjects.

Eliminated Untouchability

Apastambha Dharma Sutra III, 10-26, says:

The tongue of a Shudra, who spoke evil about a Brahmin should be cut off. A Shudra who dared to assume a position of equality with the first three castes was to be flogged. If a Shudra overheard a recitation of the Vedas, *molten tin was to be poured into his ears; if he repeated the* Vedas, *his tongue should be cut and if he remembered Vedic hymns, his body was to be torn into pieces.*

After defeating the Mores at Javali, Shivaji built a fort at Bhorpya hill, and named it Pratapgad. A temple of Bhavani Mata was also built. When Shivaji arrived for the *pranpratishtha pooja,* he saw a few lower caste people standing some distance away. When questioned, he was told that they were the untouchables who had carved the idol. Shivaji asked the untouchables to perform the *pooja*. The *poojari* objected, but Shivaji reasoned that:

'if these untouchables could carve the idol, how would that idol be desecrated by their performing the pooja?'

Elimination of Casteism

His personal attendant was a *mehter*, Madari. His bodyguard when he went to meet Afzal Khan was a barber, Jiva Mahale. His look alike who hoodwinked Siddi Johar was also a barber, Shiva Kashid.

"Devadhinam jagat sarvarm mantradhinam ta devata tam mantram Brahmandhinam Brahmana nam devata."

Meaning:

"The universe is under the power of gods, The gods are under the power of the mantras, *The* mantras *are under the power of the Brahmins. Therefore, the Brahmins are our gods."*

Abbe J.A. Dubois's, *Hindu Manners, Customs and Ceremonies, Oxford, Third Edition, 1906, p. 139, see also p. 93.*

Again, *Manu*, 167-272 says:

"Let the king never slay even a Brahmin, though he may have committed all possible crimes.

Yet during the attack on Afzal Khan, when his lawyer Krisha Bhaskar raised his sword to strike a blow on Shivaji's head, Shivaji said, *"So what if you are a Brahmin?"* and he killed him. This was the only scar on Shivaji's body by which he was identified later, both by Fazal Khan at Panhala and his mother, after the escape from Agra.

Stopped Conversions

Shah Jahan (1630 C.E.-1658 C.E.) was the son of a Hindu princess, Jagat Gosain (a wife of Jehangir), and the grandson of another Hindu Rajput princess, Jodhabai (an influential wife of Akbar and mother of Jehangir), yet in 1632 Shah Jahan ordered all recently constructed or partially-constructed Hindu temples obliterated. Seventy-six temples were destroyed in Benares and ten thousand inhabitants were executed by being "blown up with powder, drowned in water or burnt by fire". As a result of this campaign, four thousand were taken captive to Agra where they were tortured to try to convert them to Islam. Only a few apostatised; the remainder were trampled to death by elephants.

Aurangzeb's frenzy continued for several years. Cart-loads of idols were taken also from Jodhpur to the capital to be trodden upon by the faithful. The *Jaziya* was reimposed. Hindu fairs and festivals were prohibited. Hindus were forbidden to wear arms and fine dresses, and to ride well-bred horses, elephants, and to go in palanquins, According to the law, two-and-a-half per cent customs duty should be taken from Musalmans and five per cent from Hindus.

Jadunath Sarkar, whose 1928 biography of Aurangzeb in four volumes suggested that Aurangzeb intended nothing less than to establish an Islamic state in India, an objective that could not be fulfilled without 'the conversion of the entire population to Islam and the extinction of every form of dissent'; and to render this scenario more complete, he proposed that the *jaziya* (poll-tax) on non-Muslims, which Aurangzeb had re-instituted in 1679, was aimed at forcibly converting Hindus to Islam.

The Portuguese government passed a number of laws for the propagation of Christianity which caused considerable harassment to the people. A book called *Livro Do Pai Dos Critados*, a compilation of the copies of various laws made by the Portuguese in this respect, is preserved in manuscript form in the archives of Goa. The Portuguese, who had cultivated hatred against Maharashtra Dharma, that is Hindu Dharma, according to a few contemporary Marathi sources imposed various restrictions on the religious practices of the Hindus. Hindus were prohibited from building temples and Muslims from erecting mosques. The presence of a Portuguese official at every marriage as a witness was made compulsory. No Hindu was allowed to perform any religious function at home and if he was found guilty of that, his house was plundered and he was sent to Goa for a period of two to three years as punishment. He was not allowed to keep a chamber of gods—*dezara* in this house and offer worship on auspicious days. Even the raising of *tulsi* plant and its worship was not permitted. When a person died, leaving behind him only a minor son without any close relation except the widow of the deceased person, the boy was converted to Christianity. People were, therefore, appealing to the Marathas to undo the work of the Portuguese and enhance the prestige of Maharashtra Dharma, a term which found a place in the subsequent treaties with the Portuguese. They often captured a number of innocent Maratha women and children from the Maratha villages and put them under captivity with a constant threat of conversion. To bring pressure on the Marathas, Portuguese had issued Inquisition in Goa and were forcibly converting Hindus to Christianity, well before Shivaji's birth. He defeated Portuguese for the first time in 1667. The reasons of this policy were not only political, but theological too.

The Portuguese persecutions of the Hindus mostly in the 16th century are described in Da Chuna's *Bassein and Goeaz.* Hindu temples and Muslim mosques were demolished for building churches. In famine years, the Catholic fathers used to buy Hindu children from their guardians and make them converts. Particularly Hindu and Muslim orphans were considered as wards of the states, fed and brought up as Christians. When Shivaji demanded the restoration to his hands of any Hindu boy convert at the prayer of the boy's former guardian, the Portuguese governor declined on the ground that it was against the rules of his state to deliver any Christian to pagan authority for the purpose of being made a Pagan again. This was the real cause of the friction. A Portuguese book '*The Vergel de Plantas* ... written before 1680, states that, in 1667, there were counted in Bardes by the favour of the Viceroy the Conde de S. Vicente, 46,450 Christians converted by the Padres of the province of St. Thomas and 7,000 Hindus, out of whom 4,000 have been baptised; as for the remaining 3,000 they are labouring with great zeal for their conversion with the likely hope of success. The words 'favour of the Viceroy' do not mean force, but only the probihtion of the sale of Hindus as slaves to other than the Christian fathers, who converted them.

Started Reconversion to Hinduism

Who was Shivaji/Govind Pansare/53

In the times of Shivaji, Dharma preached that*'a person who was converted from Hinduism to Islam was as good as dead. If he was dead, how could he be made alive again? Still worse for commiting this sin, he would be born as an ant or a bug.'*

The lowest of the Hindu would not condescend to eat food with a Muslim or a Christian, one of the reasons being they ate beef.

One of the first acts of conversion from Hindu to Muslim was to make the neo convert to eat beef.

How could such a person ever be taken back into Hinduism?

But Shivaji was far ahead of his times in this respect too.

Netaji Palkar

After Shivaji's escape from Agra, Aurangzeb, as a revenge, ordered Mirza Raja Jaisingh I to arrest Netaji Palkar. He was then forcibly converted to Islam. His wives were thereafter brought to Delhi and also converted for him to remarry them in the Islamic way. Taking up the name of Muhammed Kuli Khan, Netaji Palkar was appointed as garrison commander of the Kandahar fort. Hc tried to escape, but was traced and trapped at Lahore. Thereafter, on the battlefields of Kandhar and Kabul, he fought for the Mughals against rebel Pathans and utterly defeated them. Thus, he gained the good faith of Aurangzeb and was sent to the Deccan along with Commander Diler Khan to conquer Shivaji's territory. However, after entering Maharashtra, Netaji joined Shivaji's troops and went to Raigad. Thus, after a decade, Netaji turned up at the court of Shivaji, asking to be taken back into the Hindu fold.

Shivaji arranged for reconversion of Netaji at Raigad, even though it was strongly opposed by many of the orthodox Brahmins.

Similarly, Baji Nimbalkar, who had been forcibly converted by Afzal Khan for supposedly leaking his plans to Shivaji, was reconverted to Hinduism. To show his solidarity with Bajaji, he married his daughter Sakhubai to Bajaji's son Mahadji.

The Arya Samaj used the example of Shivaji to strengthen its plea that all mankind were entitled to be admitted within the Hindufold.

Farming and Revenue

About Shivaji's policy of encouraging agriculture, Sabhasad writes:

New cultivators who will come (to settle in our dominions) should be given cattle. Grain and money should be given (to them) for (proving themselves with) seeds. Money and grain (should be) given for their subsistence (also and) the sum should be realised in a couple of years according to the means (of the cultivator). In this manner, should the cultivators be supported? In every village, from each individual cultivator should the *karkum* (i.e. the civil authority) realise, according to the assessment, rent in grain from the crops (at the time of each harvest)."

That this policy was actually adopted is borne out by Shivaji's letter dated 5th September, 1676 to Ramaji Anant, the Subadar of Prabhavali district. It reads:

"His Majesty had kindly appointed you the division. You have taken a solemn oath that you will not appropriate anything for yourself and shall serve His Majesty loyally. Accordingly, act justly without yearning for even the discarded stem of a leaf of vegetable (that does not belong to you). Execute the work of sowing, storing and realisation of government dues at the proper time. Revenue settlement by sharing is adopted in the country. See to it that the cultivator gets his (proper) share and the government its dues. Bear in mind that even slight injustice and oppression on the people would displease His Majesty.

"Secondly, there are no orders to take cash instead of corn. Do not take cash instead of corn. Revenue should be realised in corn which should then be sold so as to fetch a high price and prove beneficial to the state. Revenue should be realised and stored in (proper) time. Then it should be sold in the proper season. Coconut, copra, betel nut and pepper should be sold out in such a season that, on the one hand, they would not be spoilt in storage and, on the other, would fetch a good price.

"Encourage the cultivators and promote cultivation. Exert yourself and go from village to village. The cultivators in the village should be assembled. If a cultivator has the manpower, oxen and grain to cultivate (his) piece of land, well and good. Then he can cultivate the land on his own. But if a cultivator has the ability and manpower to cultivate (his piece of) land, but does not have the oxen, plough and grain and is, therefore, to remain idle, then he should be given cash and made to purchase two or four oxen. He should be given a *khandi* (a unit of measurement) or two of grain for his subsistence. You should get him to cultivate the land according to his ability. The money advanced for oxen and grain should subsequently be realised gradually and according to his ability without charging any interest. You are authorised by His Majesty to spend up to two hundred thousand *Laris* for this purpose—to make inquiries about the peasants, support them, bring waste lands under cultivation and increase the revenue.

"If a cultivator is ready to exert himself, but is unable to pay arrears of dues and is, therefore, in dire straits, then the realisation of the dues should be suspended and report made to His Majesty about the promotion of agriculture as well as about the cancellation of such dues. Then His Majesty would issue a decree about the remission (of the dues in such cases).

Non-payment of revenue was not punished by slavery as we shall see below.

□

Shivaji and Slavery

Slavery begins to appear in explicit and extensive reference in surviving historical records following the raids of Mahmud of Ghazni in the 11th century. Many chroniclers claim that his campaign of 1,024 in which he sacked Ajmer, Nehrwala, Kathiawar, and Somnath was particularly successful in garnering more than 1,00,000 Hindu slaves for the Muslim general.

Qutub Minar remains one important example of the use of slave labour to erect monuments under Muslim rule. It is located in South Delhi. It was built by Qutb-ud-din Aybak of the Slave dynasty, who took possession of Delhi in 1206. It is one of the first monuments built by a Muslim ruler in India.

Slavery under Arabic and Turko-Afghan Invaders

Probably, the greatest factors contributing to the increased supply of Indian slaves for export to markets in Central Asia in this period were the military conquests and tax revenue policies of the Muslim rulers in the subcontinent. According to the Persian historian Firishta, after the Ghaznavid capture of Thanesar, (c. 1014), "the army of Islam brought to Ghazna about 200,000 captives, and much wealth, so that the capital appeared like an Indian city, no soldier of the camp being without wealth, or without many slaves," and that, subsequently, Sultan Ibrahim's raid into the Multan area of north-western India yielded 1,00,000 captives.

Slavery under the Turko-Afghan Delhi Sultanate

'Slave-king' Balban (r. 1266-87) and Sultan Alauddin Khilji (r.

1296-1316) are similarly reported to have legalised the enslavement of those who defaulted on their revenue payments.

Export of Indian Slaves to International Markets

There was a high demand for skilled slaves of India's advanced textile industry. After sacking Delhi, Timur enslaved several thousand skilled artisans, especially the masons for use in the construction of the Bibi-Khanym Mosque in Samarkand. Young female slaves fetched higher market price than skilled construction slaves, sometimes by 150 per cent.

At the time of Muhammad bin Qasim's invasion of Sindh, the head of the state was the Caliph and prisoners taken in Sindh were regularly forwarded to him. Kufi, the author of the Chachnama, *rightly sums up the position. Out of the total catch, four-fifths was the share of the soldiers; "what remained of the cash and slaves was sent to Hajjaj (the Governor of Iraq) for onward transportation to the Khalifa."*

Amir Timur, who invaded India in 1399, and took a large number of prisoners, writes: "I ordered that all the artisans and clever mechanics, who were masters of their respective crafts, should be picked out from among the prisoners and set aside, and accordingly some thousands of craftsmen were selected to await my command. All these I distributed among the princes and amirs *who were present, or who were engaged officially in other parts of my dominions (to take care of them). I had determined to build a Majid-i-Jami in Samarkand, the seat of my empire, which should be without rival in any country; so I ordered that all builders and stone-masons should be set apart for my own special service."*

Ziyauddin Barani records regulations regarding sale of 'horses, slaves and quadrupeds' under one category. T.P. Hughes quoting the Hidayah *says that slaves, male and female, are treated merely as articles of merchandise, and 'very similar rules apply both to the sale of animals and bondsmen.' A milch buffalo cost 10-12 tankahs, a working girl was cheaper. The price of a good quality horse was 90-120 tankahs, that of a* ghulam *was 100 on an average. A handsome boy could be had for 20 to 30 tankahs. It is, therefore, a matter of some satisfaction that under the Khaljis, the value of humans in terms of price was not less than that of horses and buffaloes.*

Islamic civilisation did indeed practice castration of slaves on an unprecedented scale. Several cities in Africa were real factories of eunuchs; they were an expensive commodity as only 25 per cent of the victims survived the operation. Hindu Kush (Hindu-killer) mountain is so named because thousands of enslaved Hindus died in crossing it.

Slavery in America

About 6,00,000 slaves were imported into the US, or 5 per cent of the 12 million slaves brought across from Africa. The great majority went to sugar colonies in the Caribbean and to Brazil, where life expectancy was short and the numbers had to be continually replenished. Life expectancy was much higher in the US (because of better food, less disease, lighter workloads, and better medical care), so the numbers grew rapidly by excesses of births over deaths, reaching 4 million by the 1860 Census. From 1770 until 1860, the rate of natural growth of North American slaves was much greater than for the population of any nation in Europe, and was nearly twice as rapid as that of England.

By 1750, Georgia authorised slavery in the state because they had been unable to secure enough servants as labourers, since economic conditions in England began to improve in the first half of the eighteenth century. During most of the British colonial period, slavery existed in all the colonies. People enslaved in the North typically worked as house servants, artisans, labourers and craftsmen, with the greater number in cities. The South depended on an agricultural economy, and it had a significantly higher number and proportion of slaves in the population, as its commodity crops were labour intensive. Early on, slaves in the South worked primarily in agriculture, on farms and plantations growing indigo, rice, and tobacco; cotton became a major crop after the 1790s. The invention of the cotton gin enabled the cultivation of short-staple cotton in a wide variety of areas, leading to the development of the deep South as cotton country. Tobacco was very labour intensive, as was rice cultivation. In South Carolina in 1720, about 65 per cent of the population consisted of slaves. Planters (defined by historians as those who held 20 slaves or more) used slaves to cultivate commodity crops. Backwoods subsistence farmers, the later wave of settlers in the 18th century who settled along the Appalachian mountains and backcountry, seldom owned slaves.

In the 17th century, Quaker and evangelical religious groups condemned slavery as un-Christian; in the 18th century, rationalist thinkers of the Enlightenment criticised it for violating the rights of man. Though anti-slavery sentiments were widespread by the late 18th century, they had little immediate effect on the centres of slavery: the West Indies, South America, and the Southern United States. The Somersett's case in 1772 that emancipated slaves in England, helped launch the movement to abolish slavery. Pennsylvania passed an Act for the Gradual Abolition of slavery in 1780. Britain banned the importation of African slaves in its colonies in 1807, and the United States followed in 1808. Britain abolished slavery throughout the British Empire with the Slavery Abolition Act, 1833, the French colonies abolished it 15 years later, while slavery in the United States was abolished in 1865 with the 13th Amendment to the US Constitution.

Prohibition of Slave Trafficking

The following paragraph shows how much Shivaji was ahead of the so-called progressive countries. The historian Ravindra Ramdas refers to a trade treaty with the Dutch:

In the letter of assurance dated 26th August, 1677, which Shivaji granted to the Dutch company, traffic in slaves was specifically prohibited. The relevant passage states:

"In the days of the Moorish (Muslim) government, it was allowed for you to buy male slaves and female slaves here (the Karnataka), and to transport the same, without anyone preventing that. But now you may not, as long as I am master of these lands, buy male or female slaves, nor transport them. And in case you were

to do the same, and would want to bring (slaves) aboard, my men will oppose that and prevent it in all ways, and also not allow that they may be brought back in your house; this you must observe and comply with."

In this letter, Shivaji had granted the Dutch company all the privileges they had enjoyed during Sher Khan's rule except the right to buy and transport slaves, "since", comment Jager and Clement in their letter dated 29th August 1677 from Trinamal to Devanampattinam: "(Shivaji) he established (as) a fundamental rule of his government, that none of his subjects may be made into slaves, let alone be sold or transported, in order not to lack any inhabitants, with which these new conquests are sparsely enough provided, even though this tyrannical rule has already made the best inhabitants leave."

As we have seen above, the 'slave-king' Balban (r. 1266-87) and Sultan Alauddin Khilji (r. 1296-1316) are reported to have legalised the enslavement of those who defaulted on their revenue payments.

On the other hand, Shivaji was clear that the *ryots* were his children and he was the *karta* of the family of subjects. His attitude to agriculture and revenue have already been discussed above and can be briefly put down as:

"See to it that the cultivator gets his (proper) share and the government its dues. Bear in mind that even slight injustice and oppression on the people would displease His Majesty.

"Secondly, there are no orders to take cash instead of corn. Do not take cash instead of corn. Revenue should be realised in corn."

For such a noble king, enslavement for non-payment of revenue dues was unthinkable.

□

Shivaji and His Father

When Shah Jahan revolted against his father Jehangir, he had come to Maharaja Shahaji for help. Maharaja Shahaji had sheltered and protected Shah Jahan for about eight months, during which Mughal forces weren't able to catch hold of Shah Jahan.

In 1648 Mustafa Khan, an Adilshahi *Wazir*, had laid siege to Gingee in Tamil Nadu. Shahaji was one of the *mansabdars* under his command. In the middle of the siege, Shahaji requested permission to withdraw with his force to his *jagir*. Mustafa Khan refused. Adilshah asked Mustafa Khan to arrest Shahaji but Mustafa Khan had pledged friendship with Shahaji and even sworn by his son's (Atish) head. He, therefore, diplomatically used Baji Ghorpade to arrest him when he was sleeping after a night of merriment.

Four factors contributed to Shahaji's arrest: his friction with Mustafa Khan, his increasing hold over the *mansabdars* in Karnataka, his own ambitions and aspirations. However, it would be correct to say that Shivaji capturing Kondana in 1647 was the proverbial last straw.

But what is significant here is that it was Afzal Khan who took Shahaji in chains from Gingee to Bijapur. In this interim period, Shivaji gave up the Kondana fort and Adilshah took a benevolent view. Shahaji was put in prison and not killed.

A very reliable Persian history of Bijapur, viz., *Basatin-us-salatin*, supplies the following information: "Shahaji, withdrawing his head from obedience to the Nawab Mustafa Khan, began to oppose him, till, at last, the *nawab* decided to arrest him. One day he made Bajirao Ghorpade and Jaswant Rao get their forces ready and sent them very early in the morning to Shahaji's camp. Shahaji, having passed the preceding night in mirth and revelry, was still sieeping in bed. As soon as the two Raos arrived and he learnt of their purpose, he in utter bewilderment took horse and galloped away from his house alone. Baji Ghorpade gave chase, caught him, and brought him before the *nawab*, who threw him into a confinement. His contingent of 3,000 cavalry was dispersed, and his camp was thoroughly looted. Adil Shah, on hearing of it, sent from his court Afzal Khan to bring Shahaji away and an eunuch to attach his property.

The captive Shahaji, on his arrival at Bijapur, was to be cast into prison, but was handed over to the care of a brother of first eminence, Ahmad Khan (Mulla Ahmad of Kalian) with instructions to conciliate him every possible means. Terms were soon settled. This act of kindness and leniency on the part of the king astonished the residents and gentry of Bijapur, and it began to be said, *"Shahaji Raja is fit to be executed, not kept in prison. Because he has been imprisoned, it seems he will be pardoned and let off."* The possibility of Shahaji's release was not approved by many counsellors of the court because they were apprehensive that the 'wily fox' would lose no opportunity to resume his old tricks or so they felt... According to them, releasing Shahaji was like 'knowingly stepping on a snake's tail, straightening the scorpion's sting, regarding thorns as a heap of flowers or resting with a beehive as one's pillow.'

The all-merciful king then put Shahaji in the charge of Sar-i -Sarnaubat Ahmad Khan, and told him that Shahaji could expect pardon, release and re-instatement if he agreed to peaceably hand over the unimaginable Kondhana fort that had come into (his) possession during the interregnum in the Nizamshahi, Bangalore and the fort at Kundurpi to Adilshahi officials. Shahaji wrote to his two sons—Sambhaji to restore Bangalore (along with 40 miles east of Chittaldurg) and Shivaji to restore Kondana to the Bijapuri officers. They obeyed at once and on 16th May, Shahaji was called by Adilshah to an audience, vested with a robe of honour and set free with the restoration of all his estates and the dignities. A son and heir had been born to Muhammad Adilshah on 5th May 1649, and this joyous event was diplomatically used as a plea for the 'pardon' of Shahaji.

Shahaji realised that 'the thorny shrub of his ill deeds had, by the king's grace, sprouted white flowers. The territories that were in his possession prior to his arrest were restored to him'. p. 144 to 145 (*Shivaji—His Life and Times*)

When Shahaji was thrown in prison because of the rebellion of Shivaji, Shivaji did give up the Kondana fort but it is interesting to note the discussion that followed between him and Sonopant Dabir: (loose translation)

"Shivaji: *Were it not for my father, I would not have given up this fort. And no one would have the guts to take it from me by force.*

"Sonopant: *A fort is not important. Your father is more important. It is, therefore, right that you gave up the fort. Because if you have surrendered the fort to release your father, it is as though you have not surrendered the fort. This enemy has foolishly equated Kondana and Bengaluru to the Meru Parvat of Shahaji. That is not an act to be proud of."*

(Meru Parvat was the highest peak in the Himalayas used by the gods and demons to churn the ocean and produce *amrit*—nectar of eternal life using the Wasuki snake as a rope.)

In conclusion, it is important to note that the elder son Sambhaji was killed during an expedition due to the treacherous role of Afzal Khan. Baji Ghorpade had arrested Shahaji when he was sleeping after a night of merriment. Afzal Khan had taken Shahaji in chains from Gingee to Bijapur.

Shahaji never forgot this insult by Baji Ghorpade and Afzal Khan and wrote to Shivaji, urging revenge, *'If you are my true son'.*

Later, Shivaji killed Afzal Khan. Similarly, Shaista Khan had defeated Shahaji in his second attempt. Shivaji in a daring attack severed three of Shaista's fingers and forced him to retreat. Shivaji also killed Baji Ghorpade in 1664, proving to be a true son of his father.

□

Shivaji and His Brother

Shivaji Meets Vyenkoji

As seen above, the elder brother of Shivaji, Sambhaji was killed during an expedition due to the treacherous role of Afzal Khan. Shivaji took his revenge by disembowelling Afzal Khan.

Shivaji had a half brother, Vyenkoji, son of Shahaji and his second wife Tukabai. Like Shahaji, Vyenkoji remained loyal to Adilshahi till the end in spite of Shivaji's request to join him.

We have already discussed that Shivaji wanted a safe haven in the South. Accordingly, he left Raigad on Dashera in 1676 and halted at Hyderabad for a month between February-March 1677. After defeating Sher Khan on 5th July, 1677 he met his brother Vyenkoji at Tirumalavadi. However, they could not come to terms on the estates left by their father Shahaji Raje and Vyenkoji left the camp without informing Shivaji. Shivaji started his return journey on 27th July, 1677.

Vyenkoji Attacks Forces of Shivaji

Having learnt of Shivaji's departure, Vyenkoji began to conspire with petty local chieftains for eviction of Shivaji's forces from Karnataka. Though they did not respond to this plan, he assembled his own force, comprising 4,000 cavalry and 10,000 infantry, crossed the Coleroon and, on 16th November, 1677, attacked the Maratha army under Santaji and Hambirrao which numbered about 6,000 infantry and 6,000 cavalry. In a letter, which he later sent to Vyenkoji, Shivaji himself says that the battle was fought near Valikandapuram. The *Jedhe Chronology* calls the place Ahiri. According to St. George letter of 20th/29th November 1677, Santaji was initially forced to withdraw, but he turned back during the night, surprised Ekoji's camp and scattered his army. The booty, according to this letter, included 1,000 horses, tents and all the baggage.

When Shivaji learnt of Vyenkoji's defeat, he wrote an emotional letter to Vyenkoji which illustrates the fact that to Shivaji, it was always family first:

"As we have much work to do in Raigad province, we kept Santaji Raja, Raghunathpant and Hambirrao in that (i.e. the Gingee) province and arrived in the district of Torgal. There we learnt that misguided by the Turks (Muslims), you assembled and sent your army against our men. They arrived at Valikandapuram. When your men advanced (against our men), a great battle was fought between your men and our men. Your men were defeated. Pratapji Raja, Bhivji Raja and Shivaji Dabir, these three were captured and many were killed. Many fled in rout. This we have learnt. Having heard this, we wondered how in spite of your being a son of the Maharaja (Shahaji), you do not reflect and do not discriminate between sin and righteousness. Then there is no wonder that you will be brought to distress. You would ask what you should think. (We would answer) you should have thought that 'we have enjoyed the entire *jagir* for thirteen years. Now, we should give him half the share which he (i.e. Shivaji) is demanding and should be happy'. You should have thought 'he (Shivaji) is blessed by Shri Mahadeo (Shiva) and Goddess Bhavani. He kills the wicked Turks (Muslims). How could I win (against him) when my army also has Turks? How would the Turks hope to escape with their lives?' You should have thought thus and should not have brought upon open hostilities. But you cherished (wicked) intentions like Duryodhan and caused unnecessary loss of life. Now let bygones be bygones. Do not be adamant hereafter. You have enjoyed the entire *jagir* for thirteen years. Now we have taken what is ours. Now give up to my men the place like the forts of Arni, Bangalore,

Kolar, Hoskote and Shiralkot (Shire), other minor places and Tanjore which have reminded in your hands. Also give up half the share of cash, ornaments, elephants and horses and make peace with us with an open mind. We shall give you an estate of three hundred thousand hons in the province of Panhala on this side of the Tungabhadra. Or, if you do not want an estate from us, we shall request the Qutbshah and shall secure for you an estate (with an annual income) of three hundred thousand (hons) from him. Both the alternatives have been written to you. Choose any one of these two; do not be adamant. There is no need to quarrel among ourselves and become disheartened. At least, hereafter, aim at maintaining peace between you and us and settle the matter of division and be happy. Family feud is not good. As an elder, we have told you (these things) till today and now we again tell you that it is well and good if you would listen (to this advice), else you will fall into distress. What can we do (then)?'

Shivaji Rebukes a Depressed Vyenkoji

That Vyenkoji was close to Shivaji is proved from the fact he shared his worst fears with him, when Sambhaji had gone over to Diler Khan and later came back. Shivaji wrote: *"I conciliated him as is proper in family affairs."*

A few days before his death Shivaji received a letter from Raghunathpant that Vyenkoji, his younger brother, had given himself to gloom and melancholy. Besides, he refused to dispose of any administrative work, had grown indifferent to food and drink and adopted the habits of a religious recluse. Upon this, Shivaji wrote to Vyenkoji the following letter:

"Many days have elapsed," quotes Prof. Takakhav, "without my receiving any letter from you and in consequence, I am not in comfort. Raghunathpant has now written that you having placed melancholy and gloom before yourself, you do not take care of your person or in any way attend to yourself as formerly, nor do you keep any great days or religious festivals. Your troops are inactive and you have no mind to employ yourself on state affairs. You have become a *bairagi* and think of nothing but to sit in some place accounted holy, and let times wear away. In this manner, much has been written to me and such an account of you has given me great concern. I am surprised when I reflect that you have our father's example before you—how did he encounter and surmount all difficulties, perform great action, escape all dangers by his spirit and resolution, and acquired a renown which he maintained to the last? All he did is well known to you. You enjoyed his society, you had every opportunity of profiting by his wisdom and ability. You also know, and have seen, how I have established a kingdom. Is it then for you, in the very midst of opportunity, to renounce all worldly affairs and turn *bairagi*—to give up your affairs to persons who will devour your estate, to ruin your property and injure your bodily health? What kind of wisdom is this? What will it end in? I am to you as your head and protector; from me you have nothing to dread. Give up, therefore, all this and do not become a *bairagi*. Throw off despondency, spend your days properly, attend to fasts, feasts, and customary usages, and attend to your personal comforts. Look to the employment of your attention to affairs of moment. Make your men do their duty; apply their services properly in your quarter, and gain fame and renown. What a comfort and happiness it will be to me to hear the praise and fame of my younger brother... Hold together for your mutual support, and you will acquire celebrity and fame. Above all things, be not slothful; do not allow opportunity to slip past without receiving some returns from your army. This is the time for performing great actions. Old age is the season for turning bairagi. Arouse! Bestir yourself. Let me see what you can do."

□

Shivaji and His Sons

Shivaji had two sons and three daughters. His elder son Sambhaji was born of his first wife Saibai and younger son Rajaram was born of second wife Soyarabai.

Shivaji's aim was to take into possession most of the important strongholds in the South so that in times of stress and difficulty, the government of Maharashtra could move into them. Jinji, Gingree or Chenjee, in South Arcot (Tamil Nadu), was one such powerful fort.

In 1678, Shivaji decided to divide his kingdom between his two sons.

The homeland Maharashtra would be ruled by the delicate eight-year-old Rajaram under the guidance of the *ashtapradhan*.

The southern part, i.e. Mysore to Jinji would be ruled by the vigorous grown-up Sambhaji by himself, especially since there was a rift between him and the *ashtapradhan*.

The *Anupuran* of Devadatta, although a partisan account speaks of the complaints which Shivaji's ministers made about Sambhaji's behaviour. The ministers said, *"We pay the same respects to the prince (Sambhaji) as we pay to you. But the prince ridicules us by saying, 'See, these crafty men are coming.'* They also complained that Sambhaji sided with the *ryots* with the result that taxes could not be collected in full. Obviously, Shivaji seems to have realised that were Sambhaji to stay at Raigad, the rift between him (Sambhaji) and the council of ministers would only widen; and would in no way be conducive to good administration. After all, Moropant and Annaji were seasoned administrators and would have liked to work in freedom.

It is also possible that there was no harmony between Sambhaji and his stepmother Soyarabai, the mother of the young prince Rajaram.

In any case, Shivaji entrusted the administration to his ministers. Sambhaji was asked to go and stay at Shringarpur in Konkan. He was also asked, if the *Anupuran* is to be belived, to administer the province of Prabhavali.

While embarking on this campaign, Shivaji made very careful arrangements for the administration of the kingdom. The Peshwa Moropant was in charge of the northern territory. The southern region was under the control of Annaji Datto, while the central region comprising of Panhala was administered by Dattaji Trimbak. Rahuji Somanath was to stay at Raigad and carry on the day-to-day administration.

It is clear that Sambhaji was not left at Raigad to administer the kingdom during his father's absence in the South. Rahuji Somanath was the man in-charge.

Perhaps this was the last straw. Sambhaji rebelled and joined forces with Diler Khan.

Together they attacked Bhupalgad, the commander giving up the fort rather than fire cannons on the crown prince.

Then they besieged Bijapur but could not take it. Next they went to Athni which Diler plundered and imprisoned the inhabitants to be sold as slaves. Sambhaji objected but was over-ruled by Diler. Many from the Mughal camp, including his brother-in-law, censured Sambhaji for deserting Shivaji.

Sambhaji at last saw the light and chose to return to his father. In a letter to Vyenkoji, Shivaji wrote of the 'return of the prodigal son'.

"Sambhaji Raja had gone to the Mughals. We employed various means to bring him back. He too realised that in the (Mughal), empire or in the Badshahis of Bijapur or Bhaganagar (Hyderabad) things will not be done to his liking. So, in response to our letter, he came and met us. I conciliated him as is proper in family affairs."

Sambhaji also seemed to show some amount of humility and

remorse. *"I am only worthy of Saheb's feet. I shall be satisfied with whatever (*doodh-bhat*/rice and milk) is offered to me."*

Shivaji fell ill in February 1680, but he did not know that he would die in a month's time. By the time he knew his illness was fatal, it was too late. Both Moropant and Annaji Datto were away. Shivaji knew that it was high time that he made a clear will about the division of his kingdom. He did so in the presence of six Brahmins and eight Marathas. That such a will was definitely made is in keeping with Shivaji's overall attitude. A man who planned each campaign to the last detail could not possibly leave a kingdom he had put together over a life-time to just wither away or drift aimlessly.

However, as ill-luck would have it, Hambirrao reached Panhala where Sambhaji was under house arrest long before Annaji Datto and Moropant arrived with the will. And the result was a rampaging and raging Sambhaji who went on a revenge spree, killing his step-mother Soyarabai, Annaji Datto and Moropant.

History tells us that Sambhaji chose to disobey his father, insisted on the throne at Raigad and paid the price by a horrible death at the hands of Aurangzeb.

But had he obeyed him, Rajaram and all the *ashtapradhan* would have resisted Aurangzeb while he would have been safe at Jinji and the history of India would have been different.

Shivaji's foresight in building a second Maratha capital deep in the South was of immense value to the national cause after his death. The capture and murder of his eldest son, Sambhaji, by Aurangzeb in March 1689 and the defeat of the Maratha forces in all theatres of war, in contrast to their resounding successes against their enemies during his life-time threatened to annihilate his hard-won realm. But the fugitive Rajaram, his second son, saved it from falling into tearful ruins by seeking asylum in Jinji. Zulikar Khan put a siege on Jinji for nine years, starting 1890, but he could get Jinji only after he reached an understanding with Rajaram in 1897. (Stgm/hss/686)

□

Shivaji and Justice

The Khandoji Khopde Episode

As we have discussed earlier, justice is a part of equality, and needless to say, Shivaji was a true protagonist of this idea.

When Afzal Khan came with his army, Khandoji Khopde, sure of the Khan's success, was one of the first Maratha *sardars* to join him in return for the *deshmukhi* of Utroli. Contrary to his expectations, Shivaji disembowelled the Khan. Khandoji Khopde knew that soon Shivaji would come after him. He requested his father-in-law Haibatrao Shilimkar, a staunch supporter of Shivaji, to request Kanhoji Jedhe to secure a pardon from Shivaji. Kanhoji Jedhe was one of the first *jagirdars* to join Shivaji along with his five sons. (I pour water over my *jagir*)

Shivaji could not refuse Kanhoji Jedhe and he pardoned Khandoji Khopde. But every time he saw the traitor, he was consumed with anger. And one day he gave orders to cut Khandoji Khopde's right hand and left leg. When Kanhoji Jedhe naturally asked Shivaji why he went back on his word, Shivaji replied *"I cut off the hand that raised a sword against swarajya and the leg that took him to the enemy. But as per my promise, I pardoned his life."*

So what if You are a Brahmin?

The letter that Shivaji wrote to Jivaji Vinayak, the governor of Prabhavali, reveals the strict discipline that Shivaji expected from his officials:

"The Peshwa Moropant issued a draft on your region for the

supply of money and provision to Daulat Khan and Daryasarang. It is understood that you have not complied with the same. It is surprising. There would be very few such inefficient simpletons like you. You might have thought that your falts would be overlooked if you were able to send provision and cash to some other place. We have built the fort of Padmadurg and created a second Rajpuri. The fort must get assistance, water, provision and other materials. The fleet must receive them quickly. This has not happened. The Abyssinian troops must have reduced Padmadurg to great straits. By not sending supplies, you will cause delay to the movement of the fleet. This is treachery. Do you think that by sending in future, you can get your faults condoned? Do you think that we will overlook your conduct? Possibly, the Abyssinians have bribed you and taken you in their service. That is why you must be behaving like this. We must deal with such servants sternly and fittingly.

Who will care for the consideration that you are a Brahmin? Arrange for supplies immediately as instructed by Moropant. Let not the fleet complain against you. With supplies in their hands, the fleet will move to the assistance of Padmadurg. Should any further complaint be received against you, you will not be spared. Considering you as a servant of the enemy, we will look upon you as our enemy. You will receive the fate you deserve."

The words, *"Who will care for the consideration that you are a Brahmin?"* were perhaps uttered for the first time in Maratha history.

Sambhaji

As we saw earlier, while embarking on the Jinji campaign, Shivaji made very careful arrangements for the administration of the kingdom. Rahuji Somanath was to stay at Raigad and carry on the day-to-day administration.

It is clear that Sambhaji was not left at Raigad to administer the kingdom during his father's absence.

Perhaps this was the last straw. Sambhaji rebelled and joined forces with Diler Khan. Sambhaji at last saw the light and chose to return to his father.

Shivaji ruled that the southern part, i.e. Mysore to Jinji would be ruled by the vigorous grownup Sambhaji since there was a rift between him and the *ashtapradhan.*

It is also a fact that Shivaji did not send for Sambhaji on his deathbed.

The reason is simple—if Shivaji could not bring himself to forgive the likes of Khandoji, there was no way he would forgive his son for the treachery of defecting to Diler Khan.

However, Sambhaji changed into a very different person after his father's death. The courageous manner in which he lived and died won him the respect of every Maratha.

Devdanda, Rajdanda, Jatidanda

In its judicial sense, the Maratha state was a triune state and not a unitary one. The three main instiutions were: 1-(a) raja and *huzur hazir majlis* or *rajsabha* or *harmasbha,* (b) *deshadh kali* and *gotasabha* at the district level, 2-*dharmadhikari* and *brahmasabha*. 3-*jatisabha,* purely for caste purposes.

The ruler was merely an executive authority of society and polity. He was not a legislator, but a symbol of power and Dharma. He was to follow the awards decided in an assembly *majlis* or *sabha* of government officers (*diwan*) and of the people gathered in the *gota* or territorial community of communities (classes, castes and other groups), his jurisdiction over religion and caste was limited. The *brahmasabha* and the *jatisabha* were the final authorities in religious and social matters. But he could interfere with their decisions, if necessary, as controlling, co-ordinating and corrective authority. The strength of the judicial institutions where human life, liberty and property were concerned was essentially based on their democratic composition and procedure, though there were tests of divine ordeals for want of evidence. Even here the democratic conception included not merely the seen government and people, but also the unseen God, the three sources or elements of authority, political, religious and social. But the king's presence as a symbol of authority was essential. He was the representative of the Dharma of the community as a whole.

The *dharmasabha* or the *paragana* or the '*tarf majlis*' of the Maratha and pre-Maratha period is a democratic body like the Witenagemot, Shiremoot and Hundredmoot of the Anglo-Saxons. There can be no justice without where the king, his officers and nobles and local representatives have to be present. The local government officers set the judicial machinery in motion and saw that all cases were tried properly by the *gota* in the *majlis.* As executive officers, they were only to enforce the decision passed by *majlis*. They could not interfere with the decision of the *majlis*.

It is a noteworthy feature of the system that, in cases of crime, after going through the punishment ordered by the government, the offender was required to purge himself of the sin he had committed by performing penance, which was called *devdanda* and to give dinner to the people of the caste to qualify himself for social intercourse. This was called *jatidanda*. This threefold system of punishment seems to have checked the tendencies in crime and Elphinstone once rightly remarks that the country was peculiarly free from crime.

The Witenagemot

'Meeting of wise men', also known as the witen *(more properly the title of its members) was a political institution in Anglo-Saxon England, which operated from before the 7th century until the 11th century. The Witenagemot was an assembly of the ruling class whose primary function was to advise the king and whose membership was composed of the most important noblemen in England, both ecclesiastic and secular. The institution is thought to represent an aristocratic development of the ancient Germanic general assemblies, or* folkmoots. *In England, by the 7th century, these ancient* folkmoots *had developed into convocations of the land's most powerful and important people, including ealdormen, thegns, and senior clergy, to discuss matters of both national and local importance.*

□

Shivaji's Close Associates

As mentioned earlier under guerrilla warfare, the Spartans and Athenians (500 B.C.) were the precursors of the Centurions of Rome (100 B.C.), who, in turn, were the precursors to the Templar Knights (1000 A.D.), who fought against the Hashashins and reached a stalemate. The tactics and strategy were learnt through warfare by Timur and Chenghis Khan who were the precursors of the Mughals. The Mughal army consisted of Rajputs besides the Mughals.

A recent episode on History Channel proved that the Rajputs were better than the Roman Centurions.

Shivaji's army successfully fought against the combined forces of the Rajputs and the Mughals.

Some of Shivaji's close associates were also his primary army chieftains and have entered folklore along with him, e.g. Baji Prabhu, Tanaji Malusare, Jiva Mahala, Yesaji Kank, Murar Baji, etc.

Prataprao Gujjar 'Charge of the Light Brigade'

The following description will illustrate how highly Shivaji's officers rated him.

In 1674, Prataprao Gujar, the then commander-in chief of the Maratha forces, was sent to push back the invading force led by the Adilshahi general, Bahlol Khan. Shivaji had directed Prataprao to finish off Bahlol Khan, who had proved to be treacherous in the past. The Maratha army surrounded the camp of Bahlol Khan at the village of Nesari. Prataprao's forces defeated and captured the opposing general in the battle after cutting off their water supply by encircling a strategically-located lake, which prompted Bahlol Khan to sue for peace. In spite of Shivaji's specific warnings against doing so, Prataprao released Bahlol Khan. Days after his release, Bahlol Khan started preparing for a fresh invasion.

When Shivaji heard of Prataprao's decision, he was greatly displeased and sent a letter to Prataprao refusing him audience until Bahlol Khan was re-captured. Prataprao realised the full extent of his strategic error and was so upset about it that he now desperately wanted to redeem himself. In the ensuing days, he learnt of Bahlol Khan having camped nearby. Prataprao decided to confront Bahlol Khan at Nesari near Kolhapur.

The potential battle would have had Gujar with 1,200 troops facing Khan with 15,000. Given the uneven match, Prataprao reasoned that there was no point in leading his 1,200 cavalrymen into a suicide charge. So, in a fit of desperation and anguish and in an over-reaction to Shivaji's letter, he left by himself, without asking his cavalry to accompany him. It was his personal honour at stake, not his army's. On seeing their leader head to certain death, six other Maratha *sardars* joined him in the charge. They attacked the enemy camp and were cut down before they could reach Bahlol Khan.

Anandrao Mohite, though, stayed back. The seven Maratha officers were Prataprao Gujar, Visaji Ballal, Dipoji Rautrao, Vithal Pilaji Atre, Krishnaji Bhaskar, Siddi Hilal and Vithoji. It was an impulsive and seemingly irrational decision, and the loss of Prataprao Gujar was a big loss to the Marathas. Anandrao Mohite managed to withdraw the army to safer areas.

This event was retold in the Marathi poem '*Saat*' (Seven). The poem was written by a well-known poet, Kusumagraj and was also sung by the great Indian singer, Lata Mangeshkar.

Shivaji's army then avenged the death of their general, by defeating Bahlol Khan and capturing his *jagir* (fiefdom) under the leadership of Anaji and Hambirao Mohite. Shivaji was deeply grieved on hearing of Pratprao's death. He arranged for the marriage of his second son, Rajaram, to the daughter of Prataprao

Gujar, who was later to be the Queen of the Maratha Empire, Maharani Tarabai. Anandrao Mohite became Hambirrao Mohite, the new *sarnaubat* (commander-in-chief of the Maratha forces).

Yesaji Kank, My 'War Elephant'

Abu Hussein invited Shivaji to Hyderabad and consented to be a vassal at an annual tribute of one lakh hon. For several days, there was a round of feasting and banqueting. One day, when Shivaji expressed astonishment at the size and gorgeous trappings of the elephant of Golconda, Abu Hussein said, "But have you no war elephant of your own." Shivaji turned and pointed to some of his guardsmen who stood behind him and said, "These are my war elephants" Abu Hussein smiled and began to tell stories of how his elephant was regarded by everyone with terror. Shivaji nodded to one of his captains, Yessaji. "You will find him more than a match for your elephant," he said, "Let us see," said Abu Hussein. The war elephant's *mahout* slid off his back and the stable hands incited it to fury. Yessaji advanced, his sword drawn. The elephant trumpeted and rushed towards him. Yessaji stepped aside and with a single blow, severed the brute's trunk.

The stunned Abu Hussein asked for the services of Yessaji, but Shivaji declined.

Shivaji likened his comrades like pearls in a stringed necklace. The loss of one of them and the necklace was incomplete

Like any other general, Shivaji's men were willing to die for him. When Shivaji was in prison at Agra, not a single officer deserted him. Not a single officer revolted against him in all his life.

More importantly, they were willing to accept Shivaji's code of ethics in war even under the utmost provocation.

Shiva Kashid, a Barber

We have already discussed the siege of Panhala and the roles of Shiva Kashid and Baji Prabhu Deshpande.

While Shiva Kashid, as an imposter of Shivaji, left by the main door of the fort, the real Shivaji along with about 600 members of the Bandal community left by a side exit (chor dindi) and proceeded towards Vishalgad, about 40 kms north-west of Panhalgad.

Shiva Kashid's palanquin reached Siddi Jauhar's camp and there was great rejoicing. But Jauhar soon realised the person presenting himself as Shivaji was actually look-alike. His victorious moment turned to dismay. Shiva Kashid was killed by a spear thrust in his chest.

Perhaps this is the most unique case in the history of a barber, willing to go to a sure death, without being able to strike a single blow in defence, justifying his inclusion with the likes of Baji Prabhu and Tanaji Malusare.

It is important to understand that Shiva Kashid was not a solitary or fluke incident, but instead illustrates a very important facet of Shivaji's personality. Let us analyse the situation. Shivaji conquered Panhala on 28th November, 1659. Shiva Kashid was killed in July 1660. This means that like any other local resident of Panhala, Kashid had perhaps heard of Shivaji and his initial exploits but certainly had not seen him, let alone met or spoken to him before November 1659. That means in a short span of six to seven months, Shivaji had fired the imagination of every single person in and around Panhala. Remember Kashid was a simple barber and not a part of the Kshatriya Maratha community, like Baji Prabhu or Tanaji Malusare. Fighting and killing and dying was not something that had been drilled into him as a glorious tradition. Perhaps he had never held a sword or spear in his hand. His only tools were a scissor and a razor.

And he was not alone. Shivaji's concept of *swarajya* seemed to have fired the imagination of each and every person living in Maharashtra. Each and everyone was willing to fight and die with pride. Before he came, the Marathas were mere hirelings or glorified suicide troops. Shivaji was the first to challenge the mighty Bijapur and Delhi and teach his countrymen that it was possible for them to be independent leaders in war. He taught the contemporary Hindus to shake off their despondency and frustration and to rise to the full stature of their growth. The saga of Shiva Kashid should not be seen as an example of a soldier who was willing to die for his general, but as a supreme sacrifice made by an insignificant patriot for a larger dream of independence. With this view in mind, the story of Shiva Kashid is not merely a footnote in history of Shivaji, but illustrates the real reason behind the success of Shivaji.

The Common *Ryots*

These were common people, farmers and artisans, big and small, having their own petty aims and aspirations, which they put aside for the greater glory of *swarajya*. Che Guevra asks and answers the question himself:

"Why does the guerrilla fighter fight? We must come to the inevitable conclusion that the guerrilla fighter is a social reformer, that he takes up arms responding to the angry protests of the people against their oppressors, and that he fights in order to change the social system that keeps all his unarmed brothers in ignominy and misery."

Shivaji did not have the support of the powerful Kshatriya community. In fact, they despised him for one of Shivaji's diktats was that no *sardar* could build a *gadhi* (castle), maintain an army or collect taxes. These were the perks that the *sardars* had enjoyed perhaps for centuries from the Mughals or Adilshahi.

First Shivaji made little people big, then these little people made Shivaji very big and then, both Shivaji and his people together created something very, very big.

□

Death of Shivaji and After

Reporting the death of Shivaji, the English write from Bombay to Surat: "We have certain news that Shivaji Raja is dead. It is now twenty-three days since he deceased, it is said, of bloody flux being sick for twelve days."

The *Masire Alamgiri* states that "news came from the Deccan that on Friday the 4th of April, 1980/24 Rabiussani, Shivaji after returning from a journey dismounted from his horse, vomited blood twice due to excess of heat and died (went to hell). The Persian words are '*as sawari amada ba istilai garmi do martaba khoon rau karda wa ba qare jahanum pharau raft.*'

It is interesting to see the comments made by Shivaji's contemporaries on his death.

The Portuguese Viceroy, Antonio de Paes Sande reported to the King of Portugal on 24th January, 1681, "The state of India is presently at peace with its neighbours and the death of Shivaji has relieved us from an enemy who was more to be feared while at peace than during open hostilities. He died on 4th of April of last year."

When Aurangzeb came to know of Shivaji's death, he said:

"Shivaji was a great warrior. He alone had the capacity to establish a new independent kingdom. It has been my constant endeavour to destroy all the old kingdoms. For 19 years, my armies have been fighting him. In spite of that, his kingdom kept on increasing." Shivaji: the Great Maratha, p. 936

But the greatest crisis came after his death when Aurangzeb invaded the Deccan from 1680 to 1707. The English factors verily observed that he is so inveterate against Raja Sambhaji that he hath thrown off his *pagri* and sworn never to put it on again till he hath either killed or taken or routed him from his country. But, by a strange irony of fate, despite the destruction of Sambhaji and the rout of Rajaram and the capture of Shahu, it was Aurangzeb's empire and not that of the Marathas that was undermined by his ceaseless war for over forty years.

The saviours of the legacy of Shivaji and the heritage of Maharashtra at that time were the *saptarishi* (seven sages) who were the braintrust of Maharashtra. Their courage, wisdom, resourcefulness, perseverance, patriotism, loyalty, selflessness and devotion to duty saved Maharashtra.

Their names are:

1. Ramchandra Bavdekar *Amatya*
2. Shankaraji Narayan
3. Parsuram Trimbak
4. Santaji Ghorpade
5. Dhanaji Jadhav
6. Kandho Ballal *Chitnis*
7. Prahlad Niraji

Manucci writes in 1700: "Aurangzeb left Ajmer in September 1681. His object was war with Sambhaji unmindful of his fate, namely this departure was forever, that there would be no return for him either to Agra or Delhi. He is now in camp for seventeen years without affecting anything against the Marathas. Till this day, he has not been able to accomplish the enterprise he intended (as he said) to finish in two years. He marched, carrying with him three sons, Shah Alam, A'zam Tara, Kam Bakhash, and also his grandsons. He had with him great treasure, which came to an end so thoroughly during this war that he was compelled to open the treasure houses of Akbar, Nurjehan, Jehangir and Shah Jahan. Besides this, finding himself with very little cash owing to the immense expenditure forced upon him and because the revenue payers did not pay with the usual promptitude, he was obliged at Aurangabad to melt down all his household silverware. In addition to all this, he wanted to empty the great store-houses filled with goods left by deceased persons or with property collected in Akbar's, Jehangir's and Shah Jahan's time from men, great and small, who had been servants of the state. But, afterwards, he ordered these storehouses not to be opened, for he rightly feared that, he being absent, the officers would embezzle more than half." The Great Mughals, Bamber Gascoigne Constable and Co., London 1998

At last, the conventional piety, which had always filled his letters, gives way under the twin pressures of approaching death and a guilty conscience to genuine personal anguish. "I know not to what punishment I shall be doomed," he writes with unusual simplicity to one of his sons and he bewails an old man's lack of close friend and his own particular shortage of good officers in a letter to his third son Azam which is almost a poetic lament for the frailty of human affairs. "*My child, my soul life and prosperity of my life, Behrehmund is sick, Mukhlis Khan, etc. are disgusting. Hammed-ed-Deen is a cheat, Siadat Khan and Mohammed Amen Khan in the advanced guard are contemptible. Zul Fikir Khan is impetuous cheat, Kulich Khan is worthless, Firoze Jung is at the head of affairs in equal authority with Umdet-ul-Mulk. The* mansabdars, *great and small from the dearness of grin, are almost ready to desert Mirza Sudder-Ed-Deen; Mohammed Khan is expert in every business. Sirberah Khan, the* kotwal, *is a thief squeezing pickpocket. Yarali Khan and Munaim Khan are untruly jesters, Arshi Khan gets drunk and swills with wine. Muherrim Khan is vicious. The Deccaners are at loggerheads. Abdul Hukk and Multefit Khan are veteran soldiers, Murid Khan without men serves as a simple horseman. Meer Khan, the fatherless, is distressed for a coat and turban. Innaiyet Ullah is entirely possessed by the thought of his departure. The brother of Munsoor Khan is acting against the accursed Marathas and you are employed in diffusing liberalities. Akbar is a vagabond in the desert of infamy. Shah Alam and his sons are far distant from the victorious army. Kam Bakhsh is perverse and regardless of what is said to him. Your son is obedient to the advice of his illustrious father. I myself am forlorn and destitute and misery is my ultimate lot.*"

Stanley Wolpert writes in his *New History of India* that:

The conquest of the Deccan, to which Aurangzeb devoted the last 26 years of his life, was in many ways a pyrrhic victory, costing an estimated hundred thousand lives a year during its last decade of futile chess game warfare...The expense in gold and rupees can hardly be accurately estimated. (Aurangzeb)'s moving capital alone—a city of tents 30 miles in circumference, some 250 bazaars, with a half million camp followers, 50,000 camels and 30,000 elephants, all of whom had to be fed, stripped peninsular India of any and all of its surplus grain and wealth... Not only famine, but bubonic plague arose... Even Aurangzeb had ceased to understand the purpose of it all by the time he was nearing 90... "I came alone and I go as a stranger. I do not know who I am, nor what I have been doing," the dying old man confessed to his son in February 1707. Short History of Aurangzeb, p.305-310

The next two letters illustrate the depths of despondency and depression that Aurangzeb had sunk to.

Aurangzeb's Last Letter to Azam

'Peace be on you!'

'Old age has arrived and weakness has grown strong; strength has left my limbs. I came alone and am going away alone. I know not who I am and what I have been doing. The days that have been spent except in austerities have left only regret behind them. I have not all done any (true) government of the realm or cherishing of the peasantry.

'Life, so valuable, has gone away for nothing. The Master has been in my house, but my darkened eyes cannot see His splendour. Life lasts not; no trace is left of the days that are no more; and of the future, there is no hope.

'My fever has departed, leaving only the skin and husks behind it. My son Kam Bakhsh, who has gone to Bijapur, is near me. And you are nearer even than he. Dear Shah Alam is farthest of all. Grandson Muhammad Azim has, by order of the great God, arrived near Hindustan (from Bengal).

'All the soldiers are feeling helpless, bewildered, and perturbed like me, who having chosen to leave my master, am now in a state of trepidation like quicksilver. They think not that we have our Lord Father (ever with us). I brought nothing with me (into the world), and carrying away with me the fruits of my sins. I know not what punishment will fall on me. Though I have strong hopes of His grace and kindness, yet in view of my acts, anxiety does not leave me. When I am parting from my own self, who else would remain to me?

Whatever the wind may be,
I am launching my boat on the water.

'Though the lord cherisher will preserve His slaves, yet from the point of view of the outer world, it is also the duty of my sons to see that God's creatures and Muslims may not be unjustly slain.

'Convey to my grandson Bahadur (i.e. Bidar Bakht) my parting blessing. At the time of going away, I do not see him; the desire of meeting remains (unsatisfied). Though the Begum is, as can be seen afflicted with grief, yet God is the master of hearts. Shortness of sight bears no other fruit than disappointment."

'Farewell! Farewell! Farewell!

Aurangzeb's Last Letter to Kam Bakhsh

'My son, (close to my heart like my liver)! Although, in the days of my power, I gave advice for submission to the will of God and exerted myself beyond the limits of possibility, God having willed it otherwise, none listened to me. Now that I am dying, it will do no good. I shall carry away with myself the fruits of all the punishment and sins that I have done. What a marvel that I came (into the world) alone and am (now) departing with this (large) caravan! Where I cast my eyes, no caravan-leader save Good comes into my view. Anxiety about the army and camp-followers has been the cause of (my) depression of mind and fear of final torment. Although God will undertake the protection of his people, yet it is also obligatory on Muslims and my sons. When I was full of strength, I could not at all protect them; and now I am unable to take care of myself! My limbs have ceased to move. The breath that subsides, there is no hope

of its return. What else can I do in such a condition than to pray? Your mother Udipuri (Begum) has attended me during my illness; she wishes to accompany me (to the next world). I consign thee and thy children to God. I am in trepidation. I bid you farewell... Worldly men are deceivers (literally, they show wheat as sample but deliver barley); do not do any work in reliance on their fidelity. Work ought to be done by means of hints and signs. Dara Shukoh made unsound arrangements and, hence, he failed to reach his point. He increased the salaries of his retainers to more than what they were before, but at the time of need, he got less and less work out of them. Hence he was unhappy. Set your feet within the limits of your carpet.

'I have told you what I had to say and now I take my leave. See to it that the peasantry and the people are not unjustly ruined, and that Muslamans may not be slain, lest punishment should descend on me.'

Aurangzeb's Last Will

A few relevant points of Auranzeb's will are enumerated here:

'Praise be to God and blessing on those servants of Him who have become sanctified and have given satisfaction to Him.

I have (some instructions to leave as my) last will and testament: First, on behalf of this sinner sunk in inequity (i.e. myself) cover (with an offering of cloth) the holy tomb of Hasan (on HIM BE PEACE!), because those who are drowned in the ocean of sin have no other protection than seeking refuge with that Portal of Mercy and Forgiveness. The means of performing this great auspicious act are with my noble son, Prince Alijah (Azam); take them.

Second, four rupees and two annas, out of the price of the caps sewn by me, are with Aia Beg, the *mahaldar*. Take the amount and spend it on the shroud of this helpless creature. Three hundred and five rupees, from the wages of copying the Quran, are in my purse for personal expenses. Distribute them to the *faqirs* on the day of my death. As the money got by copying the Quran is regarded with respect of the Shia sect. Do not spend it on my shroud and other necessaries.

Fourth, bury this wanderer in the Valley of Deviation from the Right Path with his head bare, because every ruined sinner who is conducted bareheaded before the grand Emperor (i.e. God) is sure to be an object of mercy.

Fifth, cover the top of the coffin on my bier with the coarse white cloth called *gazi*. Avoid the spreading of a canopy and innovations like (procession of) musicians and the celebration of the Prophet's nativity (*maulud*).

Twelfth, the main pillar of government is to be well informed in the news of the kingdom. Negligence for a single moment becomes the cause of disgrace for long years. The escape of the wretch Shiva took:

If you learn (the lesson), a kiss on your wisdom.

If you neglect it, then alas! Alas!

The last clause in Aurangzeb's will amply illustrates that till the very end of his life, Aurangzeb was obsessed with Shivaji.

□

Shivaji and Freedom Struggle

Prediction of British Conquest of India

Ramchandra Nilkanth, the progenitor of the Amatya family of Bavdain Kolhapur district, was a man of great vision and sagacity. He had been Shivaji's youngest minister, was trained directly under Shivaji and, therefore, knew well the art of promoting concord and concerted action among the self-willed leaders of the government. He was himself not a man of the sword, but he was gifted with the rare spirit of rousing others to great heights of heroism. Santaji Ghorpade and Dhanaji Jadhav were conspicuous among his lieutenants who shattered the imperialists' dream of conquest. Rajaram's warm tribute to Ramchandrapant presents the true measure of Amatya's valuable services to the nation. "The Maratha kingdom," declared Rajaram, "is a gift from the gods. Ramchandrapant saved it from a grave crisis by creating a band of leaders in its defiance after a careful appraisal of their individual abilities. He made the best use of the nation's resources for protecting it from the aggression of the imperialists. Providence has crowned his endeavours with success, while defeating the designs of the enemy."

Most important he wrote the *Adnyapatra* or royal edict through which we know the thoughts of Shivaji. It is interesting to note what Shivaji says about the foreign merchants through the *Adyapatra*.

'Among the merchants, the Portuguese and the English and the Dutch and the French and the Danes and other hat-wearing (i.e. European) merchants also do carry on trade and commerce.

But they are not like other merchants. Their masters, every one of them, are ruling kings. By their orders and under their control, these people have come to trade in these provinces. How can it happen that rulers have no greed for territories? These hat-wearers are amibitious of increasing their territories and establishing their religion. Moreover, this race of people is obstinate. Where a place has fallen into their hands, they will not give it even at the cost of their lives. Their intercourse should, therefore, be restricted to the extent only of their coming and going for purposes of trade.

They should strictly be given no places to settle in. They should not at all be allowed to visit sea-forts. If some places has sometimes to be given to factory, it should not be at the mouth of an inlet or on the sea-shore; they would establish new forts at those ports with the help of their navy to protect them. Their strength lies in their navy, guns and ammunition.

As a consequence, so much territory would be lost to the kingdom.

Therefore, if any place is at all to be given to them, it should be in the midst of two or four great towns, eight to sixteen miles distant from the sea, just as the French were given lands at Rajapur. The place must be such as to be low-lying and within the range of control of the neighbouring town, so as to avoid troubling the two. Thus, by fixing their place of habitation, factories might be permitted to build. They should not be allowed to erect strong and permanent houses. If they live in this way by accepting the above conditions, it is well; if not, there is no need of them. It is enough if they occasionally come and go, and do not trouble us; nor need we trouble them'.

One is amazed at this diktat in the *Adnyapatra* because it is almost as if Shivaji had a sixth sense of the Act passed in then British Parliament which aimed at strengthening the power of the East India Company. King Charles II provisioned the EIC (in a series of five Acts around 1670) with the rights to autonomous territorial acquisitions, to mint money, to command fortresses and troops and form alliances, to make war and peace, and to exercise both civil and criminal jurisdiction over the acquired areas.

□

Shivaji Festival and Tilak

Lokmanya Tilak organised the first Shivaji Festival at Raigad in 1896.

The collector of Colaba rightly observed:

"The object of the celebration is obviously to arouse if it exists, or create if it does not exist, a nationalist feeling among the Marathas."

The next Shivaji festival was held in Pune in 1897, where Tilak gave a speech praising the killing of Afzal Khan by Shivaji. Within ten days, two British officers, Rand and Ayrest were shot dead by the Chaphekar brothers.

Tilak was arrested on charges of seditious writings in *Kesari* which included the rhetorical poem on Shivaji's utterances. The Abhinav Bharat group headed by V.D. Savarkar was taking secret oaths in front of Shivaji's portrait. His portrait was also distributed by Sardar Swaran Singh (Ajit Singh's brother) in Punjab.

The Shivaji Festival was held in high acclaim by total of 128 newspapers incuding *Ahmedabad Times, Gujarat Deshi Mitra* SURAT; *Deshbhakta,* BARODA; *Gulbarga Samachar,* HYDERABA.D.; Kalidas, DHARWAD; *Karnataka Vaibhav,* BIJAPURj; *Kathiawar Times,* RAJKOT; *Navsari Prakash,* NAVSARI; *Phoenix,* KARACHI; *Prabhat,* SINDH; the rest being from Maharashtra (The Shivaji Commemoration Movement, Maharashtra Archives Bulletin No. 13 & 14)

During the First and Second World Wars, his war cry of '*Har Har Mahadev*' was heard wherever the Maratha troops fought under the allied banner.

Even now it is the war cry of some of the Indian regiments.

□

Comparison with Foreign Warriors

Abbe Carre was a French traveller who visited India around 1670; his account was published as *Voyage des Indes Orientales mêlé de plusieurs histories curieuses* at Paris in 1699. Some quotes:

"Hardly had he won a battle or taken to town in one end of the kingdom than he was at the other extremity causing havoc everywhere and surprising important places. To this quickness of movement, he added, like Julius Caesar, a clemency and bounty that won him the hearts of those his arms had worsted... "In his courage and rapidity, he does not ill resemble the King of Sweden, Gustavus Adolphus.

"With a success as Caeser's in Spain, he came, he saw, he overcame and is reported to have taken so vast a treasure in gold, diamonds, emeralds, rubies and wrought coral that have strengthened his arms with very able sinews to prosecute his further designs.

"He being no less dexterous there at (conquests) than Alexander the Great was for, by the agility of his winged men (himself terming them birds) he took in less than eight months what he had delivered to Jaysing. (English Records on Shivaji, vol. 2, p. 120 dt 15 Jan. 1677/78)

"But it is well known that Shivaji is as second sertorous, and comes not short of Hannibal for strategems." (English Records on Shivaji, vol 2, p. 153, dt. 14 Feb. 1677/78)

Shivaji the Great Maratha, p. 307, H.S. Sardesai)

He had the vision of Mazzini, the dash of Garibaldi, the patriotism, perseverance and intrepidity of William the Orange, He did for Maharashtra what Fredrick the Great did for Germany and Alexander the great did for Macedonia. (Shivaji: the Great Maratha p. 413/4 H.S. Sardesai)

His nimbleness and agility in war have been commented upon by many a writer. Guarda remarks, *'Sevagy often sent expeditions to different places at the same time and in all of them, he was convoked and he was in command. The question is still unsolved whether he substituted others for himself or he was a magician or the devil acted in his place.'*

Oxinden's observation on the same subject is even more dramatic: *"Sevagy is so famously infamous for his notorious thefts that report hath made him an airy body and add wings or else it were impossible he could be at so many places as he is said to be at all at one time."*

Guarda had to admit that *'in a short time, he reached a position which was then regarded as a great wonder. With a justice administered equally to all of it without impartially, he made subjects ever happy and his fame rose to such a height that throughout Hindustan, it became as dreaded as it was cherished.'*

Barthelemy Carre in his two volumes, *Voyage des indes orientales mele de plusieures histories curieuses* testifies to the respect and administration in which the Maratha hero was held not only by his officers and subjects, but also by his adversaries. He commences his *History of Sevagy* by affirming that '*Shivaji was one of the greatest men the East has ever seen in courage. The rapidity of his conquests and his great qualities he does not ill resemble that great King of Sweden, Gustavus Adophus. Carre spoke of Shivaji's liberality as verging on extravagance and possessing qualities of a great general and above all, a clearness of resolution and unusual activity almost always prove decisive in affairs of war.'* He added that *'Shivaji's valour was like a rushing torrent which carried every place he fell upon. Hardly had he won a battle or taken a town extremity causing havoc everywhere and surprising important places. To this quickness of movement, he added like Julius Caesar, a clemency and bounty that won him the hearts of those his arms had worsted.'*

In his sequel to the *History of Sevagy*, written after his second visit to India in 1672, Carre paid a visit to Shivaji's governor of Chaul who drew the best portrait (of him) in the world. Continuing in the same vein, he said,

'Ever destined to conquer a part of the world, he had studied with extreme care everything about the duty of a general and that of a soldier; above all, (the art of) fortification, which he understood better than the ablest engineers, and geography, of which he had made a special study, and which he had mastered and to such an extent as to know not merely all the cities including the smallest townships of the country, but even the lands and the bushes of which he had prepared very exact charts.

Adept at making friends, like his wealth, his friends were innumerable; they sent him information every hour. Concluding the chapter, Carre remarks, *'I understood that valour has its rewards and that great men find praise even in the mouth of their enemies.'*

John Francis Gamelli Careri:

"This Sevage, whom his subjects call Raja, which signifies petty king, is so powerful that he maintains war at one and the same time with the great Mughal, and the Portuguese. He brings into the field 50,000 horses, and as many or more foot, much better soldiers than the Mughals; for they live a day upon a piece of dry bread, and the Mughals will march at their ease, carrying their women, abundance of provisions, and tents, so that their army looks like a moving city. All the coast from Chaul to Goa, for the space of 250 miles belongs to him, and from thence to Visapor, he has several forts, most of them among inaccessible mountains, besides cities and towns, defended both by art and nature." (Shivaji: the Great Maratha, p. 422, H.S. Sardesai)

Francois Martin, the governor of Pondicherry (1664-1696): *'According to the assurances given by Shivaji, the French were allowed to stay in complete security at Pondicherry so long as they refrained from taking the side of either party, Sivagy caused a formal* firman *for our security.'* Henry Gary, writing in 1678, admitted: *'with a success as happy as Caesar in Spaine he came, saw and overcame and reported so vast a treasure in gold diamonds, emeralds, rubies and wrought coral that have strengthened his armies with very able sinews to prosecute his future victorious designs president.'*

Bhushan praised Shivaji as the universal man.

Shivaji was as strong as the Russians,
Expert swordsman like the Khurasens.
Wise and tactful in victory like the British.
Self-respecting like the Romans,
Treacherous killer of enemies like the Habsis,
Religious like the Arabs
Respectful and grand in behaviour like Iranians.
When angry like the Turans
Tricked the enemy like the French,
Self-sacrificing like the Kshatriyas of India,
To these we must add Shivaji was

Administrator, businessman, fort builder, litterateur, chivalrous, ship-builder, freedom fighter, environmentalist and hero as king.'

□

Nation-Builder

Did Shivaji merely Found a Krieg-staat*?

Was he merely an entrepreneur of rapine? A Hindu edition of Alauddin Khilji or Timur? I think it would not be fair to take this view. For one thing he did not have peace to work out his political ideas. The whole of his short life was one struggle with his enemies. (1646-74), a period of preparation rather than fruition All his attention was necessarily devoted to meeting daily dangers with daily expedients and he had not the chance of peacefully building up a well-planned political edifice 1674-80. *(a government that lives and grows only by wars of aggression.)

Shivaji was a unique combination of the best of the mature materialism of Islam and the sublime spiritualism of Hinduism.

Shivaji made a preparatory demand for *chaut* from Surat. 'As your emperor has forced me to keep an army for the defence of my country, that army must be paid by his subjects.'

The loot of Surat by Shivaji was a subscription for home rule, the only difference being that if Shivaji had asked for a subscription, he would have been thought to be mad. So, he had to take it by force.

Prof. Takakhav in his book, *'life of Shivaji Maharaj'* (p. 370), writes it will again be no exaggeration to say that it will be hard to find a parallel either in ancient or modern history to the extraordinary skill with which he evolved his methods and principles of government. To the qualities of a successful general and conquerer, he joined an administrative genius and statesmanship which have seldom proved so fruitful of active benevolence. (Shivaji: the Great Maratha, p. 456 H.S. Sardesai)

Shivaji, a Statesman

No blind fanatic or mere brigand can found a state. That is the work of a statesman. And statesmanship has been defined by the right hon'ble H.A.L. Fisher as the power of correctly calculating and skilfully utilising the forces of one's age and country so as to contribute to the success of one's policy. The great Italian statesman, Count Cavour, has rightly defined statesmanship as tact des chooses possible or the instinctive perception of what is possible under the circumstances. (House of Shivaji, Jadunath Sarkar, p. 103)

The holy man, Ramdas's influence on Shivaji was spiritual and not political. After the capture of Satara, 1673, Shivaji installed his guru in the neighbouring hill-fort of Parli or Sajjangarh, and guides still point out to the credulous tourist the seat on the top of Satara Hill from which Shivaji used to converse with the saint across four miles of space!

A charming anecdote is told that Shivaji could not understand why Ramdas used to go out daily on his begging tour, though his royal dispel had made him rich beyond the dreams of avarice, and that he next day placed at his feet a deed making a gift of all his kingdom to the saint. Ramdas accepted the gift, appointed Shivaji as his vicar and bade him rule the realm thenceforth, not as an autocratic owner, but as a servant responsible for all his acts to a higher authority. Shivaji then made the red ochre-coloured robe of a Hindu *sannyasi* his flag, *bhagwa jhanda*, in order to signify that he fought and ruled in the livery of his ascetic lord paramount. (Shivaji and His Times, Jadunath Sircar, p. 289)

Shivaji, a Constructive Genius

I regard him as the last great constructive genius and nation-builder that the Hindu race has produced. His system was his own creation; he took no foreign aid in his administration. His army was drilled and commanded by his own people. What he built lasted long.

Before he came, the Marathas were mere hirelings or glorified suicide troops. Shivaji was the first to challenge Bijapur and Delhi and teach his countrymen that it was possible for them to be independent leaders in war. Then he founded a state and taught his people that they were capable of administering a kingdom in all its departments. He has proved by his example that the Hindu race can build a nation, found a state, defeat enemies, can conduct their own defence, can protect and promote literature and art, commerce and industry, can maintain navies and ocean trading fleets on their own, and conduct naval battles on equal terms with foreigners. He taught the modern Hindu to rise to the full stature of their growth. (Shivaji and His Times, Jadunath Sirkar, p. 304)

"Shivaji possessed every quality requisite for success in the disturbed age in which he lived; cautious and wily in council, he was fierce and daring in action; he possessed an endurance that made him remarkable even amongst his hardy subjects, and an energy and decision that would in any age raise him to distinction." (Warriors and Statesmen in India, Sir E. Sullivan)

(Shivaji: the Great Maratha, p. 971 H.S. Sardesai)

Shivaji's political ideals are such that we can almost accept them today without any change. He aimed at giving his people peace, universal tolerance, equal opportunities for all castes and creeds, a beneficent, active and pure system of administration, a navy for promoting trade, and a trained militia to guard the homeland. Above all, he sought for national development through action and not by lonely meditation. Every worthy man, not only his natives of Maharashtra, but also recruits from other parts of India who came to Shivaji were sure of being given some task which would call forth his inner capacity and pave the way for his own rise to distinction, while serving the interests of the state. The activities of Shivaji's government spread in many directions and this enabled his people to aspire for a happy and varied development, such as all modern civilised states aim at.

How anxious Shivaji was to protect his people from the

harassment of the Mughals is evident from the letter he wrote to Sarjerao Jedhe on 23rd October, 1962:

"News has been brought that the Mughals are likely to raid your region. Immediately on receipt of this letter, you issue a warning to all the villages in the *taluka*. Send all the *ryots* to a safe place below the *Ghats* where the enemy will not harm them. Do not delay. Act immediately. If you fail in your duty and the Mughals arrest our people and take them away, all the blame will fall on you. Work day and night and send our people to (safe) places in the *Ghats*. Do not delay by even one hour in carrying out these measures."

Shivaji did not have the classical appreciation needed to spend over 20 crore rupees and hold deprived subjects with strokes of hunter to build a Taj Mahal even as famine was claiming over hundreds of thousands of lives; nor was he pious enough to erect temple after temple while India was being systematically consumed by the British.

The Construction of the Taj

The plinth and tomb took roughly 22 years to complete. The Taj Mahal was constructed using materials from all over India and Asia, and over 1,000 elephants were used to transport building materials. The translucent white marble was brought from Makrana, Rajasthan, the jasper from Punjab, and jade and crystal from China. The turquoise was from Tibet and the lapis lazuli from Afghanistan, while the sapphire came from Sri Lanka and the carnelian from Arabia. In all, twenty-eight types of precious and semi-precious stones were inlaid into the white marble.

A labour force of twenty thousand workers was recruited across northern India. Sculptors from Bukhara, calligraphers from Syria and Persia, inlayers from southern India, stonecutters from Baluchistan, a specialist in building turrets, another who carved only marble flowers.

In fact, he did not even build a marble palace for himself. Other kings and emperors built towers (Kutub Minar) or archways

(Buland Darwaza), Shivaji did no such thing because he felt that every single '*mavla*' had a role in victory. Even though Tanaji died while taking Kondana, Shivaji did not name the fort after him. He named it Singhad.

Unlike Alexander, who not only named a string of cities after himself, but also named one after his horse Bucephalus, (Bucephala) (or Aurangzeb who named Khirki after him—Aurangabad, Shivaji did not name a single city or fort after himself or his family.

Europe, 200 years before Shivaji had entered 'the age of activity', to quote the words of the limitless Leonardo da Vinci, Galileo's telescope, Kepler's treatise on Mars, astronomical discoveries of Copernicus, Gilbert's findings in electricity and magnetism. Harvey's researches in the circulation of blood and Vesalius' researches in anatomy laid the foundation for a major techno-scientific revolution in Europe. Francis Drake and Walter Raleigh had performed navigational feats and expanded trade. The East India Company came into existence on the last day of 1600.

Shivaji was unaware of all this because he had no foreigners staying for long periods at his court. This was because he was always on the move and at war.

Akbar, the greatest and wisest of the Mughals, on the other hand, had many foreigners staying for long periods at his court. When he was presented a copy of a printed Bible by a Jesuit father Monsserate, he could not comprehend its importance. As we know, he was more interested in starting a new religion.

Had this printed copy been presented to Shivaji, perhaps the history of India would have changed. After all, knowledge was and is power.

□

Great Men/Greatness Theory

You must admit that the genesis of a great man depends on the long series of complex influences which have produced the race in which he appears, and the social state into which that race has slowly grown....Before he can remake his society, his society must make him Herbert Spencer. The Study of Sociology, societal, economic, technological and environmental factors are seen as just as or even more significant than political factors or the impact of single persons in shaping history. The is true of the background of Shivaji.

Dorris' core argument is that, those who become 'great' are those who start out with sufficient genetic potential and then are able, over two or more decades, to obtain matches/fits with 'the right kind of problems' to extend the development of these genetic biases into what Dorris terms 'key characteristics'. These are the intellectual, personality, and self characteristics which eventually turn out to be required to solve a key generational problem in their field and/or society. This is true as seen by the religious persecution by Aurangzeb.

Cox found that the perceived eminence of those with the highest IQs was higher than that of those attaining lower IQ estimates, and that those with higher IQs also exhibited more versatility in their achievements. For example, da Vinci, Michelangelo, Descartes, Benjamin Franklin, Goethe, and others with IQs in the mid-160s or above were superior in their versatility to those attaining lower scores, such as George Washington, Palestrina, or Philip Sheridan. This is again true as can be seen from the fact that Shivaji excelled as a warrior, general, administrator, fort-builder, ship-builder and reformer.

They are seen as extremely influential individuals who use their personal charisma, intelligence, wisdom, powers of persuasion, or other gifts to achieve significant historical impact. This is true because it can be said that what Shivaji started, Gandhiji completed and what Aurangzeb started, Jinnah completed.

The Scottish Victorian Historian, Thomas Carlyle (1795-1899) says, "The history of the world is but the biography of great men." Sivaji symbolises this view. The history of Maharashtra and later India, is but the history of Shivaji and his heirs.

Winston Churchill, considered the greatest Briton of all times sees it (greatness) as a responsibility: "*Responsibility is the price of greatness.*" This is true of Shivaji as can be seen from his letter to his soldiers on the guidelines he laid down on their behavour during war to show how he felt a responsibility towards his countrymen.

Gandhi considered great men great because of this commitment *'to the greater good'. His dictum was "Be the change you wish to see in the world."* Shivaji did exactly that. He wanted to instill courage in his comrades and took on Afzal Khan single-handedly. He put his life on the line to prove his point.

Greatness has a moral dimension, a willingness to be good. William Shakespeare guides us, *"He is not great who is not greatly good."* This is perhaps the most important of all the prerequisites of greatness for it is well known that Shivaji was a man with no weakness. (Shivaji: the Great Maratha, p. 459)

Takakhav asks, 'Who is a great man?' In our opinion, a great man is one who possesses an extraordinary degree of ability, skill, character, intelligence and whose deeds greatly influence the events of his time.

Shivaji's deeds not only influenced the events of his time, but the events of all times.

□

Biography of Each Warrior

Akbar the Great

Early Life

Abul-Fath Jalal-ud-din Muammad Akbar (born 15th October, 1542, Umarkot, Sindh (India) descended from Turks, Mongols, and Iranians—the three people who predominated the political elites of northern India in medieval times. Among his ancestors were Timur (Tamerlane) and Chenghis (Genghis) Khan. His father, Humayun, driven from his capital of Delhi by the Afghan usurper Sher Shah Suri, was vainly trying to establish his authority in Sind. Soon Humayun had to leave India for Afghanistan and Iran, where the Shah lent him some troops. Humayun regained his throne in 1555, 10 years after Sher Shah's death. Akbar, at the age of 13, was made governor of the Punjab.

Humayun had barely established his authority when he died in 1556. Within a few months, his governors lost several important places, including Delhi itself, to Hemu, a Hindu minister who claimed the throne for himself. But a Mughal force defeated Hemu on the historic battlefield of Panipat, which commanded the route to Delhi, thus ensuring Akbar's succession. The battle was going in Hemu's favour when an arrow pierced Hemu's eye, rendering him unconscious. The leaderless army soon capitulated and Hemu was captured and executed.

At Akbar's accession, his rule extended over little more than the Punjab and the area around Delhi, but under the guidance of his chief minister, Bairam Khan, his authority was gradually consolidated and extended. The process continued after Akbar forced Bairam Khan to retire in 1560 and began to govern on his own—at first still under household influences, but soon as an absolute monarch. After a dispute at court, Akbar dismissed Bairam Khan in the spring of 1560 and ordered him to leave for Hajj to Mecca.

Imperial Expansion

Akbar first attacked Malwa, a state of strategic and economic importance, commanding the route through the Vindhya range to the Deccan plateau and containing rich agricultural land; it fell to him in 1561.

Towards the zealously independent Hindu Rajputs (warrior ruling class) inhabiting rugged, hilly Rajasthan, Akbar adopted a policy of conciliation and conquest. Successive Muslim rulers had found the Rajputs dangerous, however weakened by disunity. But, in 1562, when Raja Bihari Mal of Amber (now Jaipur), threatened by a succession dispute, offered Akbar his daughter in marriage, Akbar accepted the offer. The Raja acknowledged Akbar's suzerainty, and his sons prospered in Akbar's service. Akbar followed the same feudal policy towards the other Rajput chiefs. They were allowed to hold their ancestral territories, provided they acknowledged Akbar as emperor, paid tribute, supplied troops when required, and concluded a marriage alliance with him. The emperor's service was also opened to them and their sons, who offered financial rewards as well as honour.

The 'Sabat' at Chittor

However, Akbar showed no mercy to those who refused to acknowledge his supremacy as seen in the case of Chittor.

Akbar planned to use two-man methods of assault mining and a device called *sabat* or covered way. At first, two mines were completed in one month, but when their fuses were lit, they did not blow up simultaneously, but there was a time lag between the explosions. The assault troops expecting only one explosion surged forward when the second charge went up. Two hundred Mughals were killed, among them several of Akbar's favourite officers. In concept, it was a steadily growing fortification designed to provide the attackers with defensive cover almost identical with that enjoyed by the defenders, while moving them slowly near their prey. It consisted of a covered way, wide enough for ten men to ride abrest and high enough for a man on an elephant with a raised spear to pass along, with side walls of rubble and mud which could resist cannon balls and a wooden roof held together with hides. The front end was permanently under construction and was an extremely dangerous place to work in. But as the perilious work progressed nearer and nearer the wall of the fort, the advantage steadily shifted to the attackers. It is much easier to fire guns at a sharp angle upwards than at a sharp angle downwards while remaining effectively under cover. Akbar's *sabat* was a treacherous armoured snake writhing with infinite slowness towards the point where it could latch its jaws onto Chittor's walls and nibble. (*The Great Mughals*, Bamber Gascoigne, Constable and Company, London, 1998, p. 90)

But before that, a bullet fired from the sabat (Akbar) and killed Jaimal, the commander of the fort. Soon *jauhar*, the Rajput custom of burning their women, started and the warriors came out to fight to death.

The Mughal army surrounded the fortress in October 1567 and it fell in February 1568 after a siege of four months. The fort was then stormed by the Mughal forces, and a fierce resistance was offered by members of the garrison stationed inside, as well as local peasants who came to their assistance. Over 30,000 unarmed inhabitants were massacred by the Mughal army.

Akbar measured his success in battle by the quantity of cordons of distinction (*janeu* or the sacred thread) collected from the fallen Rajput soldiers and other civilians of Chittor and which amounted to seventy-four and half *man (a unit of weight in India equalling 40 kg)* by weight. To eternise the memory of this deed, the number 74.5 is accursed and marked on a banker's letter in

Rajasthan; it is the strongest of seals, for 'the sin of the sack of Chittor' is invoked on him who violates a letter under the safeguard of this mysterious number. The fortress was completely destroyed and its gates were carried off to Agra, while the brass candlesticks taken from the Kalika temple after its destruction were given to the shrine of Moinuddin Chishti in Ajmer.

Akbar, bolstered by his success, was looking forward to widespread acclamation as a great conqueror of Islam and his vigorous Islamic policy is illustrated by *Fatahnama-i-Chittor* issued by him after the conquest of Chittor at Ajmer, where he stayed for some time en route to Agra, on Ramazan 10,975/March 9,1568, where the infidels (Hindus) are reviled:

"...the Omnipotent one who enjoined the task of destroying the wicked infidels (Hindus) on the dutiful *mujahids* through the blows of their thunder-like scimitars laid down: 'Fight them! Allah will chastise them at your hands and He will lay them low and give you victory over them.'

"This is of the grace of my Lord that He may try me whether I am grateful or ungrateful—we spend our precious time to the best of our ability in war (*ghiza*) and *jihad* and with the help of Eternal Allah, who is the supporter of our ever-increasing empire, we are busy in subjugating the localities, habitations, forts and towns which are under the possession of the infidels (Hindus), may Allah forsake and annihilate all of them, and, thus, raising the standard of Islam everywhere and removing the darkness of polytheism and violent sins by the use of sword, we destroy the places of worship of idols in those places and other parts of India."

Even though Mewar did not submit, the fall of Chittor prompted other Rajput *rajas* to accept Akbar as emperor in 1570 and to conclude marriage alliances with him, although the state of Marwar held out until 1583. After Akbar's conquest of Chittor, two major Rajput clans remained opposed to him—the Sisodiyas of Mewar and Hadas of Ranthambore. The latter, reputed to be the most powerful fortress in Rajasthan, was conquered by the Mughal army in 1569, making Akbar the master of almost the whole of

Rajputana. As a result, most of the Rajput kings, including those of Bikaner, Bundelkhand and Jaisalmer submitted to Akbar. Only the clans of Mewar continued to resist Mughal conquest and Akbar had to fight with them from time to time for the greater part of his reign. Among the most prominent of them was Maharana Pratap who declined to accept Akbar's suzerainty and also opposed the marriage etiquette of Rajputs, who had been giving their daughters to Mughals. He renounced all matrimonial alliances with Rajput rulers who had married into the Mughal dynasty, refusing such alliances even with the princes of Marwar and Amer until they agreed to sever ties with the Mughals.

When Rana Pratap in exile was facing the prospect of actual starvation, he wrote to Akbar indicating his readiness to negotiate a treaty. Pratap's first cousin (his mother's sister's son) Prithviraj Rathod, who was one of Akbar's courtiers, heard of this overture. He is said to have grown despondent and wrote thus to his cousin Pratap:

"The hopes of the Hindu rest on the Hindu *surya*, yet the Rana forsakes them. But for Pratap, all would be placed on the same level by Akbar; for our chiefs have lost their valour and our females their honour. Akbar is the broker in the market of our race; he has purchased all but the son of Udai (Singh II of Mewar); he is beyond his price. What true Rajput would part with honour for *nauroza* (the Persian new year's festival, where Akbar selected women for his pleasure); yet how many have bartered it away? Will Chittor come to this market? Though Patta (an affectionate name for Pratap Singh) has squandered away wealth (on warfare), yet he has preserved this treasure. Despair has driven men to this market, to witness their dishonour: from such infamy, the descendant of Hammir (Maharana Hammir) alone has been preserved. The world asks, from where does the concealed aid of Pratap emanate? None but the soul of manliness and his sword. The broker in the market of men (Akbar) will one day be surpassed; he cannot live forever. Then will our race come to Pratap, for the seed of the Rajput to sow in our desolate lands. To him all look for its preservation, that its purity may again become resplendent. It is as much impossible for me to believe that Pratap has called Akbar his emperor as to see the sun rising in the west. Tell me where do I stand? Shall I use my sword on my neck or shall I continue my proud bearing?"

One of the notable features of Akbar's government was the extent of Hindu, and particularly Rajput, participation.

Akbar adopted a generous attitude towards Hindus and has been praised to the skies for that. But, it is an elementary rule that a stable government is impossible if the majority of the subjects are unhappy. Akbar was courteous to them who, as a community, were raising his kingdom and stabilising it for him. The Hindus he treated well were a majority in his empire and were enriching his treasury through their taxes. The Hindus had no history of invasions. They had not destroyed *masjids*. They had not celebrated genocides of Muslims. They had not defiled Muslim women or imposed forced conversions. These were the people Akbar was generous to. On the contrary, Muslims were a minority community in Shivaji's empire. It was not the mainstay of his taxes. (Akbar and Hindus, Shriman Yogi)

Akbar was a follower of Salim Chishti, a holy man who lived in the region of Sikri near Agra. Believing the area to be a lucky one for himself, he had a mosque constructed there for the use of the saint. Subsequently, he celebrated the victories over Chittor and Ranthambore by laying the foundation of a new walled capital, 23 miles (37 km) west of Agra in 1569, which was named Fatehpur ('town of victory') after the conquest of Gujarat in 1573 and, subsequently, came to be known as Fatehpur Sikri in order to distinguish it from other similarly named towns. Palaces for each of Akbar's senior queens, a huge artificial lake and sumptuous water-filled courtyards were built there. However, the city was soon abandoned and the capital was moved to Lahore in 1585. The reason may have been that the water supply in Fatehpur Sikri was insufficient or of poor quality.

The Kacchwaha Rajput, Raja Bharmal, of Amber, who had come to Akbar's court shortly after the latter's accession, entered into an alliance by giving his daughter Harkha Bai in marriage to the emperor. Harkha Bai became Muslim and was renamed Mariam-uz-Zamani. After her marriage, she was treated as an outcaste by her Hindu family and for the rest of her life never visited Amer. She was not assigned any significant place either in Agra or Delhi, but rather a small village in the Bharatpur district. She died in 1623. A mosque was built in her honour by her son Jehangir in Lahore. Bharmal was made a noble of high rank in the imperial court, and, subsequently, his son Bhagwant Das and grandson Man Singh also rose to high ranks in the nobility.

Rathore Kalyandas threatened to kill both Mota Raja Rao, Udai Singh and Jehangir because Udai Singh had decided to marry his daughter to Jehangir. Akbar on hearing this, ordered imperial forces to attack Kalyandas at Siwana. Kalyandas died fighting along with his men and the women of Siwana committed *jauhar*.

The Mughal empire acquired its first access to the sea after Akbar's conquest of Gujarat in 1572, and for the first few years, conscious of the threat posed by the presence of the Portuguese, remained content with obtaining a *cartaz* from them for sailing in the Persian Gulf region. At the initial meeting of the Mughals and the Portuguese during the siege of Surat in 1572, the Portuguese, recognising the superior strength of the Mughal army, chose to adopt diplomacy instead of war, and the Portuguese Governor, upon the request of Akbar, sent him an ambassador to establish friendly relations. Akbar accepted the offer of diplomacy, in order to facilitate the safe passage of the members of his harem on their projected pilgrimage to Mecca. In 1573, he issued a *firman* directing his administrative officials in Gujarat not to disturb the Portuguese in their adjoining territory of Daman. The Portuguese, in turn, issued passes for the members of Akbar's family to go on Hajj to Mecca. The *cartaz* thus issued made mention of the extraordinary status of the vessel and the special status to be accorded to its occupants. Akbar never thought of making an attempt to have a navy of his own.

Akbar's Hindu generals could not construct temples without

the emperor's permission. In Bengal, after Man Singh started the construction of a temple in 1595, Akbar ordered him to convert it into a mosque. He gave two villages for the upkeep of a mosque and a *madrasa* which was set up by destroying a Hindu temple. During the early part of Akbar's reign, his army was responsible for the demolition of rich Hindu temples which had gold deities in the Doab region.

Akbar adopted an attitude of suppression towards Muslim sects that were condemned by the orthodoxy as heretical. In 1567, on the advice of Shaikh Abdu'n Nabi, he ordered the exhumation of Mir Murtaza Sharifi Shirazi—a Shia buried in Delhi because of the grave's proximity to that of Amir Khusrau, arguing that a 'heretic' could not be buried so close to the grave of a Sunni saint, reflecting a restrictive attitude towards the Shia, and which continued to persist till the early 1570s.

In 1575, he built a hall called the Ibadat Khana (House of Worship) at Fatehpur Sikri, to which he invited theologians, mystics and selected courtiers renowned for their intellectual achievements and discussed matters of spirituality with them. However, a leading noble of Akbar's court, Aziz Koka, wrote a letter to him from Mecca in 1594, arguing that the Din-i-Ilahi promoted by Akbar amounted to nothing more than a desire on Akbar's part to portray himself as 'a new prophet'. To commemorate Din-e-Ilahi, he changed the name of Prayag to Allahabad (pronounced as *Ilahabad*) in 1583.

Akar started a new religion, '*din-e-ilahi* 'The emperor enlisted selected members of his nobility as his disciples. Each initiate swore to accept four degrees of devotion to Akbar.' The unhesitating willingness to sacrifice one's life (*jan),* property (*mal*), religion (*din*) and honour (*namus*) in the service of the master, i.e. Akbar. Throughout the ceremony, the neophyte placed his head on Akbar's feet in an extreme form of prostration known as *sijdah*. Akbar placed a new turban upon his head and gave him a symbolic representation of the sun embossed on a medallion and a tiny portrait of Akbar to wear on his turban.

Akbar also placed a robe brocated in gold and silver first on his own body and then personally draped them on the recipient. By this devices, the notion of one body in service to the ruler and nobles was promulgated. (*The Cambridge History of India, The Mughal Empire,* John Richards, Cambridge University Press, p. 47, 49)

The lord of half a million swords does not feel happy unless he can flatter himself that he is not as other men are, that he is a kin to gods and that he rules by divine right.

Though illiterate, he secured his own recognition as the *mujtahid* or infalliable interpreter of the *quran* and of all disputed points of Islamic theology. 1579 I quote from his court flatterer Abdul Faiz: 'Men of all nations look upon offering a vow to His Majesty as the means of solving all their difficulties... His Majesty gives satisfactory answers to everyone and applies remedies to their religious perplexities. Not a day passes but people bring cups of water to him, beseeching him to breathe upon it. Many sick people whose disease the most eminent physicians pronounced incurable have been restored to health by this divine means. (*Mughal Administration,* J. Sarkar, Orient longman Ltd., p. 99-121).

'Every morning, at dawn, he stood at an open window to be seen and revered by the people. The Hindu *darshanias* or men who did not begin their days without first gazing on the emperor's face as on an idol in the morning, formed another set of his worshippers, and they have another set of rules.'

Another legend is that Akbar's daughter Meherunnissa was enamoured by Tansen and had a role in his coming to Akbar's court. Tansen converted to Islam from Hinduism, apparently on the eve of his marriage with Akbar's daughter.

After his daughter Meherunnissa's marriage with a Hindu musician Tansen, Akbar issues a **Firman** ***that in future no Mughal princess/daughter of Mughal would be ever allowed to marry. Any girl born into Mughal royalty would remain unmarried for life, until her death.***

Though the Quran retricts the number to four, Akbar had technically three wives—a Hindu, a Muslim and a Christian. But the actual number of women in the harem could have exceeded 5,000 as in the case of...

The harem was a cage full of idle but pretty women in which only the cock of the roost was seen or heard. No doubt, much of the time was spent in self-adornment or in looking at one's own face in the mirror about an inch in diameter, which each lady wore on her right thumb, but the harem was also a beehive of business activity and intrigue.

If there were 5,000 women and the emperor had sex with one woman every night with no break, then a woman would have her chance of sex 5,000 divided by 365 = 13.69 i.e. once every 13.69 years.

These circumstances gave rise to situations described below.

When a doctor had to see a lady too ill to be moved to the outer gate in the harem, the precautions taken were elaborate. Francois Bernier writes, 'a Kashmere shawl covered my head, hanging like a large scarf down to my feet and a eunuch led me by my hand, as if I were a blind man.' When the doctor reached the patient, the shawl would be removed. She would be lying out of sight behind a curtain. If she needed to be bled or to have a minor wound dressed, the appropriate hand or leg would appear through the curtain. If some further inspection was required, the doctor was allowed to put his hand through the curtain, and Manucci describes the stimulating dangers and the need to keep a straight face, when the patient was only pretending illness for the sake of being visited. There are some who from time to time pretend being invalid, simply that they may have the chance of some conversation with and have their pulse felt by the (male) physician who comes to see them. The (male) physician stretches out his hand inside the curtain; he may hold it, kiss it and softly bite it. Some, out of curiosity, apply it to their breast, which has happened to me several times; but I pretend not to notice, in order to conceal what was happening from the eunuchs and matrons present there and arouse their suspicions. So great is the jealousy and wickedness of the eunuchs that they do not allow any virile-shaped vegetables like radishes and cucumbers (unless cut) so that they may not be put to some unnatural abuse..." (*The Great Mughal,* Bamber Gascoigne, Constable and Co., 85, 162)

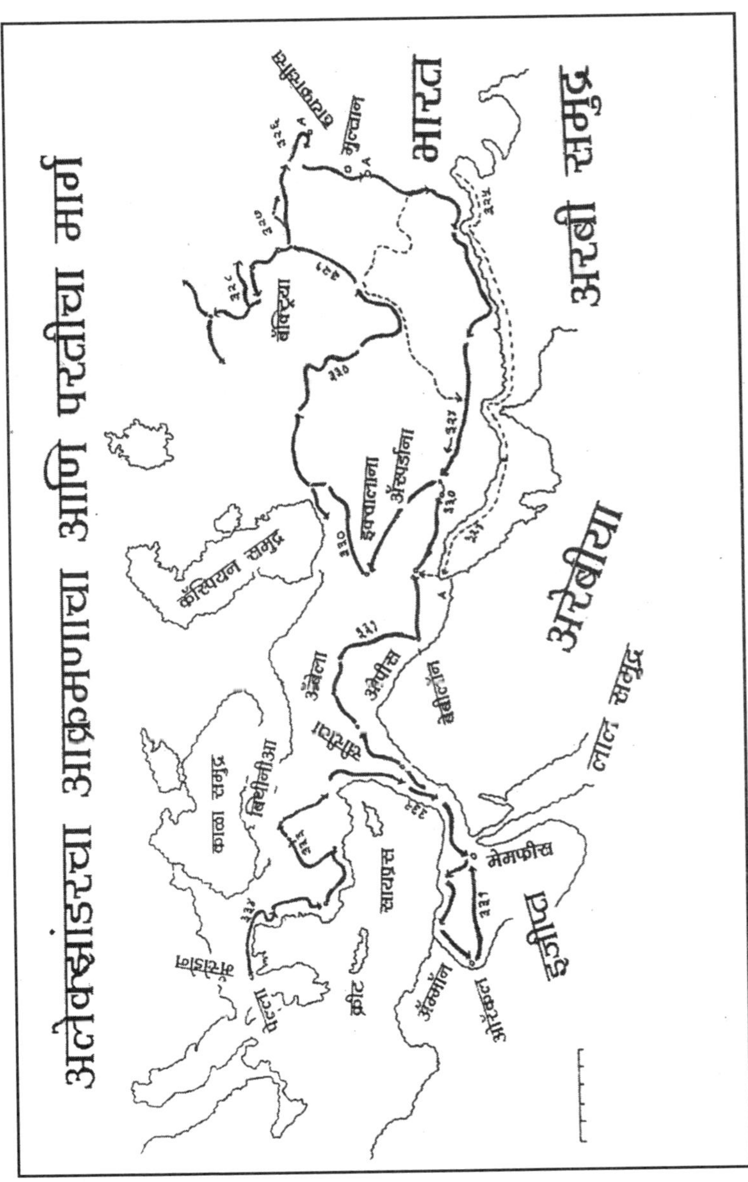

Description of the Ten Great Warriors

Shivaji's contemporaries, such as the English, have compared him with many great warriors and emperors. Though comparisons among great men are never worthwhile, they do bring out something that is extraordinary even amongst equals.

Alexander the Great

Alexander (born in Pella in 356 B.C.) lived only a short thirty-three years and is believed to be a direct descendant of the God Zeus.

His father, Phillip II of Macedon, left his young son Megas an entire kingdom that included hundreds of small city-states. With the military training and learning from the teacher and philosopher Aristotle, young Alexander would have the proper rearing to become one of Macedon's greatest rulers. Then, after the assassination of his father at a wedding ceremony, Alexander was named the next ruler and agreed upon by all the head military officials.

Upon his succession, the city of Thebes attempted twice to secede from the Union that his father Phillip II had made. With impressive military force that led to tens of thousands of deaths, the entire city was finally conquered and all its citizens either killed or sold into slavery. With Thebes now under control, Alexander the Great decided he should also continue with his unprecedented military marvel to the Persian Empire. At Gordian, he cut the proverbial Gordian knot. In Persia, Alexander moved his way down the coast, taking over one city after another, victory after victory, to eventually control the entire peninsula. He took the Persian title 'king of kings' (*shahanshah*), adopted the Persian custom of proskynesis, either a symbolic kissing of the hand, or prostration on the ground. The Greek regarded the gesture as the province of deities and believed that Alexander meant to deitify himself by requiring it and mutinied at the town of Opis.

Alexander then moved towards Egypt, where he was actually welcomed as a liberator. He visited the Oracle of Ammon and claimed his divinity. While there, he founded Alexandria, which would become one of the most prosperous cities in the entire world. In a matter of months, Alexander also marched upon Assyria and then onward to Babylon, where he took over its surrounding lands in three years' time.

In his travels and with his hopes of fusing his empire, Alexander encouraged those countries, cities, and states to join his merchant armies and to crusade with him. He also encouraged his armies to marry women of other lands and to bear children with them, so that his empire would be better united and not of one race. Additionally, he promoted high-ranking officials in the places he conquered to join an equally high position in his dynasty. He was successful in much of his attempts to unite his people.

Alexander went on to take over northern India. Before his death, he took over other parts of India and other areas of what is now known as the Middle East. With his massive armies consisting of soldiers and infantrymen of both Greek and Persian origin, he was able to continue his imperialistic endeavours without recourse. And, while it is debated whether poison, infection, or disease took his life, Alexander lived to become known as one of the bravest military leaders and kings of all time. He died of war wounds at the age of 32. He had given detailed instructions to be carried out after his death but were not.

Julius Caesar

With a formal education due to his lineage, Caesar studied some of the most prominent works of the day. He abhorred how opposing factions were tearing the republic of Rome apart. Some favoured an electoral government, while others wanted a leader for life. At that time, young Caesar didn't know he was to become Rome's most prominent leader, emperor and deity.

After being forced to go into hiding with the reign of Sulla, Caesar and his family had to muster a plan to take on Sulla's proclaimed dictatorship. Caesar soon joined the army, but did not dare travel back to Rome. He was scared for his own life, even if he and his family's titles had been restored. Caesar would rise to power quickly, obtaining the civic Crown for his brave efforts in battle.

Sulla, the ruler at the time, gave the government back to the people and dismantled his rule. Walking freely about in the streets, just as any other man, he then retired away to his own private estate and was not involved in politics again. When Sulla died, Caesar returned to Rome, where he would await his chance to become one of the possible candidates to be voted into office.

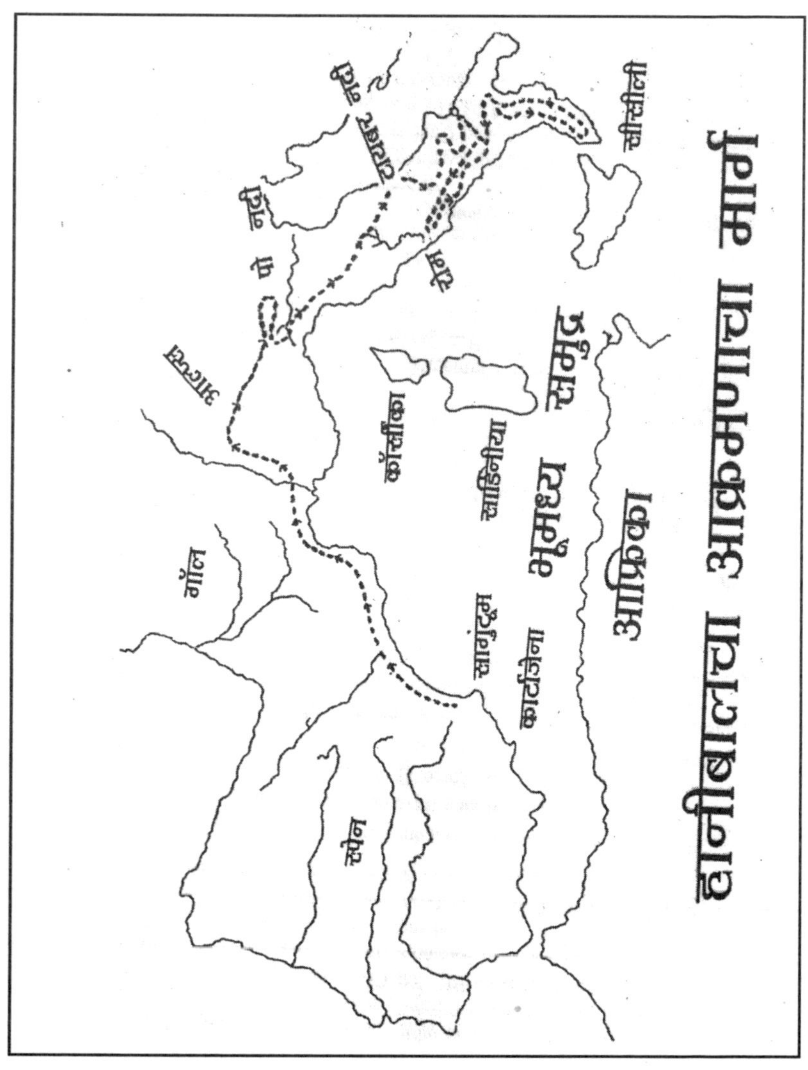

He organised the first triumvirate with Pompey and Crasus but later broke up. He conquered large parts of Europe some quite easily (I came, I saw, I conquered). It wasn't until 60 B.C. that Caesar was elected Consul of the Roman Republic. Caesar then was appointed to various posts throughout the Republic where he fought and won many strategic battles that did not go unnoticed by other council members in Rome. Caesar started another civil war that would eventually see him rise to be appointed dictator over Rome.

He then began his life-long involvement with Cleopatra, who he could not marry due to Roman law. He also travelled to the Middle East, where he secured even more territory for Rome. It was through Caesar's direct hand that Rome had evolved from a republic to an empire. He was recalled to Rome, made dictator for life, father of the fatherland, the month of Quintilis was renamed July in his honour, was granted a golden chair in the senate house, was made dictator for life, was offered a crown but, a month later (on the Ides of March) was assassinated by 60 of his fellowmen including Brutus, to whom the last words were 'You too, child' or 'Et tu Brutus'.

He was declared a deity by the senate. His name would become the title of every Roman leader who followed.

Hannibal

Hannibal ('Mercy' or 'favour of Baal'), Carthaginian general and statesman, son of Hamilcar, was born in 249 or 247 B.C. Destined by his father to succeed him in the work of vengeance against Rome, he was taken to Spain, and while yet a boy, gave ample evidence of his military aptitude. Upon the death of his brother-in-law Hasdrubal (221), he was acclaimed commander-in-chief by the soldiers and confirmed in his appointment by the Carthaginian government. In 219, attacked Saguntum (modern Murviedro), which was under the special protection of Rome. Hannibal executed a daring plan of carrying the war into the heart of Italy by a rapid march through Spain and Gaul and reached the Rhone and by autumn arrived at the foot of the Alps. His passage over the mountain chain, was one of the most memorable achievements of any military force of ancient times. In December of the same year, he had an opportunity of showing his superior military skill when the Roman commander attacked him on River Trebia (near Placentia In 217, Hannibal reached Rome, but realising that without siege engines, he could not hope to take the capital. A large Roman army advanced into Apulia in order to crush him, and accepted battle on the site of Cannae. Thanks mainly to brilliant cavalry tactics, Hannibal, with much inferior numbers, managed to surround and cut to pieces the whole of this force; moreover, the moral effect of this victory was such that all the south of Italy joined his cause. In 207, he succeeded in making his way again into Apulia, where he waited to concert measures for a combined march upon Rome with his brother Hasdrubal. On hearing, however, of his brother's defeat and death at the Metaurus, he retired into the mountain fastnesses of Bruttium, where he maintained himself for the ensuing years. Hannibal was recalled from Italy by the 'patriot' party at Carthage. After leaving a record of his expedition, engraved in Punic and Greek upon brazen tablets, in the temple of Juno at Crotona, he sailed back to Africa.

In 202, Hannibal, after meeting Scipio in a fruitless peace conference, engaged him in a decisive battle at Zama. Unable to cope with his indifferent troops against the well-trained and confident Roman soldiers, he experienced a crushing defeat which put an end to all resistance on the part of Carthage.

Seven years after the victory of Zama, the Romans, alarmed at this new prosperity, demanded Hannibal's surrender. Hannibal thereupon went into voluntary exile. First he journeyed to Tyre, the mother-city of Carthage, and from there to Ephesus, where he was honourably received by Antiochus III of Syria.

In 190, he was placed in command of a Phoenician fleet, but was defeated in a battle off River Eurymedon.

From the court of Antiochus, who seemed prepared to surrender him to the Romans, Hannibal fled to Crete. Once more the Romans were determined to hunt him out, and they sent Flaminius to insist on his surrender. Prusias agreed to give him up, but Hannibal did not choose to fall into his enemies' hands. At Libyssa, on the eastern shore of the Sea of Marmoura, he took poison, which, it was said, he had long carried about with him in a ring. The precise year of his death was a matter of controversy. If, as Livy seems to imply, it was 183, he died in the same year as Scipio Africanus.

He had indeed bitter enemies and his life was one continuous struggle against destiny. For steadfastness of purpose, for organising capacity and a mastery of military science, he has perhaps never had an equal.

Attila

Attila (434 to 453) was a chieftain who brought the Huns to their greatest strength and who posed a grave threat to the Roman Empire.

The Huns first appear in European records at the end of the 4th century A.D., when they descended from the Steppes and attacked the Germanic tribes on the north-eastern edge of the Roman Empire. Rua, the man responsible for much of this unity, died in 434 and left the kingdom to his nephews Attila and Bleda. For 10 years, they ruled jointly and threatened the Eastern Roman Empire on several occasions. In 435, a 'peace' was signed with the Romans, which among other things guaranteed the Huns an annual payment of 700 pounds of gold. In 441, the Huns attacked the provinces across the Danube. In 443, Attila so severely defeated the Roman general Aspar that the Romans had to purchase peace with an annual tribute of 6,000 pounds of gold.

In 445, Attila murdered Bleda and united all the Huns under his own leadership. The Roman Priscus, an eyewitness who was an ambassador to Attila's court, describes him as short with a broad chest, flat nose, and beard sprinkled with grey. Attila 'Scourge of God' ruled with absolute authority, his power based in a large part on the extensive wealth from his conquests.

War with the Eastern Empire was renewed in 447, and the Romans were defeated in the bloody battle of Marcianopolis. In the peace treaty of 448, they were forced to cede extensive territory along the Danube. Attila then turned his attention to the Western Empire. Geiseric the Vandal urged Attila to attack the Goths so as to remove their pressure on the Vandals, and Attila moved to attack the Visigoths. At the same time, the sister of the emperor Valentinian III, Honoria, asked Attila to rescue her from an unwelcome marriage. This gave Attila the excuse to move against Rome. Aëtius, the strongman of the Western Empire and one-time hostage of the Huns, created an alliance of Romans and Visigoths, and when the Huns invaded Gaul in 451, he defeated them on the Catalaunian Plains in Champagne.

Although defeated, the Huns escaped destruction and the next year attacked Italy. The important city of Aquileia was destroyed, but Attila did not attack Rome. An embassy from Pope Leo I was credited with dissuading him, but the growing fear of plague and famine probably determined the decision. In 453, while planning another attack on the Eastern Empire, Attila died suddenly from a haemorrhage, reportedly the result of excessive drinking at a wedding. Some historians say that "Attila died, pierced by the hand and blade of his wife."

After his death, his sons divided his 'empire' and the power of the Huns was soon destroyed by internal strife. Attila proved to be a major threat to Rome in his life-time, but left no permanent power to challenge the empire.

Richard the Lionheart

Younger Years

Richard the Lionheart was born on 8 September, 1157, in Oxford, England. He was generally considered to be his mother's favourite son, and has been described as spoiled and vain because of it.

Richard the Lionheart was the third son of King Henry II and Eleanor of Aquitaine, and although his eldest brother died young, the next in line, Henry, was named heir. Thus, Richard grew up with little realistic expectations of achieving the English throne. In any case, he was more interested in the family's French holdings than he was in England; he spoke little English, and he was made Duke of the lands his mother had brought to her marriage when he was quite young: Aquitaine in 1168, and Poitiers three years later.

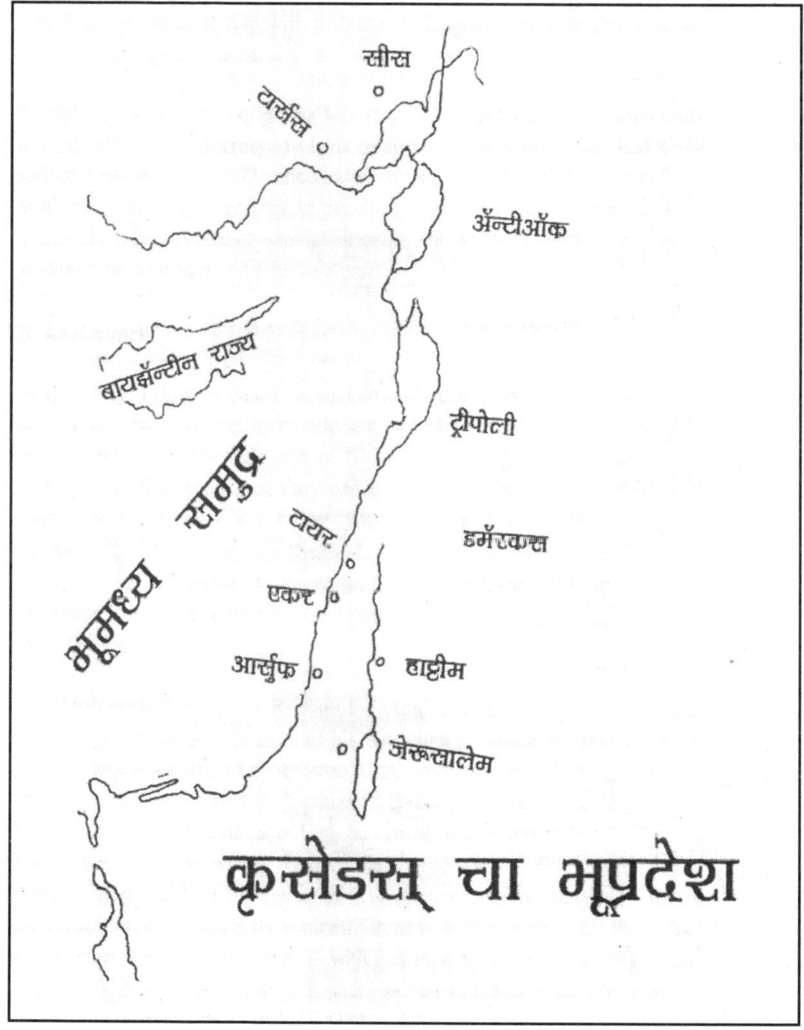

In 1169, King Henry and King Louis VII of France agreed that Richard should be wed to Louis's daughter Alice. This engagement was to last for some time, although Richard never showed any interest in her; Alice was sent from her home to live with the court in England, while Richard stayed with his holdings in France.

Brought up among the people he was to govern, Richard soon learned how to deal with the aristocracy. But his relationship with his father had some serious problems. In 1173, encouraged by his mother, Richard joined his brothers Henry and Geoffrey in rebelling against the king. The rebellion ultimately failed; Eleanor was imprisoned, and Richard found it necessary to submit to his father and receive a pardon for his transgressions.

Duke Richard

In the early 1180s, Richard faced baronial revolts in his own lands. He displayed considerable military skill and earned a reputation for courage (the quality that led to his nickname of Richard the Lionheart), but he dealt so harshly with the rebels that they called on his brothers to help drive him from Aquitaine. Now his father interceded on his behalf, fearing the fragmentation of the empire he had built (the 'Angevin' Empire, after Henry's lands of Anjou). However, no sooner had King Henry gathered his continental armies together than the younger Henry unexpectedly died, and the rebellion crumpled.

As the oldest surviving son, Richard the Lionheart was now heir to England, Normandy, and Anjou. In light of his extensive holdings, his father wanted him to cede Aquitaine to his brother John, who had never had any territory to govern and was known as 'Lackland'. But Richard had a deep attachment to the duchy. Rather than give it up, he turned to the king of France, Louis's son Philip II, with whom Richard had developed a firm political and personal friendship. In November of 1188, Richard paid homage to Philip for all his holdings in France; then joined forces with him to drive his father into submission. They forced Henry—who had indicated a willingness to name John his heir—to acknowledge

Richard as heir to the English throne before hounding him to his death in July 1189.

Richard the Lionheart: Crusader King

Richard the Lionheart had become king of England, but his heart wasn't in the sceptred isle. He spent only six months of his ten year reign in England, claiming it was 'cold and always raining'. He cared little for England and during the period when he was raising funds for his Crusade, Richard was heard to declare, "If I could have found a buyer, I would have sold London itself." Ever since Saladin had captured Jerusalem in 1187, Richard's greatest ambition was to go to the Holy Land and take it back. His father had agreed to engage in Crusade along with Philip, and a 'Saladin Tithe' had been levied in England and France to raise funds for the endeavour. Now Richard took full advantage of the Saladin Tithe and the military apparatus that had been formed; he drew heavily from the royal treasury and sold anything that might bring him funds—offices, castles, lands, towns, lordships. In less than a year, after his accession to the throne, Richard the Lionheart raised a substantial fleet and an impressive army to take on Crusade.

Philip and Richard agreed to go to the Holy Land together, but not all was well between them. The French king wanted some of the lands that Henry had held, and that were now in Richard's hands, which he believed rightfully belonged to France. Richard was not about to relinquish any of his holdings; in fact, he shored up the defences of these lands and prepared for conflict. But neither king really wanted war with each other, especially with a Crusade awaiting their attention.

In fact, the Crusading spirit was strong in Europe at this time. Although there were always nobles who wouldn't put up a farthing for the effort, the vast majority of the European nobility were devout believers of the virtue and necessity of Crusade. Most of those who didn't take up arms themselves still supported the Crusading movement any way that they could. And right now, both Richard and Philip were being shown up by the septuagenarian

German emperor, Frederick Barbarossa, who had already pulled together an army and set off for the Holy Land.

In the face of public opinion, continuing their quarrel was not really feasible for either of the kings, but especially not for Philip, since Richard the Lionheart had worked so hard to fund his part in the Crusade. The French king chose to accept the promises that Richard made, probably against his better judgement. Among these pledges was Richard's agreement to marry Philip's sister Alice, who still languished in England, even though it appeared he had been negotiating for the hand of Berengaria of Navarre.

During the Crusade arguments arose over who would be the king of Jerusalem because of which King Philip of France and Leopold of Austria quit the Crusade. In Acre, the third Crusade reached a stalemate and Richard realising that even if he could capture Jerusalem, he could not hold it. Therefore, a three-year truce was agreed with Saladin who promptly renegaded on it. Richard in fury had 3,000 prisoners slaughtered before sailing from Acre.

On his way back, he was shipwrecked and was ransomed for1,00,000 marks which he paid (from taxes in London).

He was wounded in the siege of Castle of Chalus Chabrol and died 11 days later.

William Wallace

William Wallace (c. 1270-1305) was the son of Sir Malcolm Wallace, a descendant of Richard the Welshman of the royal Stewart family. Sir Malcolm Wallace was murdered and William was brought up by his uncles who were priests. William Wallace's efforts to free Scotland from England's grasp came just a year after his country initially lost its freedom, when he was 27 years old.

In 1296, England's King Edward I forced Scottish king John de Balliol, already known as a weak king, to abdicate the throne, jailed him, and declared himself ruler of Scotland. Resistance to Edward's actions had already begun when, in May 1297, Wallace and some 30 other men burned the Scottish town of Lanark and killed its English sheriff. Wallace then organised a local army and attacked the English strongholds between the Forth and Tay rivers.

Battle of Sterling Bridge

On 11th September, 1297, an English army confronted Wallace and his men at the Forth river near Stirling. Wallace's forces were vastly outnumbered, but the English had to cross a narrow bridge over the Forth before they could reach Wallace and his growing army. With strategic positioning on their side, Wallace's forces massacred the English as they crossed the river, and Wallace gained an unlikely and crushing victory.

He went on to capture Stirling Castle, and Scotland was briefly nearly free of occupying English forces. In October, Wallace invaded northern England and ravaged Northumberland and Cumberland countries, but his unconventionally brutal battle tactics (he reportedly flayed a dead English soldier and kept his skin as a trophy) only served to antagonise the British even more.

Battle of Falkirk

When Wallace returned to Scotland in December 1297, he was knighted and proclaimed guardian of the kingdom, ruling in the deposed king's name. But three months later, Edward returned to England, and four months after that, in July, hc invaded Scotland again.

On July 22, Wallace's troops suffered defeat in the Battle of Falkirk, and as quickly as that, his military reputation was ruined and he resigned his guardianship. Wallace next served as a diplomat and, in 1299, attempted to garner French support for Scotland's rebellion. He was briefly successful, but the French eventually turned against the Scots, and Scottish leaders capitulated to the English and recognised Edward as their king in 1304.

Capture and Execution

Unwilling to compromise, William Wallace refused to submit to English rule, and Edward's men pursued him until August 5, 1305, when they captured and arrested him near Glasgow. He was taken to London and condemned as a traitor to the king and was hanged, disembowelled, beheaded and quartered. He was seen by the Scots as a martyr and as a symbol of the struggle for independence, and his efforts continued after his death.

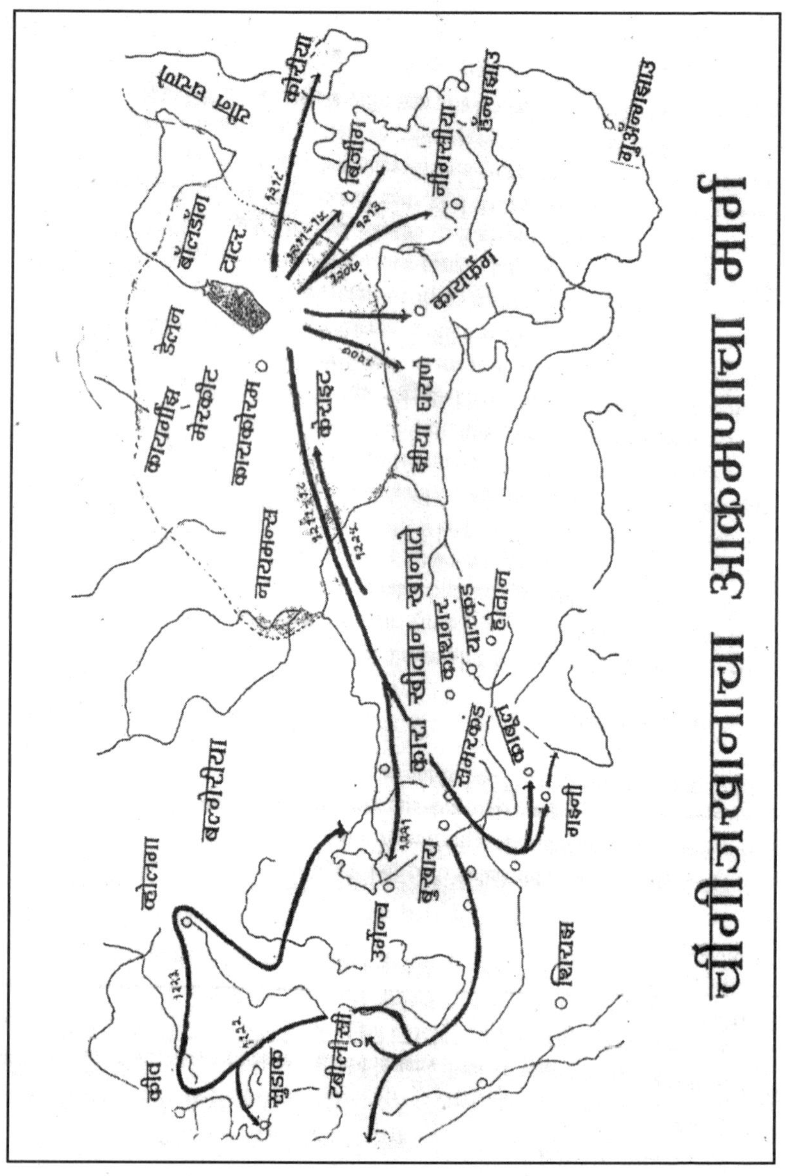

Genghis Khan

Early Life

Genghis Khan was born in north central Mongolia and named 'Temujin'. Temujin was born with a blood clot in his hand, a sign in Mongol folklore that he was destined to become a leader. His mother, Hoelun, taught him the grim reality of living in turbulent Mongol tribal society and the need for alliances.

When Temujin was nine, his father died and Temujin returned home to claim his position as clan chief. In a dispute over the spoils of a hunting expedition, Temujin quarrelled with and killed his half-brother Bekhter, confirming his position as head of the family.

The Universal Ruler

His campaigns are shown in the figure alongside. The early success of the Mongol army owed much to the brilliant military tactics of Genghis Khan and his understanding of his enemies' motivations. He employed an extensive spy network and was quick to adopt new technologies from his enemies. The well-trained Mongol army of 80,000 fighters coordinated their advance with a sophisticated signalling system of smoke and burning torches. Large drums sounded commands to charge, and further orders were conveyed with flag signals. Every soldier was fully equipped with bow, arrows, shield, dagger and lasso. He also carried large saddlebags for food, tools and spare clothes. The saddlebag was waterproof and could be inflated to serve as a life-preserver when crossing deep and swift-moving rivers. Cavalrymen carried a small sword, javelins, body armour, a battle-ax or mace, and a lance with a hook to pull enemies off their horses. They were devastating in their attacks. Because they could moeuver a galloping horse using only their legs, their hands were free to shoot arrows. The entire army was followed by a well-organised supply system of oxcarts carrying food for soldiers and beasts alike, as well as military equipment, shamans for spiritual and medical aid and officials to catalogue the booty.

Following the victories over the rival Mongol tribes, other

tribal leaders agreed to peace and bestowed on Temujin the title of 'Genghis Khan', which means 'universal ruler'. And, later 'Mongke Koko Tengri' (the 'Eternal Blue Sky'), the supreme God of the Mongols. To defy the Great Khan was equal to defying the will of God. He said, "I am the flail of God. If you had not committed great sins, God would not have sent a punishment like me upon you."

Major Conquests

In 1219, Genghis Khan personally took control of planning and executing a three-pronged attack of 2,00,000 Mongol soldiers against the Khwarizm dynasty. The Mongols swept through every city's fortifications with unstoppable savagery. Those who weren't immediately slaughtered were driven in front of the Mongol army, serving as human shields when the Mongols took the next city. No living thing was spared, including small domestic animals and livestock. Skulls of men, women and children were piled in large, pyramidal mounds. City after city was brought to its knees, bringing an end to the Khwarizm dynasty in 1221.

The empire was governed by a legal code known as Yassa. Developed by Genghis Khan, the code was based on Mongol common law, but contained edicts that prohibited blood feuds, adultery, theft and bearing false witness. Also included were laws that reflected Mongol respect for the environment, such as forbidding bathing in rivers and streams and orders for any soldier following another to pick up anything that the first soldier dropped. Infraction of any of these laws was usually punishable by death. Advancement within military and government ranks was not based on traditional lines of heredity or ethnicity, but on merit.

He fathered hundreds, if not thousands, of children raping several women every night. 8 per cent of the men in a large region of Asia (about 0.5 per cent of the world total) and in Mongolia alone, as many as 2,00,000 of the country's 2 million people could be Khan's descendants The sacking of Urgench is considered one of the bloodiest massacres in human history. During his reign he massacred 30,000,000-60,000,000 people i.e. 7.5-17 per cent of the world's population. He is known to have said, "The greatest pleasure is to vanquish your enemies and chase them before you, to rob them of their wealth and see those dear to them bathed in tears, to ride their horses and clasp to your bosom their wives and daughters,"

Genghis Khan's Death

Genghis Khan died of fatigue and injuries in 1227. He was buried without markings. According to legend, the funeral escort killed anyone and anything they encountered to conceal the location of the burial site, and a river was diverted over his grave to make it impossible to find.

Before his death, Genghis Khan and his empire was divided among his sons. Among the many descendants of Genghis Khan is Kublai Khan, who was the son of Tolui, Genghis Khan's youngest son. He was made Great Khan and emperor of the Yuan Dynasty of China.

Adolphus Gustavus

Gustavus II. the eldest son of Charles IX of Sweden and Christina of Holstein-Gottorp, was born on 9th December, 1594. On 15th August, 1609, he made his first speech to the Estates when he dismissed them after a stormy session, for his father was incapacitated by a stroke from which he never completely recovered. He henceforth was co-regent until his father's death in October 1611.

Early Days

When the young king took over, the country was at war with Russia, Poland and Denmark. Consequently, a peace treaty was signed at Knäred in January 1613, whereby Sweden agreed to pay Denmark one million riksdaler within six years and give up all claims to certain disputed Arctic regions. Älvsborg Fort and the surrounding region were to be occupied by the Danes as pledge for payment. All other boundaries were to remain the same. Sweden did, however, retain exemption from the tolls at the Sound.

The struggle with Russia was aided by succession problems in the Muscovite state known as the 'Time of Troubles'. Playing off various succession candidates, Gustavus was able to conclude on 27th February, 1617, at Stolbova, a favourable peace treaty which excluded Russia from the Baltic. In autumn of that year, Gustavus's long-delayed coronation took place in the Cathedral of Uppsala. On 25th November, 1620, he married Maria Eleanora of Brandenburg and thereby achieved 'his first victory on German soil'.

Domestic Affairs

The Charter of 1617 sanctioned all former privileges of the nobility and stipulated that all important crown offices be reserved for the nobility. No commoner could be employed in the central administration or serve as a judge or diplomat. By the Statutes of the Nobility of 1626, grades in the nobility were defined and it became the right and the duty of the upper class to enlist in the civil service of the country. The nobility, however, was not a closed caste and was constantly recruited from below. Commoners with conspicuous abilities as soldiers and administrators were given the title commensurate with their positions. As time passed, a cleavage developed between the new aristocracy of service and the aristocracy of land and family. Furthermore, Gustavus gave the Estates considerable power and balanced the lower estates against the upper. The meetings of the Estates gradually were transformed into orderly discussions as opposed to the stormy and highly dramatic meetings held by earlier sovereigns. There were complaints over taxes, but the successful foreign policy of the king usually kept the Estates loyal.

Gustavus and his able chancellor Oxenstierna worked tirelessly to create a central organisation to meet the country's administrative needs. Their efforts reached fruition in the 1634 acre? Regeringsform (Constitution). It was this machinery that made it possible for government to function during the long absences of Gustavus and during the minority of Christina. Sweden was also fortunate in the number of able leaders it had to fill posts provided under the new arrangements.

War and Diplomacy

For Gustavus, Adolphus war and diplomacy intermingled. It has been said that he was the first man in modern times to reduce war to a system and to secure brilliant results by strict application of that system. He was skilled in military engineering and cartography and was a student of the scientific side of war. Some of his officers were trained by Maurice of Orange and Gustavus took the tactics of the brilliant Dutchman and gave them his own twist by combining them with the best of the Spanish school. Consequently, there developed through his efforts a general European system of fighting—formation in line.

Gustavus developed naval superiority since campaigns across the Baltic were impossible without it. The backbone of his army was Swedish and Finnish regiments drafted from each province, but a number of Germans and Scots served under him. His armies were usually outnumbered, but he substituted manoeuvreability for size. His highly mobile army was supplied with light up-to-date equipment with large stores of supplies kept in readiness for their needs. His artillery was capable of rapid fire and his units coordinated the various arms into an organic whole possessing superior-striking power. Gustavus paid close attention to detail and to instructing his officers personally. Consequently, he developed a school of generals which included Swedes, Germans and Scots.

In 1621, Gustavus captured Riga and soon the rest of Livonia. Later, in 1629 in Poland, after much soul-searching, Gustavus decided to espouse the Protestant cause, motivated by religion highly mixed with a concern for Sweden's well-being.

On 19 May, 1630, Gustavus formally took leave of the Estates, realising he might never return to Sweden. On 24 June, he landed at Rügen.

In 1632, when he received news that Wallenstein was

threatening Protestant Nuremberg, Gustavus began a successful invasion of Bavaria. On 6 Novemver, 1632, the two met at Lützen. The Swedish troops won the battle, but lost their king. Gustavus fought without armour because it irritated old wounds and was uncomfortable because of his weight. Somehow in the mists, the nearsighted king became detached from his troops and was slain. There was no one to take his place, and, henceforth, neither Catholics nor Protestants were able to gain a complete mastery over the other. Gustavus is said to be founder of *Stormaktstiden—'the era of great power'.*

We shall describe two more warriors, Napolean and Spartacus.

Napoleon Bonaparte

Although France was left in an economic state similar to that before his rule, Napoleon Bonaparte was a revered military genius and rose in rank to become Emperor of France and King of Italy. The Little Corporal, as he was known, was to have great might in all his endeavours and has become one of the most studied personages of the 18th and 19th centuries.

Young Napoleon was born in Corsica. During his military training in France and while serving as a lieutenant and captain in their forces, he often returned to Corsica to be with family and friends. At the age of 16, while Napoleon was in France training, his father died of cancer and Napoleon became the family's caretaker. Napoleon and his family fled to Corsica to live in France when Paoli came to power and declared his rule of dictatorship over the island—and thereafter declared independence from France.

Napoleon Bonaparte climbed rank quickly in the armed forces due to his familial connections and his uncanny military knowledge, which he gained through dedicated reading. He also was influenced by the writings of Voltaire and did not practise much in the way of religion. Although he was a Roman Catholic, he often thought about becoming a Muslim after visiting Egypt.

When a riot occurred in Paris, in hopes of stopping a national convention, Bonaparte was reinstated to second in command and took care of the situation by shooting those who began marching on the capital. With his actions, he was said to have alone saved the newly found government of France and was quickly appointed the commander of the Army of the Interior. The new government was known as the Directory. With his new command, he led France to several military triumphs in Austria, Italy, the French, colonies, and the Alps.

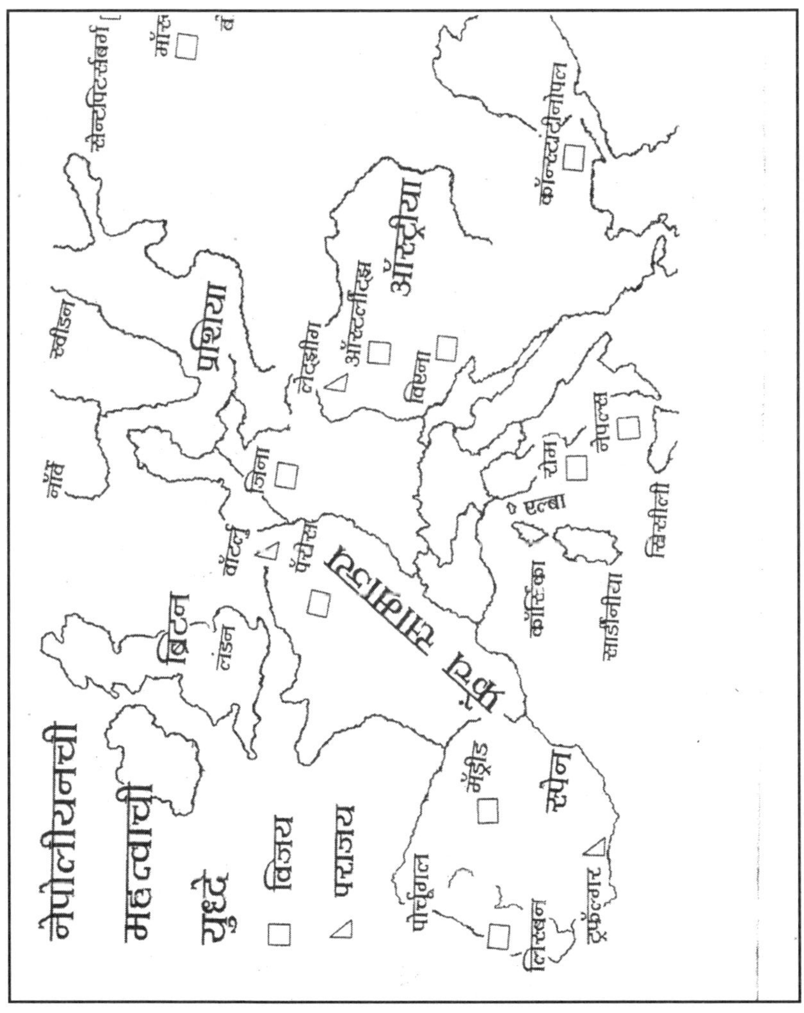

Napoleon was away from Paris for long periods due to battles and victories. In his absence, the Royalists began gaining power. In order for them to not take over, Napoleon proclaimed himself dictator of France and had the full support of the military. When he first took power, peace was restored for a time. However, during these peaceful times, Napoleon carried on his attempts at imperialism, which made Great Britain nervous. The two countries went to war and finding no peace, Napoleon attempted to gather allies and form blockades on British goods.

Napoleon's Failings

Napoleon also made mistakes and suffered setbacks. The French navy was kept firmly in check by their British equivalent and the Emperor's attempt to tame Britain through economics—the Continental System—harmed France and her supposed allies greatly. Bonaparte's interference in Spain caused even larger problems, as the Spanish refused to accept Napoleon's brother Joseph as ruler; instead fighting a vicious guerrilla war against the French invaders.

The Spanish 'ulcer' highlights another problem of Bonaparte's reign: he couldn't be everywhere within his empire at once, and the forces he sent to pacify Spain failed, as they often did elsewhere. Meanwhile, British forces gained a toehold in Portugal, slowly fighting their way across the peninsula and drawing ever more troops and resources from France itself. Nevertheless, these were Napoleon's glory days, and on 11th March, 1810, he married his second wife, Marie-Louise; his only legitimate child—Napoleon II—was born just over a year later, on 20th March, 1811.

1812: Napoleon's Disaster in Russia

The Napoleonic Empire may have shown signs of decline by 1811, including a downturn in diplomatic fortunes and continuing failure in Spain, but such matters were overshadowed by what happened next. In 1812, Napoleon went to war with Russia, assembling a force of over 4,00,000 soldiers, accompanied by the same number of followers and support. Such an army was almost impossible to feed or adequately control and the Russians repeatedly retreated, destroying the local resources and separating Bonaparte from his supplies.

The Emperor continually dithered, eventually reaching Moscow on September 8th after the Battle of Borodino, a bludgeoning conflict where over 80,000 soldiers died. However, the Russians refused to surrender, instead torching Moscow and forcing Napoleon into a long retreat back to friendly territory. The Grande Armée was assailed by starvation, extremes of weather and terrifying Russian partisans throughout, and by the end of 1812, only 10,000 soldiers were able to fight. Many of the rest had died in horrible conditions, with the camp's followers faring even worse.

In the final half of 1812, Napoleon had destroyed most of his army, suffered a humiliating retreat, made an enemy of Russia, obliterated France's stock of horses and shattered his reputation. A coup had been attempted in his absence and his enemies in Europe were re-invigorated, forming a grand alliance, intent on removing him. As vast numbers of enemy soldiers advanced across Europe towards France, over-turning the states Bonaparte had created, the Emperor raised, equipped and fielded a new army. This was a remarkable achievement, but the combined forces of Russia, Prussia, Austria and others just used a simple plan, retreating from the emperor himself and advancing again when he moved to face the next threat.

1813-1814 and Abdication

Throughout 1813 and into 1814, the pressure grew on Napoleon; not only were his enemies grinding his forces down and approaching Paris, but the British had fought out of Spain and into France, the Grande Armée's Marshalls were underperforming and Bonaparte had lost the French public's support. Nevertheless, for the first half of 1814, Napoleon exhibited the military genius of his youth, but it was a war he couldn't win alone. On 30th March, 1814, Paris surrendered to allied forces without a fight and, facing massive betrayal and impossible military odds, Napoleon abdicated as Emperor of France; he was exiled to the Island of Elba.

The 100 Days and Exile

Undoubtedly, bored and aware of the continuing discontent in France, Napoleon made a sensational return to power in 1815. Travelling to France in secret, he attracted vast support and reclaimed his imperial throne, as well as re-organising the army and government. This was anathema to his enemies and after a series of initial engagements, Bonaparte was narrowly defeated in one of history's greatest battles: Waterloo.

This final adventure had occurred in less than 100 days, closing with Napoleon's second abdication on 25th June, 1815, whereupon British forces forced him into further exile. Housed on St. Helena, a small rocky island well away from Europe, Napoleon's health and character fluctuated; he died within six years, on 5th May, 1821, aged 51. The causes of his death have been debated ever since, and conspiracy theories involving poison are rife.

Spartacus

Origins

Spartacus (c. 109-71 B.C. was a Thracian, who had once served as a soldier with the Romans, but had since been a prisoner and sold for a Gladiator.

Spartacus was trained at the gladiatorial school (*ludus*) near Capua belonging to Lentulus Batiatus. In 73 BCE, Spartacus was among a group of gladiators plotting an escape.

The plot was betrayed but about 70 men seized kitchen implements, fought their way free from the school, and seized several wagons of gladiatorial weapons and armour. The escaped slaves defeated a small force sent after them, plundered the region surrounding Capua, recruited many other slaves into their ranks, and eventually retired to a more defensiblc position on Mount Vesuvius.

Once free, the escaped gladiators chose Spartacus and two

Gallic slaves—Crixus and Oenomaus—as their leaders. Although Roman authors assumed that the slaves were a homogeneous group with Spartacus as their leader, they may have projected their own hierarchical view of military leadership on to the spontaneous organisation of the slaves, reducing other slave leaders to subordinate positions in their accounts.

Mount Vesuvius

The response of the Romans was hampered by the absence of the Roman legions, which were already engaged in fighting a revolt in Spain and the Third Mithridatic War. Furthermore, the Romans considered the rebellion more of a policing matter than a war. Rome dispatched militia under the command of praetor Gaius Claudius Glaber, which besieged Spartacus and his camp on Mount Vesuvius, hoping that starvation would force Spartacus to surrender. They were surprised when Spartacus had ropes made from vines, climbed down the cliff side of the volcano with his men and attacked the unfortified Roman camp in the rear, killing most of them

The slaves also defeated a second expedition, nearly capturing the praetor commander, killing his lieutenants and seizing the military equipment With these successes, more and more slaves flocked to the Spartacan forces, as did 'many of the herdsmen and shepherds of the region', swelling their ranks to some 70,000.

In these altercations, Spartacus proved to be an excellent tactician, suggesting that he may have had previous military experience. Though the slaves lacked military training, they displayed a skilful use of available local materials and unusual tactics when facing the disciplined Roman armies. They spent the winter of 73-72 BCE training, arming and equipping their new recruits, and expanding their raiding territory to include the towns of Nola, Nuceria, Thurii and Metapontum. The distance between these locations and the subsequent events indicate that the slaves operated in two groups commanded by the remaining leaders Spartacus and Crixus.

In the spring of 72 BCE, the slaves left their winter encampments and began to move northward. At the same time, the Roman Senate, alarmed by the defeat of the praetorian forces, dispatched a pair of consular legions under the command of Lucius Gellius Publicola and Gnaeus Cornelius Lentulus Clodianus. The two legions were initially successful, defeating a group of 30,000 slaves commanded by Crixus near Mount Garganus, but then were defeated by Spartacus.

Alarmed by the apparently unstoppable rebellion, the Senate charged Marcus Licinius Crassus, the wealthiest man in Rome and the only volunteer for the position, with ending the rebellion. Crassus was put in charge of eight legions, approximately 40,000-50,000 trained Roman soldiers, whom he treated with harsh, even brutal, discipline, reviving the punishment of unit decimation. When Spartacus and his followers, who for unclear reasons had retreated to the south of Italy, moved northward again in early 71 BCE, Crassus deployed six of his legions on the borders of the region and detached his legate Mummius with two legions to manoeuvre behind Spartacus. Though ordered not to engage the slaves, Mummius attacked at a seemingly opportune moment, but was routed. After this, Crassus' legions were victorious in several engagements, forcing Spartacus farther south through Lucania as Crassus gained the upper hand. By the end of 71 BCE, Spartacus was encamped in Rhegium (Reggio Calabria), near the Strait of Messina.

Spartacus made a bargain with Cilician pirates to transport him and some 2,000 of his men to Sicily, where he intended to incite a slave revolt and gather reinforcements. However, he was betrayed by the pirates, who took payment and then abandoned the rebel slaves. Minor sources mention that there were some attempts at raft and ship-building by the rebels as a means to escape, but Crassus took unspecified measures to ensure the rebels could not cross to Sicily, and their efforts were abandoned. Spartacus' forces then retreated towards Rhegium. Crassus' legions followed and upon arrival, built fortifications across the isthmus at Rhegium, despite harassing raids from the rebel slaves. The rebels were now under siege and cut off from their supplies.

The Fall of Spartacus

At this time, the legions of Pompey returned from Spain and were ordered by the Senate to head south to aid Crassus. While Crassus feared that Pompey's arrival would cost him the credit, Spartacus unsuccessfully tried to reach an agreement with Crassus. When Crassus refused, a portion of Spartacus' forces fled towards the mountains west of Petelia (modern Strongoli) in Bruttium, with Crassus' legions in pursuit.

When the legions managed to catch a portion of the rebels separated from the main army, discipline among Spartacus' forces broke down as small groups were independently attacking the oncoming legions. Spartacus now turned his forces around and brought his entire strength to bear on the legions in a last stand, in which the slaves were routed completely, with the vast majority of them being killed on the battlefield.

The final battle that saw the defeat of Spartacus in 71 BCE took place on the present territory of Senerchia on the right bank of River Sele in the area that includes the border with Oliveto Citra up to those of Calabritto, near the village of Quaglietta, in High Sele Valley, which at that time was part of Lucania.

On the battle, Spartacus was killed, but his body was never found. Six thousand survivors of the revolt captured by the legions of Crassus were crucified, lining the Appian Way from Rome to Capua.

We have already discussed Leonidas during the Battle of Thermople, but his demand is that his complete story be told.

Leonidas

Leonidas's name meant 'lion-like' and he was one of three sons of King Anaxandridas II. He became one of two Spartan kings, occupying the throne at the same time in a tense but civil arrangement.

In 480 B.C., King Xerxes of Persia led a massive army against the notoriously fractious city-states of Greece. In part, it was to avenge his father, the great Darius, whose stinging defeat at Marathon, some ten years earlier, had saved the free world. In part, Xerxes wanted to attain one of his father's goals, an even larger Persian empire.

Ancient reports put Xerxes' forces at 1.5 to 2 million people, and with attendants, followers and courtesans, it was stated to have been five million. More modern estimates put it at approaching 5,00,000. The council of Sparta, noting past grievances against other Greek cities, refused to release the full army of Sparta until after the completion of an upcoming religious celebration. Knowing that time was short, King Leonidas took his own personal guard of 300 men north to the narrow pass of Thermopylae, where numbers became less important than skill at close combat. The Spartans were joined by 700 Thespians and 900 Helots, though these groups reportedly stayed on the rear and engaged only after the Spartans were in battle. The Spartans repelled wave after wave of Persian forces, including Xerxes's personal guard, the Immortals, over several days of brutal combat.

Eventually, a traitor showed the Persians a secret goat-trail around the opening allowing the foreign invaders to flank the Spartans, and killing them all. Leonidas was beheaded and crucified.

But the delay, that the Spartans caused Xerxes, and their stirring example, helped Athens, Sparta and the other city-states to unite in repelling the remaining, vast Persian army. In commemoration of their bravery, a plaque was erected which reads:

'Oh stranger, go tell the Spartans that we lie here, obedient to their word.'

□

Comparison of Shivaji with Ten Warrior Kings

No two warriors in history can be compared, especially if they have lived at dissimilar times and in different countries. All successful conquering warriors in history have distinguished themselves by their tactics, logistics, strategy and their workaholic genius and bravery in ordeal, their natural leadership and charismatic oratory, their ability to fire the imagination of their soldiers to fight against greater numbers and better equipment. They had an inherent talent to turn a losing tide of battle due to their conviction that theirs was an inspired mission backed by God. Their sheer personality dominated their kingdoms centuries after their death. There have been many warriors who have conquered more kingdoms than Shivaji and have fought greater battles than him.

But Shivaji seems to have been more virtuous and his character was without a blemish. We shall now compare Shivaji with the ten warriors described above and use fifteen criteria to do so.

Background

Alexander the Great was tutored by the famed philosopher Aristotle (himself a student of Plato). His father was so victorious that Alexander was worried that when he became king, there would be nothing left for him to conquer.

Caesar was a lawyer before he entered public life. Nearly

2,500 years ago, Rome was the first republic which means that it was far ahead of the rest of the world in the field of war, culture and arts and architecture.

Hanibal's father Hamilkar and after his death, his brother-in-law Hasrudbal were the Carthagian generals who took on the might of Rome, thereby proving that Hannibal was well equipped in the aptitude and attitude of war.

Attila was a terror to the Roman Empire and demanded a yearly bounty to stay away and not attack Rome.

Napoleon's father was a lawyer-ambassador. He studied in a military school and was a product of the French Revolution.

William Wallace's father died when he was young, but his priest-uncles brought him up.

Therefore, he must have been well educated. He was given the title of 'Sir', which means that he was financially and culturally well equipped.

Gustavus Agustus perhaps enjoyed the highest status in terms of royalty, culture, education and finance.

Chenghis Khan began as the head of a small tribe, but the Mongol fighting machine was very much in place. Mongolia was made up of fragmentary tribes, but the revolutionary Mongolian 'bow and arrow' and the tactic of shooting an arrow with the horse in full gallop had been mastered much earlier.

Akbar and Aurangzeb were royal Mughal princes and were well groomed.

Aurangzeb's father Shahjahan sat on the peacock throne perhaps the most expensive throne in the world.

King Richard the Lionheart was the son Henry II and ascended, the throne of England in 1198 after defeating his father with the help of his powerful mother.

Comparatively, Shivaji's background was one of frustration and despair. And his training as a boy was comparatively negligible.

Duel

Alexander, Casear, Hannibal, Wallace, Attila, Richard, Gastavus, Akbar, Aurangzeb and Chenghis Khan had greater victories, but, in most wars, these warriors either commanded riding on elephants or perched far away on some hill.

Neither their royal robes nor their blue-blooded bodies were even stained by the blood spilt on the battlefield. But none was engaged in a man-to-man fight, like Shivaji and Afzal Khan. This was in spite of the fact that Afzal Khan used treachery to imprison his father, to kill his brother Sambhaji at Kanakgiri, and to kill Kasturiranga after inviting him for a meeting. This, in spite of the fact that Afzal Khan was taller, stronger, heavier, meaner than him. He reduced the fight to 10,000 against one (Afzal Khan).

Last Stand at Thermopile

Alexander, Caesar, Hannibal, Wallace, Attila, Richard, Gastavus, Akbar, Aurangzeb and Chenghis Khan, all took part in major battles, but none was involved in a Thermopile-like situation as did Shivaji at Pavan Khind. Last Stands have a strong pull on human emotions and on the way we like to remember history.

As we do the three hundred Spartans at Thermopile or Baji Prabhu at Pavan Khind because they all tell the story of a brave and intractable hero leading his tiny band against a numberless foe. Even though the odds are overwhelming, the hero and his followers fight on nobly to the end and are slaughtered to a man. In defeat, the hero of the Last Stand achieves the greatest of victories, since he will be remembered for all time.

Alexander, Caesar, Richard, Gastavus, Akbar, Aurangzeb and Chenghis Khan (exceptions being Hannibal, Wallace, Attila for obvious reasons) built cities, cathedrals monuments, arches, mosques and palaces for themselves. Alexander named sixteen Alexandrias after himself but he really overdid himself by naming a city Bucephela after his horse Bucephelus. Shivaji did not name any city, palace, or fort after himself. The reason was that all the success he had, he owed to all his comrade *mavles*. All the money was spent on the creation of *swarajya*, and to him, *swarajya* meant his forts. His ministers more than once pointed out to him that he spent too much on forts. Shivaji is known to have said, *"Even if each fort holds out for one year against the enemy, swarajya will remain for 360 years."*

Alexander, Caesar, Hannibal, Wallace, Attila, Richard, Akbar, Aurangzeb and Chenghis Khan (except Gastavus) took part in general slaughter of innocents.

General slaughter was a common practice after all wars. Generals demanded that their soldiers present a tally of those killed either in the form of a count of rings or 'right ears'. Akbar, as we know weighed the *janeyus* (sacred thread) of those killed at Chithod. During his reign, Chenghis Khan massacred 30,000,000-60,000,000 people, i.e. 7.5-17 per cent of the world's population.

He is known to have said, "The greatest pleasure is to vanquish your enemies and chase them before you, to rob them of their wealth, and see those dear to them bathed in tears, to ride the horses and clasp to your bosom their wives and daughters."

Attila's atrocities earned him the title 'Scourge of God'. Richard made a pact with Saladin, who promptly renegaded on it. Richard in fury had 3,000 prisoners slaughtered before sailing from Acre.

Shivaji shunned general slaughter even under the greatest of provocations as seen in the attack on him at Surat. Shivaji practised the Geneva code long before it came into existence.

Alexander, Caesar, Hannibal, Attila, Richard, Akbar, Aurangzeb and Chenghis Khan (except Wallace and Gastavus) were warriors on a conquering spree for their personal greedy of empire and their lust for power. Their soldiers were mere pawns on a chess-board. In fact, Chenghis Khan's army had a group of suicide shock troops made up of prisoners. During his Russian campain, Napoleon's Grande Armée of 4,00,000 was assailed by starvation, extremes of weather and terrifying Russian partisans throughout, and by the end of 1812, only 10,000 soldiers were able to fight. Many of the rest had died in horrible conditions, with the camp's followers faring even worse.

But Shivaji was fighting for freedom. He was a father to his subjects.

Shivaji's orders were explicitly clear: 'They should never (pemit themselves to) be caught, but should do what they could without risk and having done so, should immediately leave with all the booty, for Shivaji said that he prized the lives of his soldiers above all the interests of the world. They delivered an assault, robbed and killed whom they met and by the time the Mughals were mounted, not a single enemy was seen and they stood stupefied listening only to the complaints of the wounded, robbed and despoiled."

Alexander had his Persian queen and was thought to be homosexual. Caesar's sexual escapade with Cleopatra is well known, Attila was killed on his wedding night (by the hand and blade of his wife). Richard was a homosexual. Akbar had his harem of 5,000. Aurangzeb killed Dara and married his widow and Chenghis Khan raped many women every night including the daughters of his soldiers. Napoleon's affairs were well known but his wife Josophines's were more famous and sensational (Wallace and Gastavus were the exceptions).

Shivaji's chivalry towards women was legendary and described by his critic Kafi Khan.

Out of Alexander, Hannibal, Richard, Caesar, Attila, Gastavus, Akbar, Aurangzeb, only Richard and Caesar were imprisioned but they paid a ransom. Chenghis Khan was imprisoned, as a child. Wallace was imprisoned but could not escape, He was tried as a traitor and executed. Napoleon escaped from Elba, but could not do so from St. Helena, where he ultimately died. Shivaji's escape is unique because it was not as if he sneaked away alone. He went on invitation to Delhi with a retinue of 1,500, and escaped with 1,498 of them. What is amazing is that he escaped with his twelve-year old son. Still more astonishing is the fact that even today, no one knows for sure what route Shivaji took from Agra to Rajgad.

The escape of Shivaji caused a life-long regret to Aurangzeb, "See how the flight of the wretched Shiva, which was due to carelessness, has involved me in all this distracting campaign (for twenty-seven years) to the end of my days."

The above analysis proves beyond doubt that Shivaji's escape ranks among the most unbelievable escapes in the world.

Alexander faced a revolt after the invasion of India. Caesar was murdered in the senate. Hannibal went into exile and committed suicide. Wallace was betrayed, Richard's French army revolted. Akbar married his *mansabdar's* daughters to prevent rebellion as did Chenghis Khan, and Aurangzeb faced a total revolt from all sides. However, Attila and Gastavus never faced a revolt or rebellion as we summarised earlier. Shivaji was one of the few warriors who was imprisoned.

Yet, it is pertinent to note that none of Shivaji's comrades ever revolted or rebelled against him even when he was imprisoned at Agra.

Alexander, Caesar, Hannibal, Attila, Richard, Akbar, Aurangzeb, Chenghis Khan and Gastavus (except Wallace) employed huge forces and money in siege technology. If the siege of Troy may be considered to be the longest siege, Shivaji's incisive commando raid on Singhad should be considered as the shortest attack on a fort.

Alexander, Caesar, Hannibal, Attila, Richard, Akbar, Aurangzeb and Chenghis Khan (except Wallace and Gastavus) used the loot from their many conquests for personal luxuries, cities, cathedrals, monuments, arches, mosques and palaces.

In fact, Shivaji used the entire loot from Surat to build the sea-fort of Sindudurg.

In fact, all the money he collected, he spent on forts. As Shivaji justified after his plunder of Surat, "Your emperor has forced me to keep an army for the defence of my people and country. That army must be paid by his subject."

Alexander, Caesar, Hannibal, Attila, Richard, Akbar, Aurangzeb and Chenghis Khan (except Wallace and Gastavus) did bring about any social or religious change. Shivaji did so when he went against the caste-ridden society of India. None changed the attitude of their times as greatly as Shivaji did when he formed the Maratha navy or when he supported re-conversion or when he prevented his mother from committing *sati* or allowed lower-caste Hindus to enter and worship in a temple.

Once a warrior or king becomes 'a lord of half a million swords', he does not feel happy unless he can flatter himself that he is not as other men are, that he is 'a kin to gods' and that he rules by 'divine right'. Four of the above developed this form of megalomania.

Alexander (insisted on prokinesis), Caesar (dictator for life), Akbar (*Din-e-Ilahi*), and Chenghis Khan (the supreme God of the Mongols). Attila called himself 'the scourge of God'. Chenghis Khan said, "I am the flail of God. If you had not committed great sins, God would not have sent a punishment like me upon you.

Hannibal, Richard, Wallace and Gastavus died suddenly.

Shivaji had no such inclination of playing God. As already discussed that Shivaji was a man with amission who drew his inspirations from history, from the classics, from the society and culture around him and from Ramdas and the saints of Maharashtra. He was clear that he was doing God's work (*heech Shreeinche ichha*) All he wanted was that his subjects be free from the tyranny of five hundred years of Muslim rule. What was remarkable was that he was one of the few who planned for 350 years of freedom.

Alexander, Caesar, Hannibal, Attila, Richard, Akbar, Aurangzeb and Chenghis Khan, Wallace and Gastavus did not ban slavery. Shivaji did so long ago.

Alexander, Caesar, Hannibal, Attila, Richard, Akbar, Aurangzeb and Chenghis Khan, Wallacc and Gastavus did not formulate a new language with an official dictionary. Shivaji is the only one who did so.

Uniqueness of Shivaji

Shivaji is unique in experiencing events of world-shaking magnitude in one life-time.

1. French revolution for liberty, equality and fraternity
2. David and Goliath
3. Thermopile
4. Great escape
5. Trojan horse
6. Formed a defence line of hill forts
7. Formation of navy

8. Geneva code
9. Charge of the light brigade
10. Banned slavery

Besides this he

A = Won all battles when leading himself
B = Planned in detail battles when not leading
C = Eliminated untouchability
D = Prevented *sati*
E = Stopped conversions
F = Started reconversion to Hinduism
G = Stopped slavery
H = Started a *rajyabhasha kosh*
I = Eliminated casteism
J = Ensured justice (Sambhaji)
K = Had himself coronated after a gap of 500 years
L = Had a vision of pan-India Hindu rule
M = Resurrected a language

But what is really remarkable is that Shivaji had no weaknesses.

(a) Respected women
(b) Respected all religions
(c) Never ordered a general slaughter
(d) Never enslaved prisoners
(e) Was a teetotaler
(f) Did not build monuments to himself
(g) Treated his subjects equally
(h) Never built a tower of skulls
(i) Respected his father, mother, brother and comrades
(j) Ruled as a caretaker of the Almighty, but did not play God.

No wonder, Ramdas described him as a 'an understanding king' and Sir Jadunath Sarkar described him as 'hero as king'.